AF270903

SWITCH

M. H. Rice

M. H. Rice

Solasta Books

SWITCH

By

M H Rice

Cover art courtesy of FrinaArt

Solasta Books

Charlotte, North Carolina

Visit the website for more novels by M H Rice, including
more books in the Switch series.
MHRicebooks.com

ISBN 978-0-9995917-1-0

For all of the ways that my family and friends have encouraged me and waited anxiously for this book series, I am eternally grateful.

My mother, Evelyn
My husband, Bill
My daughters, Elizabeth and Nina

My friends and family,
Elaine
Kimberly
Pat
Marianne
Eve
Kathy
Carolyn
Annabelle
Sadie

"Most of us see time as a set thing.
Once a minute ticks by, it's gone forever.
But that's not really the way it is..."
Jean Grant Huckaby

SWITCH SERIES:

SWITCH
FORSAKEN
RETURN (February 2018)

CHAPTER 1

Nova gripped the back of the seat in front of her as the bus turned onto Riverbank Road. She tried to focus on the meaningless banter around her, but she could already hear the rushing water over the groan of the engine. She leaned her forehead against the dingy window and squeezed her eyes shut as the sound of the wheels against the pavement changed. No matter. She could picture every beam, every cable, every inch of the flimsy guardrail. Her head pounded each time the tires ran over one of the bridge joints. There were thirty. She had counted them nearly every day for the past nine months. Twenty-seven, twenty-eight, twenty-nine…

She held her breath as the sound of the road changed from the rhythmic thumping back to the smooth pavement. Relieved, she opened her eyes and allowed the drone of the bus to drown out Delilah's endless chatter until she felt an elbow jab her in the side.

"Nova!" Delilah sounded irritated.

"Sorry. I zoned out." Nova couldn't think of anything else to say. Besides, Delilah had to be used to it by now. Nova couldn't remember what it felt like to cross the bridge without imagining plunging into the churning water below.

"I just said Ethan's a jerk, like, fifteen times."

Delilah was clearly waiting for an insightful response, but all Nova could come up with was, "Oh yeah. Of course he is."

"Well, don't strain yourself." Delilah pressed her lips together in a pout that reminded Nova of the one fish that had managed to survive Mr. Waller's attempt to teach his biology students how to clean an aquarium.

"Sorry, Dee." Nova tried to keep thinking about the fish, but she could still hear the water, even as the bus put more and more asphalt between them and the river.

"You're doing it again," Delilah complained.

"Doing what?" Nova asked.

"Zoning out." Delilah flipped her dark-blond hair over her shoulder.

Ms. Bellamy had once made the mistake of referring to Delilah's hair as "dirty blond" in PE class and found her favorite whistle in the girls' locker room toilet the next day. Delilah had never admitted to the prank, of course, but Nova had learned that it was best to stay on Delilah's good side if you didn't want your possessions to end up in a toilet, or worse.

"Sorry." Nova managed what she hoped was a sincere smile.

"Quit apologizing. I get it. Maybe therapy would help. Or a lobotomy. I've got some utensils from lunch here somewhere. I could do it myself." Delilah rummaged around her book bag and finally pulled out a slightly dirty plastic fork.

"Thanks, I'll pass." Nova smiled, grateful for Delilah's impeccable, if unintentional, timing that always managed to pull her back just as she was falling into that dark hole.

"Grief is a powerful emotion, but time will lessen the

pain," her school counselor had said on Nova's first day back after the accident.

The truth was, he'd never lost anyone. He was just spitting out rhetoric, meaningless platitudes he'd read in a correspondence course manual. He had no idea what a dark, suffocating pit grief could be. And sometimes, that pit looked exactly like a bridge.

"Just think about it." Delilah shoved the fork back in her bag. "Therapy, I mean."

"I don't need therapy. I have you."

"Okay, whatever." Delilah tugged on the hem of Nova's shirt. "I see the monster table snagged another one."

Nova jerked it away from her and stared at the hole large enough to stick her finger through. "Seriously? This is getting ridiculous! I'm not gonna have any clothes left!"

"Just out of curiosity, how do you break a kitchen table?"

"Marshall hit it with his skateboard."

"That figures. Just put tape over it or something."

"My shirt?"

"No. The *table*. Put tape over the broken spot. Jeez." Delilah snickered.

"I'll try to remember to." Nova grabbed her book bag and stood as the bus pulled up to her stop. "Call me later, okay?"

"I'll try to remember to," Delilah parroted back.

"Very funny, Dee. I'm serious. I can't stand hanging out with Mom and Marshall. It's too depressing."

The truth was that she barely saw her mother anymore, and the majority of her time with Marshall was spent trying to pretend his life didn't suck.

The rest of the time, she stayed in her room, working through the "stages of grief," as the counselor called them. The denial phase had been over for months. Then came anger, bargaining, and depression. Nova couldn't pinpoint exactly where she was in that process. Was it possible to be in all three at once? The final stage was acceptance, but that seemed like an unattainable goal. She looked back at Delilah as the driver pulled the lever to open the doors.

"Promise you'll call me?"

"Fine. I'll call you."

"Thanks, Dee. I'll talk to you later," Nova prodded hopefully.

"Yeah, okay."

Nova stepped off of the bus and stopped, staring across her backyard at the kitchen window. Her mom was peering out, watching for her. Even from this distance, Nova could see that she had dyed her hair a hideous red.

Her mom usually dyed her hair on her really bad days – the days when the numbness wore off and the wound caused by her new reality cracked open, letting every bit of pain and anger ooze out onto everyone around her, and sometimes onto inanimate objects as well. The microwave door was missing because her mother had pried if off with a crowbar when it wouldn't open on the second try. That was a bad day. The trash compactor was also broken because who knew you couldn't put a microwave door in it?

Nova's gaze darted around the yard, hoping to spot Marshall so she could run interference. Better to keep him away until she had a chance to determine just how bad a day Celeste Grant was having. Her heart sank when she reached the porch and saw her little brother's backpack at the door. Marshall must already be inside.

"Hi, Mom," she said, accidentally letting the screen door slam.

"Nova, that noise! Please be careful."

"Sorry." Nova set her book bag on the floor beside the door and surveyed the cluttered counters piled high with dirty dishes. "I can load the dishwasher before dinner."

"It's full," her mom said absently, still staring out the window.

"Oh. I can *un*load it then."

"I didn't run it." Celeste was standing over the sink with the water running, a glass in her hand. "We're out of soap," she said apologetically.

"Oh…it's okay, Mom." Nova took the glass, filled it, and handed it back to her.

"I'm sorry, honey. I just can't get organized." She looked around, seeming to notice the mess for the first time. "I'll get to the store tomorrow. I ordered pizza. It's on the table."

"You got it already? It's early."

No response. Her mother had turned back to the window, looking out at nothing, the glass of water in her hand.

"Pizza's fine. I'll just eat it in my room. I have a test to study for," Nova lied, opening the box.

Plain cheese. They used to get sausage and pepperoni packed with peppers and mushrooms. Sometimes they'd order Hawaiian with pineapple and bacon. That was Nova's favorite. But that was before. When their family was happy, oblivious to what was coming. Her mom never ordered anything but cheese anymore. Nothing extra. In a sad way, it seemed fitting.

"You haven't said anything about my hair." Celeste's hopeful expression was almost childlike. The light from the window caught her at just the right angle to reveal an orange streak on top of her head where the dye hadn't quite soaked in, or maybe it had soaked in too much.

"It looks good, Mom," Nova said, concerned about how easy it was becoming to lie.

She smiled gratefully. "It's supposed to be auburn. You don't think it's too… red?"

"No, it's not too red."

Maybe "Is it too orange?" would have been a better question. But that would've required another lie. Before her mother could ask anything else, Nova picked up her book bag, grabbed a couple of slices of pizza and made a beeline for her bedroom.

She stopped at Marshall's door. "Hey kid, you in there?"

"Yeah." He sounded younger than his nine years.

Nova tried the door, but it was locked. "I have pizza. You want some?"

"I already got it."

"Well, you want to come in my room for a while?"

There was a long pause, then, "No."

"We could play a video game or something."

"That's in the den." Marshall was obviously anxious to avoid their mother too.

"I know. It'll be okay.

Another long pause. "I'm doing something." He wasn't budging.

"Okay. If you change your mind, come get me." She waited, hoping he'd cave and come out. When she didn't hear a peep out of him she stepped into her room next to his and closed the door.

After dropping everything on the floor, she lay back on her bed and stared at the spot on the ceiling where her dad had squashed a spider last summer. If she stood on her bed and examined it closely, she could still see one detached leg about a quarter of an inch from the smudge, as if it had tried to save itself. Nova hated spiders, even dead ones. Under normal circumstances, she would have long since scraped it off, or painted over it, or nailed up a board. Anything to get rid of the spider corpse. But she couldn't bear the thought of removing the tiny carcass. It was the last time her dad had smashed a spider for her. That summer had been full of lasts. They just hadn't known it at the time.

Nova glanced at the clock beside her bed, wondering when Delilah would call, if she even did. Sometimes picking up the phone was just too much effort for Dee, which was surprising since she loved to talk so much. Nova toyed with the idea of calling her instead, but she didn't want to get stuck talking to Delilah's mother, the only person on the planet who talked more than Dee. The only difference was that Mrs. Davenport asked about a hundred questions. Nova couldn't bear the thought of another one of her well meaning but exhausting interrogations.

With time to kill, Nova tried to think of something to do that didn't involve leaving her room. She had an essay due tomorrow, but no motivation to do it. Right now she had a C in her English class. One more failed essay would probably drop her to a D. Still passing. She glanced at her National Honor Society certificate on the wall and made a mental note to take it down the next day. Another last.

She could barely remember her old life, when she had worked hard in school, hung out with friends, and spent endless hours talking over new book ideas with her dad. She hadn't fully appreciated how perfect that life was until it was ripped away.

Delilah had been her friend since elementary school, but once they'd moved into high school, Nova had formed other friendships. Delilah sometimes joined Nova's inner circle before drifting off to hang out with another group. But things were awkward after the accident, and Nova's friends had slowly slipped away. All except Delilah. She was the only person who treated Nova the same as she had before. She didn't look at Nova with pity or push her to care about school again. Delilah just let her be the new version of herself without trying to change her back. In spite of Dee's occasional shallowness and tendency to prattle on about herself, she had stayed faithful when everyone else had fallen away.

Nova pulled the pillow under her head and stared at what was left of the spider. Symbolic. She closed her eyes and drifted off.

She woke when her phone rang sometime after ten o'clock.

"What took you so long?" Nova asked, trying not to

let the annoyance she felt creep into her voice.

"I was busy." Delilah didn't sound busy. She sounded bored. Apparently, she had run out of everything else to do before calling. "How was your night?"

"The usual." Nova glanced at the plate of untouched pizza on the floor, wondering if it was still okay to eat. She leaned over the side of the bed and touched a curled up corner. It felt like a cold piece of rubber.

"You were sleeping, weren't you? I swear that's all you do anymore."

"I wasn't sleeping." Nova tried to sound more awake.

Delilah laughed. "Yes, you were. I always know."

"Yeah, you're psychic," Nova responded. "So what took you so long to call me?"

Delilah eagerly launched into a moment-by-moment replay of everything she'd done since getting off the bus. Nova had never known anyone who loved talking about herself more than Delilah, a personality trait that had proven useful over the last nine months. It meant they didn't have to talk about anything to do with the accident. Nova made herself comfortable, barely listening as Dee droned on and on. Sometime around eleven, Nova drifted off again without hanging up.

CHAPTER 2

Nova's back was stiff the next morning from sleeping propped up against her iron headboard all night. She shook off the jeans she'd slept in and stepped into a hot shower, ignoring the slightly painful temperature of the water that she figured was just below scalding – not quite hot enough to actually cause damage. For some reason, the discomfort made her feel better. After several minutes, the water gradually cooled off until nearly all the warmth was gone. Nova stepped out, shivering, and used her towel to wipe off the mirror over the sink. Her cheeks were bright red, but she could still see the dark circles under her eyes. Maybe Dee wouldn't notice since all she'd cared about lately was trashing Ethan.

After blowing her hair almost dry, Nova pulled on what she hoped were clean clothes from the laundry basket in the hallway, picked up her book bag, and headed to the kitchen.

Her mother was at the table, hunched over the local job listings with a black marker in her hand. The morning sun streaming in through the window made her orange streak more prominent. Nova thought about mentioning it but decided against it. In a couple of weeks, she'd probably dye it again anyway and the orange wouldn't matter. Nova peeked over her mother's shoulder and saw that she had circled several ads.

"Anything good?" Nova asked.

Her mom didn't look up. "Not unless you call managing a convenience store good. There's not much call for an art history major who hasn't worked in sixteen years."

"It doesn't matter, Mom. We'll be fine."

"The money from your dad's books will eventually run out, Nova." She circled another ad. This one was for a dog walker.

"Do we have to talk about this every single day?" Nova groaned, mentally shaking herself for saying that. She'd become fairly adept at holding her thoughts in, but sometimes they spilled out before she had the presence of mind to stop them.

Thankfully, her mother ignored her and circled an ad for a temporary position manning a booth at a local job fair. Nova wanted to point out the irony but managed to bite her tongue in time. She scanned the table and counters for any sign that her mom had thought about breakfast, but there was nothing.

"What is there to eat?"

"Look in the pantry." Celeste waved in the pantry's direction.

Nova pulled open the pantry door and surveyed the sparse shelves, rummaging through the mostly empty boxes of cereal until she found one that was about a quarter full.

She opened the refrigerator door and stood there a moment before closing it again. "No milk?"

"I didn't get to the store. I'll go today."

"It's okay." Nova stood there for a moment, watching her mother and trying her best to picture the old Celeste, the one before the accident. It was becoming harder and harder to form the image in her mind. Tucking the bag of cereal under her arm, Nova hesitated. "What's Marshall gonna eat?"

"Leave some for him," her mom responded absently.

"He's a little kid. He needs more than dry cereal for breakfast."

"I said I'd go to the store today. He'll be fine." She continued to circle random jobs in the paper.

Nova felt anger welling up but did her best to shove it back in its hole before it made her blurt out something she'd regret. She took a bowl from the cabinet and filled it with cereal, then rummaged through the front pocket of her book bag, pulling out a Snickers candy bar that Delilah had given her a few days earlier. She placed the bowl of cereal at Marshall's seat across the table from her mom and laid the candy bar next to it. Cereal and candy. Not the most nutritious breakfast, but at least he'd be happy about the treat. The old Celeste would never have allowed her to give Marshall candy for breakfast, but the new Celeste didn't even notice.

"Don't forget to pick up the milk, okay?" She waited a moment, hoping for a response, but Celeste was still engrossed in the paper, circling more job listings. Nova started to leave, then impulsively turned back to give her a hug. Her mother looked up, obviously affected by the sudden show of affection.

"I'm sorry. I'm not very good at this single parent thing. I'll get better," she said, turning back to her paper and circling another ad.

It's been nine months. When is she planning to get *better?* Nova wondered as she let the screen door slam behind her.

*** *

"Why are you eating dry cereal?" Delilah asked when Nova plopped down in the seat beside her on the bus.

"No milk," Nova replied.

"Jeez. You never have any food. Does your mom ever go to the store?"

Nova teared up. "Sometimes." It was bad enough that she and Marshall had to deal with their fragile mother without other people noticing.

"You can always come to my house."

Delilah waited, obviously expecting a reply, but Nova couldn't think of anything to say. She didn't want to go to Delilah's. She wanted to go home, the way it used to be.

Delilah broke the silence. "You look awful, by the way."

"Thanks."

"No, I mean, you could be gorgeous if you put a little effort in. You know, if you didn't sleep all the time and maybe wore some make up. You used to look better, that's all. Most of the girls hated you."

"Um...thanks again."

"Okay, sorry. If it makes you feel any better, Mason still thinks you're 'smokin' hot.'"

"Your brother's seventeen. He thinks half the girls at school are hot. He's basically a walking hormone."

"Yeah, his bar is set pretty low. His last girlfriend had major armpit hair. She came over to swim and I seriously thought there was an animal in the pool."

"Eww, stop. Please!" Nova succumbed to a fit of giggles. Good old Delilah.

"Just look in a mirror once in a while. It wouldn't hurt."

"Ouch." Nova tried to remember if she'd brushed her hair after blowing it dry. She took a hairband off her wrist and pulled her hair up in a ponytail. "Better?"

Delilah studied her for a moment then nodded. "Sure. Sorry to rag on you so much. I'm just in a bad mood. I saw Ethan talking to Amanda yesterday. He didn't waste any time."

"Dee, you only went out a few times and you've been

broken up for a month. Get over it."

"Yeah, well. It still pisses me off."

"Really? I never would've guessed." Nova managed a wry smile.

"You're hilarious." Delilah pulled a pad of sticky notes out of her book bag and started writing on one.

"What're you doing?"

"I'm gonna leave a note on Ethan's locker."

"No, Dee! Don't do that. You'll look desperate."

"Desperate? Thanks a lot." Delilah tore off the note and threw it on the floor of the bus. "Who cares. He's not that amazing, right?"

"Right," Nova said, wondering how Delilah would take it if she knew Ethan had asked her out three times at the beginning of the school year and she'd turned him down because she'd found it impossible to care about anything after the accident. If things had been different, would she be the one throwing wadded up sticky notes on the bus floor? Nova mentally shook Ethan out of her brain and put her arm around Delilah. "Besides, you have an awesome best friend who plans to trip him in the hall today."

Delilah laughed. "I wish you could record it! I want to hear details tonight."

"Sure." Nova glanced out the window at the approaching bridge, already anxious.

"Don't go mental on me this morning, okay? It's getting old." Delilah pulled a notebook out of Nova's book bag and held it against the dirty bus window. "There. Now you don't have to look at it."

Nova closed her eyes. "I can still hear it."

"Oh my God. Fine. I'll wait."

Nova tried unsuccessfully to shut out the sound as the wheels left the pavement.

Three, four, five…

"I'm okay. Tell me about Ethan and Amanda," she said, feigning interest so Delilah wouldn't notice her counting the bridge seams as the wheels passed over them.

Twenty-eight, twenty-nine, thirty…

Nova let out her breath and listened in earnest as the wheels hit the smooth asphalt. Delilah was still rattling on when they filed off the bus and parted ways in the hall. Nova tried to slip into her first class without making eye contact with Mrs. Chandler. It was no use. Her English teacher had taken a special interest in her since the accident. Nova was sure she meant well, but the attention only made her feel worse.

"Good morning, Nova." Mrs. Chandler smiled. "Everything all right?"

"Everything's fine, thanks." Nova busied herself shuffling through her book bag.

Mrs. Chandler stood there a moment, waiting for her to look up. When she did, the teacher leaned over her desk and whispered, "I'm concerned about your grades, Nova. You were my best student last year. I know how hard things must be. Is there anything you'd like to talk about?"

"No." Nova could feel her face turning red.

Mrs. Chandler leaned in closer. Nova noticed a trace of red lipstick on her front teeth. "How's your mother?"

"She's good." Nova tried to swallow, but her throat had gone dry.

"Well, if you ever need to talk, I'm here, honey."

"Thanks." Nova tried to sound *normal,* but she felt as if she was trying to talk with a mouthful of sand.

The classroom started filling up, so her teacher walked back to the front and began talking about the day's assignment as other students took their seats. Relieved, Nova pulled out her notebook.

Delilah had written on the cover, "Don't forget to trip him."

Nova smiled. Glancing up, her eyes met Mrs. Chandler's. *Give it a rest, lady.* Looking away quickly, Nova licked her thumb and rubbed it against the notebook cover, trying to erase Delilah's note. All that did was smear the words a little. She could still read them just fine.

Delilah was still seething about Ethan and Amanda at lunch, nearly spitting out her taco when they sat down together two tables away. "Why don't they sit somewhere else?"

"Dee, let it go. All the other tables are full."

"Whose side are you on?" Delilah snapped.

"Yours, of course." Nova glanced over at Ethan and caught him watching her with his intense blue eyes.

"Is he staring at you?" Delilah demanded.

"I don't think so," Nova lied. The turkey sandwich she'd managed to shove down started working its way back up her esophagus. She grabbed her water bottle and took a big gulp.

"You're not choking, are you?" Delilah asked.

"No. I just…no." Nova swallowed hard again and felt her sandwich retreat to her stomach where it belonged.

Delilah barely noticed because she was glaring at Ethan. He glanced over again but quickly looked away.

Dee leaned forward and whispered, "Don't be surprised if he's available again soon. Maybe he's planning to dump Amanda and date you."

"I wouldn't do that." There was no way Nova would do anything to lose the only friend she had left.

"I know." Delilah pushed her chair back and stood up. "Let's get out of here. We have to do the picture thing."

"What picture thing?"

"Don't you ever pay attention anymore? The yearbook nerds want to take *candid* pictures of us doing whatever we do every day, which is totally wacked because we're not even graduating for two years, so nobody cares. Anyway, everyone has to do it and it's our turn."

Nova stared at her, clueless.

"Oh my God! Today is D through G. I'm Davenport. You're Grant. Don't you remember? They told us last week."

Delilah looked over at Ethan and Amanda, daring them to look her way.

"Oh yeah. I forgot, I guess." Nova still didn't remember.

She looked down at her unfortunate outfit choice and shook her head. Pictures. Great. Her jeans had a mustard stain from a week ago and, based on how tight it was, she was pretty sure the navy T-shirt she had on was Marshall's. Wearing your little brother's clothes seemed like some sort of line that you crossed on the path to utter humiliation. Like the naked-at-school dream. Nova shuddered. She definitely had to be more careful from now on. As they left the lunchroom, Nova could feel Ethan's eyes on her, but she refused to look in his direction.

With the exception of the thirty minutes it took the awkwardly attentive yearbook photographer to get just the right picture of Nova putting books in her locker, the day dragged on at its usual sluggish pace. When she finally stepped off the bus that afternoon, she saw Marshall sitting on the back porch. Her little brother was chewing on the strap of his backpack, visibly upset.

"What's wrong?" Nova asked, immediately on edge.

"I'm locked out and Mom's not home," Marshall cried. "I have to go to the bathroom."

"It's okay, Marsh. I have my key." Nova quickly opened the door, and Marshall practically knocked her down to get inside. She dropped her book bag on the floor just as her mother walked in the front door.

Nova snapped, "Where have you been?"

Her mom set the carton of milk on the counter. "What's wrong this time? You said we needed milk."

"Marshall was locked out! He had to go to the bathroom! You couldn't go to the store this morning and be here when he got home? And why is it up to me to say we need milk? There's no food in this freaking house! Shouldn't a mother notice that?"

"Maybe I should just let you run things, Nova. You seem to be doing that anyway," she said, resignation in her voice.

Her mother's comment had a ring of truth. Over the past nine months, she had relied more and more on Nova to run the house and take care of Marshall.

Nova burst into tears. "Why can't you get over it and be normal? I don't want to *run things*! That's your job. Did you even get anything for dinner? All I see is milk. What are we supposed to eat?"

"We're having leftover pizza from last night. We don't waste food in this house. Like I've said before—"

"Yes, I know! The money from Dad's books is going to run out. Big surprise. Just make sure Marshall eats *something*."

Marshall came in rubbing his eyes on his sleeve. "Stop fighting!"

Nova grabbed her book bag and stormed down the hall to her room, where she slammed the door and collapsed on her bed. Delilah was probably still on the bus. Nova jumped up and paced for five minutes, then she tried to reach Delilah on her private line. She didn't pick up. Nova called again and left a message for Delilah to call back as soon as possible.

Without a distraction, Nova felt as though her brain was going to explode. Why had she unloaded on her mom like that? She didn't need another reason to be depressed. Nova managed to keep it all in ninety-nine percent of the time. But the one percent that was left occasionally reared its ugly head. She needed to apologize but felt incapable of it at that moment. Better to let the one percent monster go back in its hole first.

She dropped to the floor next to her bed and pulled a notebook from her book bag. She'd tucked a pen into the binding so she could jot down her thoughts the moment they came to her. Her dad had encouraged her to keep a journal as soon as she had learned to write. She'd never had trouble getting her words out on paper, sometimes writing for hours.

Working the pen free, she opened to a blank page and wrote the date. Nova tried to collect her thoughts, her pen hovering over the page. How could she write what she felt when she couldn't form the words in her mind in the first place? Her brain was a big empty space unable to produce anything worth recording. She ripped out a sheet and scribbled, "I'm sorry, Mom," then she shoved the pen into the binding again and closed the notebook.

Sometime later, she heard her mother's bedroom door close. She'd be in there for the rest of the night. Nova opened her door quietly, crept up the hall to her parents' room, and stuck the note under the door. She waited a moment to be sure her mom wasn't coming out, then she tiptoed to her dad's office.

Gently turning the knob so as not to alert her mother, she stole silently inside and closed the door. Without turning on the light, Nova walked around the desk and carefully sat in his worn leather chair. She closed her eyes and took a deep breath. Even after nine months, it still smelled like him, a mixture of aftershave and peppermints. She sat there with her eyes closed for a few minutes, just breathing him in. He could be standing in front of her in his flannel shirt and jeans.

"What should we read today, firefly?" he'd ask.

Nova had read all of his books, but her favorite was his latest best seller, *The Journey to Always*. It was about a young man, Jonah Vincent, who woke up in another time and tried over and over to get back to his family. At the end of book one, he discovered a way back only to find that they had also left that time to find him. It was the first in a three-book series. Her dad had been almost through book two when he died. Nova had sorted through his notes for weeks after his death, trying to imagine how it all would have ended, trying to pretend he was coming back to finish it. Finally, she'd given up. The story had no ending because

Jonah had died the day that Dayton Grant went into the river.

Nova pulled the chain on the lamp, illuminating her dad's desk. His bowl of mints sat next to the lamp. His calendar was flipped to the day of the accident. Written in pencil at the bottom of the page were the words, "Tell Nova." She'd spent hours and hours trying to figure out what it was he'd planned to tell her, finally assuming he'd planned to give her some news about their upcoming research trip. But she'd never know what that was.

Papers were still strewn about the desktop – notes mostly. Nova was always careful not to disturb them too much. She needed things to stay the way he'd left them. Sometimes she almost convinced herself that he could come walking through the door any minute, loaded down with trinkets and books from some out-of-the-way place somewhere in the world. Inspiration for his next book.

"Dad, we thought you were dead," she'd say, and he would throw his head back and laugh at such a crazy idea.

She put her face down on the desk and choked back tears. He wasn't ever coming home. She'd never hear his hearty laugh again, or discuss the characters in his books as if they were real people. He'd never take her with him to exotic places to search for ideas for future novels. That life was gone, swept away. He'd taken a piece of her heart and her future with him into the water, and it was never coming back. Like his unwritten books, her pages were blank. And she had no idea how to fill them.

Her dad's flannel shirt was still draped across the arm of his chair. Nova wrapped it around her shoulders, took in a couple of ragged breaths, and sat up again. Gently sifting through the papers, she noticed a drawing peeking out from the bottom of the pile. When she carefully pulled it out, her breath caught in her throat. Why had she never noticed this before?

He had sketched a little girl with golden hair and hazel eyes. A half smile played on Nova's lips. It was a drawing of Allie, her imaginary friend when she was little. Even now Nova sometimes forgot she wasn't real, thinking instead that she'd been a childhood friend who had simply moved away. She could still picture Allie vividly, laughing and beckoning Nova to come play. Allie had been her favorite companion, until one morning when Nova overheard her parents fighting while she played in her room. She'd crept to the door and listened, frightened by the anger in her mother's voice.

"You don't find it disturbing that she has an imaginary friend that she plays with every day...named *Allie?*" she had demanded.

Later that day, her mother had taken her aside and explained to her that little girls had to eventually grow out of imaginary playmates. "You're almost six. It's time to stop pretending."

And with that, Allie was gone. No matter how hard Nova tried, she couldn't summon her. Eventually she'd forgotten about her and moved on to real friends. It hadn't been that hard. After all, Allie was someone she'd made up, like the characters in her dad's books.

Nova studied the picture again. How had he captured her little friend so perfectly when Nova couldn't remember ever telling him what she looked like? She frowned, trying to remember. She must have told him at some point. She folded the paper and tucked it under her T-shirt.

Draping her dad's flannel shirt across the arm of the chair again, she took another long look around the office, turned off the lamp, and tiptoed back down the hall to her room.

When she flicked on the lamp next to her bed, she noticed that someone had left a slice of cold pizza from the day before on the nightstand. It was probably Marshall. He was always sneaking into her room and leaving her things – a cookie from his lunch at school, a coin he found on the playground. She examined the shriveled remnant of cheese pizza. It wasn't the least bit appealing. Still, she appreciated the effort. She stepped into the hall and cracked open Marshall's door. The room was dark but she could hear her little brother breathing softly from his bed. "Marshall?" she whispered. There was no response. Nova waited a moment, just to be sure he was really asleep, then she closed his door and stepped back into her room.

Delilah finally called around nine thirty. By that time, Nova had no desire to talk about anything.

"What's up?" Delilah asked.

"Nothing."

"Sorry it took me so long to call you back. Did something happen?"

"Another fight with Mom." Nova sighed. "Nothing new."

"Don't get sucked into it. It's like me and Ethan. I just try not to think about him."

"Dee, you talk about him all the time."

"Well, he keeps pissing me off."

"No kidding."

Delilah ignored her comment. "Like the whole Amanda thing. He knows my locker's close to hers."

"I don't think he talks to her because her locker's on your hall," Nova pointed out, relieved that, once again, Delilah's preoccupation with herself was proving an effective distraction from her own miserable life.

"That's not the point. And it's not the only thing he does that bothers me…"

For the next two hours, Delilah went on to list each thing in excruciating detail. As usual, Delilah's mind-numbing monologue allowed Nova to slip into that familiar semi-conscious state where nothing mattered. She wasn't sure if she finally said good night and hung up or just fell asleep.

CHAPTER 3

When her alarm went off at seven thirty the next morning, Nova buried her head deeper into the pillow, trying to mute the incessant beeping. It was no use. She reached over and turned it off, feeling slightly nauseated as she pushed the covers back and climbed out of bed. Rubbing her stomach absently, she glanced around the room. Something seemed *off.* She stood there for a minute, her eyes making another sweep of the room.

On the surface, everything looked normal. Her canvas book bag dangled from its usual spot on the massive iron headboard that towered over her bed. She didn't remember picking it up from the floor the night before, but that was par for the course. Several discarded outfits were draped over the light blue armchair in the corner. Most of her dirty clothes were in the hamper next to her closet, the others strewn about the floor around it. Her vintage movie poster of *The Time Machine* hung slightly askew, missing one of the tacks. H. G. Wells stared back at Nova with one eye, the flap from the missing tack covering the other one. Nova had started to fix it several times, but it was another thing from her former life. Besides, one-eyed George had grown on her.

The cool wood floor felt nice against her bare feet, easing her nausea a little. Wait…where was the rug? Nova made another sweep of the room. No rug. George continued to stare with his one eye. Nova giggled even as a chill ran up her spine and the feeling that something was wrong washed over her. She shook it off. Marshall probably carried the rug into his room. He was always building elaborate forts out of blankets and boxes, anything he could come up with. Sometimes they couldn't even get into his room because his makeshift fortress covered every bit of floor space between the door and his bed. Or maybe her mom had decided to wash the rug. Once in a while, Celeste would notice that their living environment was less than pristine and she'd start randomly grabbing things from around the house and shoving them into the washer, whether those items were meant to be put in a washing machine or not. The cushions on the den couch had fallen victim to one of her cleaning sprees and after four hours in the dryer, were never the same. All things considered, Nova hoped Marshall had the rug.

The unsettled feeling stuck with her. She studied her room again. Something else was different. Nova looked George in his eye. "Shut up. You're weirding me out."

"Who are you talking to?" Marshall called from his room.

"Just talking to one-eyed George," Nova answered. At least Marshall was talking again. She waited for a response. Nothing. "He says you should come see him."

There was nothing from him for a moment, then, "He's creepy. You should call the cops and tell them you have a talking poster."

There it was – the Grant sense of humor that Marshall shared with their dad. Maybe her little brother would emerge from the fog after all.

After showering and dressing quickly, Nova hurried up the hall to the kitchen. The room was filled with a delicious aroma and there was a plate of waffles sitting in the middle of the table. Nova pulled back her chair, careful to avoid the broken place on the edge of the kitchen table since she hadn't remembered to put tape over it. She ran her hand along the rim, searching for the jagged chip. Nothing. The table was as good as new.

"Hey, how'd you fix that?" Nova asked.

"Hmm?" Her mom poured a generous helping of syrup over the waffles and looked up, smiling.

"The chip in the table. How'd you fix it? And since when do you make waffles?"

Marshall came in, dragging his backpack as if it weighed a ton. His sandy hair didn't appear to have seen a comb in days. He plopped into a chair and looked up with large hazel eyes. Nova felt a stab of pain. He looked just like her dad.

"Did you make the cinnamon ones?" he asked.

"I forgot, Marsh. I'll make some this weekend."

"Mom!" Nova exclaimed. "The chip?"

"Nova, I have no idea what you're talking about. Did you break something?"

"Very funny." Nova was getting irritated but decided to let it go rather than blow her mother's uncharacteristically good mood.

Nova studied her mom. *That'll be me in twenty years* – they had the same dark eyes and delicate features. They looked more like sisters than mother and daughter. People used to remark on it all the time, but that was before the accident, before her mom had joined the "hair color of the month" club. At least this morning her mother's hair was back to her natural dark brown.

"You should get your money back. That one didn't last two days," Nova said.

Celeste frowned. "What are you talking about?"

"Your hair? Never mind. But if my opinion matters at all, I like it better this way." Nova glanced at Marshall, who was staring at her as if she'd grown a second head.

"You're even weirder than usual." He grabbed a waffle from the platter in the middle of the table and squirted it with more syrup.

"Marshall, use a plate," Celeste scolded as he shoved the whole thing in his mouth.

He looked over at Nova, syrup running down his chin, and grinned.

"You're a slob, kid." Nova picked up her book bag from the floor. "By the way, where's my rug?"

"What rug?" her mother asked, shoving a plate under Marshall's dripping waffle.

"The one beside my bed? The one *you* gave me for Christmas?" Nova would have found her mom's blank look amusing if she hadn't been so annoyed. "Forget it. I'll find it later."

"Aren't you eating breakfast?" she asked.

"I'll just pick something up at school."

Nova didn't wait for a response before she walked out, letting the back door slam. The street curved sharply to the right after her house, so the quickest way to the bus stop was to go across the backyard to the street.

Nova stopped by the road, dropped her book bag on the ground, and sat on it, wishing that she had at least grabbed a waffle before cutting out. Closing her eyes, she tried to clear her head. It was no use. Her brain was on overdrive, thinking about the bridge, her dad, her mom's fleeting visit to normalcy…everything. As usual, she felt anger welling up. It was almost worse on the days her mother acted a little like her old self. It made the other days more unbearable.

Nova took a deep breath and let it out slowly, repeating the process several times. Feeling a little better, she glanced back at the house as she heard the back door slam again. Marshall was dragging his overstuffed backpack across the yard. When he saw her, he smiled and waved before heading off to his stop three houses down from hers.

She shook her head. Why was he in such a good mood? She noticed her mother's face in the kitchen window, watching her.

Nova turned away when she heard the familiar groan of the school bus making the turn onto her street. In a minute or so, it would appear around the bend in the road. Her eyes darted back to the now-empty kitchen window. Relieved, she stood as the bus ground to a stop and the driver jerked open the doors.

"Well, Miss Grant?"

Nova climbed the steps, losing her balance slightly when the driver slammed the doors behind her and allowed the bus to lurch forward.

"Seriously?" she muttered, grabbing the handrail.

She scanned the bus, anxious for Delilah's brain-numbing chatter. When she spotted her friend halfway down the aisle, Nova noticed that Joanna from Dee's homeroom was sitting in the seat beside her.

Nova made her way down the aisle and put her hand on the back of Delilah's seat, steadying herself. "Hey, Dee, you didn't save my seat."

Delilah had pulled her hair into a high ponytail and was using her reflection in the window to put on mascara.

Joanna looked at Nova, frowning. "Excuse me?"

"I usually sit here…obviously."

Delilah finally noticed Nova and looked her over with an amused expression. "Is there something we can do for you?" Delilah stifled a giggle.

Nova shifted her weight nervously and glanced at Joanna, who couldn't seem to wipe the scowl off her face. The other students around them had ceased their conversations and looked on with interest. Nova racked her brain, replaying her conversation with Delilah the previous night. What had she said to piss her off?

"Is everything okay, Dee?" Nova asked, keeping her voice low.

"I'm fine, but you seem a little…what's the word…*mental.*" Delilah laughed.

Nova somehow managed an awkward smile even though she felt like crawling in a hole. "Never mind, I'll just catch you later."

Delilah and Joanna exchanged looks, and someone a couple of rows back snickered. Nova continued down the aisle and found an empty seat three rows behind them. She could feel tears welling up and struggled to keep them from spilling over. The two girls looked back at her, then whispered something to each other and laughed. Nova rubbed her stomach, trying to calm her growing nausea.

As the bus lumbered along, approaching the bridge, she closed her eyes and focused on the drone of the engine. *Don't think.* Her hands gripped her book bag. She felt her house key in the front pocket, pressing through the fabric and hurting her index finger. Good. Maybe the pain would keep her mind occupied. Nova winced as the sound of the road changed to the sickening *thump, thump, thump,* sending her down into the pit again.

It wasn't fair. Not knowing to look back when her dad dropped her off that morning. Not knowing that an irritable "Now I'm gonna be late!" would be the last words she ever spoke to him. Not knowing that ten days later, an empty coffin would be lowered into the ground with precious items from his family but no body because dragging the river and searching the shore had turned up no trace of Dayton Grant.

Nova wiped her face quickly with the hem of her shirt as the bus pulled into the parking lot and everyone began to file off. Delilah and Joanna were still giggling about something, but Nova wasn't up to dealing with it. Besides, knowing Delilah, she was sure to hear in explicit detail about whatever she'd done.

A group of rowdy ninth graders nearly knocked her down as she stood, so Nova let them pass before making her

31

way down the aisle. By the time she stepped off the bus and followed the crowd through the glass double doors into Rock Springs High School, she'd lost sight of Delilah and Joanna. Nova searched the mass of students, eager to apologize for whatever she'd done to warrant the cold shoulder on the bus. She wouldn't be able to take it if she lost the only friend she had left.

Most of the students were still milling around outside or in the lobby, but she couldn't see her friend anywhere. Nova turned down the hallway to her right, pushing through the crowd, and was halfway to her first class when someone came up behind her and put his hands over her eyes, startling her.

"Guess who, hot girl!"

Nova swung around. "Ethan!"

"What's up?" He grinned, taking her book bag and hoisting it over his shoulder. "I've got this."

"Give me that!" she demanded, jerking it away from him.

"What's up with you, hot girl?"

"Hot girl? What about Delilah!" Nova sputtered, irritated by his open flirting.

Ethan's perplexed expression was almost comical. He just stood there, staring at her with his mouth hanging open. "What does Delilah have to do with anything?"

"Didn't you and Delilah split up? What makes you think I'd have anything to do with you after you dumped my best friend?" Nova glared at him.

He took a cautious step backward. "Delilah? Are you serious? Since when have I ever liked Delilah?"

"Stop it Ethan! Don't you think I know who my best friend goes out with? You're being an idiot."

"I've *never* gone out with Delilah! I don't think I've ever even talked to her."

"What's wrong with you?"

"Wrong with *me*?" His face turned bright red. "Are

you high?"

Nova's mouth hung open for a second while she tried to come up with a response. Then she managed in a much calmer voice, "I think *you're* the one who's high, and I don't care. Go bother someone else."

She took off down the hall, her heart pounding. *You're right, Delilah. He is a jerk.*

She reached her English class at the end of the hall and yanked open the door. At least a dozen students were already there, but something was definitely wrong. Several of them looked up.

One guy who looked only vaguely familiar called out, "Wake up, Nova! I think you're sleepwalking."

The room exploded with laughter. Nova stood there a second, then she stepped back out into the hallway and looked at the door again. Room 112. Mrs. Chandler's Honors English.

Ethan came up behind her. "What're you doing? I don't know what you're pissed about, but we're gonna be late."

"Late to where?" She felt as if the hallway was starting to spin.

"Economics." Ethan's face had taken on a concerned look that she found extremely irritating.

"I'm not going anywhere with you, and I don't have economics first period. I have English." She was still standing in the doorway to room 112 as other students breezed past her, but most weren't the usual ones in her class. Nova had the same feeling she'd awoken with, times ten. Everything around her was the same, yet it felt wrong, as though she was out of place.

Ethan tried to take her arm, but she jerked it away just as Mrs. Chandler walked up from behind them.

"Lovers' spat?" She frowned.

"That would be impossible!" replied Nova, feeling as if the temperature in the doorway had suddenly dropped about ten degrees. She shivered so hard that she had to clench her jaw to keep her teeth from chattering.

"Well, hold it down, you two. If you're going to break up, do it outside." Mrs. Chandler stepped into her room and closed the door.

"Mrs. Chandler, wait!" Nova wanted to reach for the door handle but couldn't seem to move. She looked at Ethan. "Break up? What's she talking about?" Nova could feel her heart pounding. "Have you been telling people we're dating?"

"What's the joke?" Ethan asked suspiciously.

"What joke? Oh my God. What's wrong with you?"

"Cut it out, Nova. We can't be late to economics again. You know Mr. Craig locks the door when the bell rings."

The hallway was mostly clear since students were already in their classes, but a few were still at their lockers.

As two girls ran past them, one looked back, laughing. "You two are gonna get locked out again!"

Nova stared after them, confused. Why would she say that? Nova looked back at the closed door to Room 112, Honors English, her first class every day for the whole school year. Except it wasn't her class. Mrs. Chandler wasn't leaning over Nova's desk, asking how she was. At least half the kids who should be there weren't. Why weren't they standing in the hall and wondering what had happened too? Why was she the only one?

"Hey, are you okay?" Ethan asked, clearly worried.

Nova looked back at him. "I feel sick."

Ethan hesitated a second, then he grabbed her by the arm and pulled her up the hallway and out the main doors, gently steering her toward the picnic table by the maintenance shed around the side of the building. It was in a shady spot out of sight of the last few stragglers coming in from the parking lot.

Nova looked at Ethan through a stream of tears. "What's

going on? What's wrong with everybody?"

He put his hands on both sides of her face and kissed her forehead, but she was too upset to care.

"It's gonna be all right," he said softly. "Seriously. Did you take something?"

"Of course not!" she choked out. She'd never even been tempted to take drugs, hating the idea of being out of control. But this must be what it felt like.

"Okay. Tell me what's wrong." His voice was soothing.

"I don't know. Everything! That's not my English class. Delilah's acting weird and so are you. Why are you even talking to me?"

"You're my girlfriend. Of course I talk to you."

"I'm not your girlfriend!"

"You're breaking up with me?" He sounded genuinely shocked.

Nova was sobbing in earnest now. "How is that possible when we're not dating?" she managed to get out between breaths.

"Okay, calm down. Let's start over. I don't know what's going on with you, but start by telling me why you think I've been going out with Delilah."

"Maybe the fact that I saw you together lots of times at school before you dumped her. Maybe because I've had to listen to the details of your breakup over and over for a month."

"Nova, I've never even talked to Delilah, much less gone out with her. She's not your friend. You've never been friends. She and Joanna have been attached at the hip since elementary school. Don't you remember? We used to make jokes about them all the time."

Nova shook her head violently. "No! I sat next to her when she first came here in fifth grade. We've been friends ever since."

"No, *I* sat next to you in fifth grade. That's when *you*

and I became friends. Delilah never said two words to us."

"That's not right and you know it! She's my best friend."

"No, she isn't. I kissed you in eighth grade when we were on that field trip to Yale. I gave you the bracelet with the bulldog charm that they sold in the gift shop. You thought it was so funny. That's when I asked you out. I've never dated anyone but you."

Nova fought to keep from throwing up as another wave of nausea washed over her. Maybe she was in the middle of some demented dream, the kind that seems real while you're having it. She put her hands over her face. *Wake up! Wake up!*

"Hey." Ethan gently pulled her hands away. "Talk to me."

"You're playing some kind of sick joke," Nova cried.

"I wouldn't do that." He sounded sincere. "I know something's wrong. I just don't know what. Did anything happen at home?"

"Home was...normal, I guess. It doesn't matter. Please stop doing this. Whatever you're up to, just stop okay?"

"I'm not up to anything. I think you're having some kind of breakdown or something. Everything was fine yesterday."

"You talked to me yesterday?" Nova wiped her eyes with her sleeve.

"Of course. I talk to you every day. I came over and played video games with Marshall."

"Marshall? You know Marshall?"

"Yeah," Ethan said, frowning.

Nova pushed him away. "Stop it! You and I don't know each other. You don't know Marshall, and you didn't come over yesterday."

Ethan's voice was calm. "Your name is Nova Eleanor Grant. You like cookie dough ice cream and old sci-fi movies. You have a *Time Machine* poster on your wall and your dad's old record collection and player under your bed. You got your braces off right before the Yale fieldtrip. That's why you let me kiss you. The bus door slammed on your hand when we were leaving to go back to school and your parents came and took you to the emergency room. You got five stitches. Anything else you want to know?"

"Ha! I've never had stitches!"

Ethan grabbed her hand and held it up. "What's this?"

A faint but distinctive scar was visible across the back of her hand. Nova felt as though she was going to pass out.

Ethan pushed her head down and gently cradled it. "Just take deep breaths."

She started to feel a little better and sat up, staring at the scar. "I don't remember this." Her voice sounded far away, as though she was eavesdropping on someone else.

She thought of a book in her dad's office – *Unbound*, a compilation of near-death experiences. Most of the people involved described floating, looking down at their lifeless bodies and feeling completely disconnected from them. That was how she felt now – disconnected, as if she were floating above and looking down at an unfamiliar reality.

This isn't a dream. I'm sitting here, outside of school, with Ethan. He thinks he's my boyfriend. So either he's crazy or I am.

"So you and I are dating? Since the eighth grade?"

"Yeah." Ethan put his arms around her, and she buried her face against his shoulder for a minute before taking a ragged breath and pushing him away again.

"Okay, let's just say for a minute that everything you're telling me is true. If it is, that means something horrible is happening to me. I'm going insane or something, because I remember being friends with Delilah. I talked to her for hours last night, mostly about you. I remember her going out with you and you dumping her. I remember sitting on the bus with her every morning for the past month, listening to her go on and on about what a jerk you are."

"You talked to her about me this morning on the bus?"

"Well, no. She was sitting with Joanna." Nova's stomach knotted up. "She was acting weird. Like you."

"I'm not acting weird. You're…" He seemed to be treading carefully, not wanting to upset her more than she already was. After a moment, he leaned in close and lowered his voice. "Nova, seriously, did you take something? You can tell me if you did. I'll help you."

"Stop asking me that! Of course not!" From inside the school, the bell rang. "This is so messed up. I can't go in there." Nova still clung to the hope that she'd snap out of whatever this was. "Something's wrong and I have to figure it out. I have to go home."

"Okay," said Ethan. "We'll wait until everybody's inside then take off."

"You're going with me?" She was alarmed at the idea of going off alone with Ethan. "I don't think that's a good idea."

He said adamantly, "I'm not letting you go alone."

"Whatever." Nova frowned, intending to keep her guard up in case he was the one who was crazy. She gave him the sternest look she could muster. "Just so you know, I took karate for two years."

Ethan gave her a tentative smile. "Okay, hot girl."

"What's this hot girl thing?" Nova asked warily.

"I've always called you hot girl. Oh yeah, you don't remember. Okay. You know, Nova…exploding star…"

"Oh, clever," she muttered.

"We'll figure this out, okay? I'll take you home."

"You have a car?" Nova's voice was barely audible.

Ethan seemed shocked by the question. "Not yet, Nova. Not until…never mind. We'll have to walk."

"Fine. Come with me. At least that way you'll see how wrong you are."

38

He waited until the parking lot was quiet, then he took her hand. "Let's go."

CHAPTER 4

They made their way around the maintenance building and slipped into the woods that bordered the school grounds. It was nearly nine o'clock. Her mother was probably on her morning run. That was the one thing that hadn't changed since the accident. She usually was home by nine thirty. What would she think when Nova showed up with Ethan?

Mom, this is my boyfriend and I've gone crazy. Of course, you probably already know that. Nova shook her head. She wasn't sure what was real anymore.

They took the path through the woods that led to Riverbank Road. Soon they would come to the bridge where a truck had veered over the line and slammed into her dad's Mustang head-on, causing it to spin around and rip apart as it plunged backward through the guardrail. The gruesome scene began playing in Nova's head, over and over, in an all too familiar loop.

"Nova!"

She realized that Ethan had said her name several times. "S-sorry."

He put his arm around her waist and pulled her back

into the trees. "We need to stay out of sight. I don't want to get busted before we even get you home."

They slowly made their way through the edge of the woods that bordered the road. As Ethan pulled her along, Nova clung to his hand, wondering how long it would take searchers to find her body if he was actually a murderous psycho playing some kind of mind game with her.

The underbrush was thick in places, making it necessary to briefly step out into the open where the cars whizzing by could see them. She could picture some commuter describing the gruesome discovery on the six o'clock news. "I thought I saw some teenagers in the edge of the woods, so I stopped to check it out, figuring they should be in school and all. That's when I found her. It was pretty awful. Looked like a nice girl."

Nova shuddered.

Ethan looked back. "You okay?"

"Sure."

Nova studied Ethan as he pulled her along, holding her hand in a firm grasp. He probably had at least thirty or forty pounds on her, but she figured an adrenaline rush would even things out. She really had taken karate, although she'd quit after six months because the instructor kept trying to set her up with his creepy nephew who always smelled like beer and Cheetos. Still, she could remember enough to defend herself if she had to. She made a mental note of Ethan's clothing so she could describe it to the cops after she beat the crap out of him. Dark jeans, gray striped t-shirt and sneakers. Nova fought off a sudden inappropriate urge to laugh.

Ethan looked back at her and smiled. Okay, she had to admit that he didn't seem like a psycho, even if he was convinced they were dating. For all she knew, he was as worried about being alone in the woods with her as she was with him, especially if he thought she was nuts. Which at this point didn't seem too far off.

As they continued along the edge of the woods, Nova

tried to concentrate on her footing to keep from falling face first into the undergrowth and dragging Ethan down with her. When they finally stepped out of the brush and into the open, her breath caught in her throat. The bridge loomed overhead.

From this angle, it should have been easy to make out the spot where her dad's car had crashed through the guardrail. But the metal had already weathered, making it impossible to tell exactly where it had broken. Shouldn't there at least be an obvious repair in the railing? How else would anyone know that something tragic had happened there? Like a marker left by family and friends on the side of the road where a loved one was killed, the shiny new rail had marked where Dayton Grant—beloved husband, father, and science fiction writer—had plummeted to his death. It had only been nine months and his marker was already gone. It didn't seem right.

Nova's grip on Ethan's hand increased as they scrambled up the steep embankment and stepped onto the bridge.

"No cars right now. Run!" yelled Ethan.

Determined not to look at the guardrail, Nova fixed her gaze on the road beyond the bridge, nearly reaching the other side before a car approached. The driver slowed to a stop and rolled down the window. Nova recognized her neighbor from the end of the street. Her name was Mrs. Wilson, or Willard. Something like that.

"Nova Grant, is that you?" the elderly woman queried, frowning when she glanced at Ethan.

Nova tried to catch her breath. "Yes, it is." She managed a weak smile, an image flashing in her mind of the old lady recounting to the news crew how she'd stopped them on the bridge and that was the last time anyone saw the poor girl alive.

"Why aren't you children in school?" she asked pointedly.

Ethan caught Nova's eye, barely hiding his amusement.

Children?

"No school today. Just exams, and we don't have one," he answered, giving Mrs. Willard or Wilson his most engaging smile. Nova could have sworn the old lady blushed.

"Hmm. What were you doing on the bridge? Didn't you hear? A car almost hit someone crossing on foot last week. It's not safe." She frowned.

"We were looking for Nova's cat. He ran away last night."

Nova thought his explanation sounded fake, but her neighbor seemed to be buying it. Ethan could be very charming. Never mind that he might be planning to murder her and she didn't have a cat.

"Well, all right. You kids be careful. I hope you find your cat, Nova." The woman sat there a minute, watching them, before she finally drove off.

Nova eyed him suspiciously. "How did you get to be such a good liar?"

"Just a natural talent, I guess." Ethan grinned, not looking anything at all like a crazy killer. He was probably exactly what he seemed. A nice guy who just happened to be *confused*. But that didn't explain all the other things that were off.

"Actually, I was just being nice. That was pathetic." Nova said.

He clutched his chest, grinning. "I'm wounded!"

She had to admit that under less bizarre circumstances, she would have found Ethan attractive. In the sunlight, his hair had a tinge of auburn, and when he looked at her with those dark blue eyes, she felt as if her knees were going to give out. Nova could see why Delilah had been so inconsolable when he broke up with her, except according to him they'd never even spoken.

A strand of hair fell slightly over Ethan's right eye, and Nova had the overwhelming urge to brush it aside. Another car whizzed by before she realized that she was standing there staring at him.

Ethan gave her a cocky smile. "Do I meet your approval?"

Nova felt her cheeks go bright red. She jabbed him in the side with her elbow and started walking again. *Stop being such a teenage girl!* she told herself.

"Don't be mad, hot girl. I check you out all the time."

Nova tried to ignore him. Nothing mattered except getting home or waking up, whichever came first. She didn't really believe that she was dreaming, but she allowed herself that possibility all the same. At least that would be easier to accept than the whole losing-her-mind thing.

They followed Riverbank for another mile or so and then turned onto Elmwood Drive. Getting home was all she could think about. Maybe she was still in bed, swept into an alternate world her sleeping mind had created. Her mom would come in and wake her. "You were having a bad dream, Nova," she'd say. They'd talk about it and everything would go back to normal. The new normal, that is. Nothing would ever make things go back to the real normal.

Elmwood was dense with trees and shrubbery that hugged the road, making it impossible to see the houses until you were practically on top of them. After they'd passed the first four or five homes, Nova broke into a run with Ethan close behind her. The Grants' house was the seventh on the right, just after the road curved. Nova could remember sitting on the driveway when she was little, waiting for her dad to return from one of his trips. She'd hear the Mustang's engine before she could actually see it.

As she rounded the curve and her house came into view, Nova stopped abruptly and gasped in disbelief. She squeezed her eyes shut and sucked in a couple of ragged breaths. When she opened them again, it was still there. Her dad's classic light blue Mustang was parked in its usual spot in the driveway, or what used to be its usual spot, before it was ripped apart and forced off the bridge into the river.

44

Nova's heart threatened to pound out of her chest. It wasn't possible. The car had been demolished. They couldn't even find all of it. A fragment of the bumper that she'd picked up from the riverbank was still in a shoebox on the top shelf of her closet. Her mom must have found an exact replica somehow. Another Mustang, just like his. That had to be it.

Nova's heart rate slowed a little, until she noticed something dangling from the car door and a chill ran up her spine. Dayton Grant hadn't been the most organized person on the planet and couldn't seem to make it anywhere on time. Part of the problem was that he never set his keys down in the same place twice, so he was forever tearing around the house at the last minute looking for them. Over her mother's objections, he'd come up with the brilliant idea of leaving them in the car door during the day if he had errands to run or appointments to keep. Even from the street, she could tell what was hanging from the door – keys.

The driveway seemed to transform into quicksand as Nova forced her feet to move. She reached the driver's side door and placed her hand against the window to steady herself before dropping to her knees.

The Friday before her dad's crash, someone had carved what looked like a lightning bolt in the door of his Mustang when it was parked outside of Mario's Italian Restaurant. He had nearly popped a vein when he'd come out and seen the mark, unaware that three days later it wouldn't matter – his car would be floating down the river, twisted beyond repair, pieces of it left behind on the bridge.

Nova leaned in, examining the spot just under the handle, all the while telling herself it wouldn't be there in spite of the gnawing feeling in the pit of her stomach. Her fingers encountered the rough place even before she saw it. Someone had painted over the scratch, but the mark was still visible – a lightning bolt.

Ethan was staring at her. "Nova, what's wrong?"

She stood up, shaking. "This is my dad's car…" Her voice was barely a whisper.

Time seemed to slow down as her eyes turned back to the driver's side window. Her dad's navy windbreaker was on the backseat where he usually kept it. His spiral notebook was tucked into the space between the front seats. He always carried it in case he had an idea for a story when he was out. Nova felt as if she was living in one of his novels right now, a made-up character in a book. Maybe he'd written her life one way and decided to change it when that storyline didn't work.

"It's okay. He's probably just in his office writing."

Nova turned to Ethan, trembling. "He's alive?"

"Why would you ask me that?" he sputtered.

"It's just…his car shouldn't be here." Her voice was barely audible, even to her.

"Nova—"

"Ethan. Is he alive or dead?"

Ethan stared at her, wide-eyed.

This time Nova found her voice. "Tell me!"

"He's alive…of course."

Nova's world started to go black. She barely felt the impact when she hit the concrete driveway.

CHAPTER 5

Nova had no idea how long she'd been out, but the first thing she saw when she opened her eyes was Dayton Grant, alive and well, kneeling beside her. His face was full of concern as he cradled her head. Nova tried to take in every detail, committing him to memory. If she was dreaming, she didn't want to forget again.

Over the past nine months, there'd been times when she couldn't quite put all the details together to form the exact picture of her dad. The vivid image of him that lived in her brain had faded a little, like a photograph that had been left in the sun. She'd try to imagine his unruly hair, his hazel eyes that sparkled with youthful mischief, the way he raised his eyebrows when he thought something was funny or ridiculous. She could manage each piece individually but couldn't seem to put them together in a way that revealed him the way he'd really been.

Nova had always taken the world too seriously, but her dad was a big kid at heart and everything about him showed it. Her mom would sometimes call him a little boy, and he would laugh – that wonderful sound that came up from his feet. His laugh could lift the sourest mood. It was amazing.

Maybe she'd died and this was heaven. It seemed natural that he would be the one to greet her. Grandma Kate was also dead, but Nova had barely known her. No, her dad would definitely be the one smiling and beckoning her to come on when she left this earth. He'd be waiting for her with open arms.

A sharp pain shot through Nova's head, jolting her back to the present. *If this were heaven, my head wouldn't hurt.* Something warm and wet was running down her cheek, pooling in her ear. She wanted to shake her head to get it out but was afraid that would make her pain worse. She squeezed her eyes shut, counted to ten, and opened them again. He was still there.

"Dad?"

Tears flowed down her cheeks, mixing with whatever the other liquid was. She could tell that something was dripping onto the driveway below her head. A frightening thought crossed her mind – maybe the wet substance was brain fluid pouring out of her cracked skull. Small quantities of glucose, sodium chloride, and protein. She'd missed that question on the pop quiz in biology. Name three substances contained in cerebrospinal fluid. Her brain had picked a weird time to finally remember the correct answer. Was she dripping small quantities of glucose, sodium chloride, and protein onto the driveway right now while her dead father held her head?

Nova started to black out again. "It's okay, baby. I'm here," was the last thing she heard before waking up surrounded by paramedics.

Her dad was still there, leaning over her, his face strained from worry.

"Dad, where have you been?"

"I've been here, baby," he answered softly, still cradling her head. His hands had to be soaking wet by now.

"How?" Nova wanted to say something else, but her

brain wouldn't cooperate.

"Your friend came to find me when you fainted."

"Ethan?"

"Yes, Ethan came to get me. Just lie still."

She tried to speak again, but the words wouldn't come out. How was he here? She closed her eyes again and willed herself to wake up, but she could still feel her dad's hands holding her head off of the concrete.

"You're going to be okay." It was his voice, soothing her the way it always had. He gently moved the damp hair from her eyes.

Nothing made sense. If he hadn't been killed in the wreck, where had he been for the past nine months? And what about his car? How was it sitting in its spot in the driveway, good as new? Nova's head was pounding. She had to be dreaming in spite of the pain. Once she'd dreamed she fell off the roof of their house and broke her leg. She'd actually felt it break before she woke up to find it had been a dream.

Somewhere behind her, Nova heard Ethan's voice. He was talking to someone, saying that she'd been confused all morning. Her dad was still leaning over her, his face racked with worry. Dayton Grant. Not in the river. Not dead. The paramedics tried to push him aside, but he refused to step away. Nova reached out and touched his face, praying silently that he was real.

"Mr. Grant, we need to get your daughter on the stretcher." It was one of the paramedics.

He let the paramedic slide his hands under Nova's head, finally relinquishing his grasp.

"I've got her. Step aside, sir," said the paramedic.

"No! Not yet!" Nova screamed, terrified that her dad would disappear again if he let go.

He leaned in and spoke softly to her, as he had when she was small. "It's all right, firefly. I'm here."

There was something off about his expression. He

looked worried, but also confused.

Nova was gently lifted onto the stretcher and loaded into the ambulance with the paramedic beside her. As soon as she was in securely, her dad climbed in and took her hand, giving it a reassuring squeeze.

"Dad, why are you here?" she said barely above a whisper.

He frowned and glanced at the paramedic.

"It's the concussion talking, sir. We'll get her to the hospital and see what's going on."

Her head cleared a little, and she started to panic. "Dad, I'm okay. I don't want to go anywhere. Can't I just stay home with you?" The pain in her head intensified, and she groaned. "Don't make me go."

"You have a good-sized cut on your head and it's bleeding pretty badly. We need to get you stitched up. Please don't be upset," he said carefully.

"Why do I need an ambulance for stitches?" She was quickly approaching hysteria. "I want to stay home!"

"They need to see what else is going on. You've been a little confused today, haven't you? We just want to figure out why."

He leaned in closer, and his familiar scent of aftershave and peppermints filled her nostrils. She tried to control the storm raging in her brain so she could get the words out, anything that would make sense. *Dad, how are you alive? Where were you for the past nine months? Why isn't your car in a landfill somewhere? WHERE HAVE YOU BEEN?*

"Hey, Nova." Ethan stood awkwardly at the ambulance door, his hands shoved in his pockets. "I'll talk to you later, okay?"

Her dad turned and said something to the paramedic, but she couldn't make it out. Then he looked at Ethan. "You know what to do. Call the number I gave you and tell my wife to meet us at the hospital."

Ethan nodded.

"Dad, don't go away," Nova managed.

"I'm not leaving you," he answered softly.

Someone slammed the ambulance door, and the siren started to wail as they pulled out onto the road. Nova began to slip away into a place between sleep and consciousness. She could still hear her dad talking to the others, but she couldn't focus enough to make out what they were saying. All she could connect with was the sound of his voice. *Dad's alive,* she repeated over and over in her head.

She felt the ambulance jostling her as it slowed through intersections and made turns. The ride seemed to be taking forever, and Nova wondered where they were taking her since there was a hospital just a few miles from their house. It didn't occur to her to ask. The inside of the ambulance seemed to close in as she drifted further away.

"Try to stay awake, Nova."

Who said that? She couldn't be sure.

She woke to the sound of her monitor beeping, the shrill pitch making her head throb. She reached up to touch the painful spot on the side of her skull and felt a thick bandage covering it. Fluorescent lights glared overhead, making it impossible to open her eyes.

"Where am I?" she called.

It was her mother who came to her side. She stroked Nova's cheek gently. "It's okay, Nova. I'm here. You're at the hospital in New Haven. You got a nasty bump on the head, but the doctors said you'll be fine."

"Mom." Nova started to cry again. "I saw Dad. His car was in the driveway when I got home. He rode in the ambulance with me."

"It's okay, honey," her mother said, turning the light off over the bed. "He's here."

With the bright fluorescents turned off, Nova could open her eyes. Her dad was sitting in a chair to the right of the hospital bed. When she saw him, a wave of relief washed over her.

He grinned. "How's my girl?"

Nova reached her hand out to touch him, but she pulled it back when she noticed blood on it. She tried to wipe it off on the bed sheet, but it had already dried.

"Don't worry, honey. We'll get you cleaned up. Just rest now." Her mom went to the sink in the room and came back with a damp washcloth, which she gently dabbed against the blood on Nova's hand. "You're going to be fine."

Nova stared at Dayton. "Dad, you're here."

"Of course I am." He leaned forward, frowning slightly.

Nova tried to pull herself together. "Can I go home? I don't need to be in the hospital."

Her parents exchanged looks.

"Honey, the doctor wants to do an MRI, just as a precaution. He doesn't expect to find anything, but it's standard procedure with a head wound."

Celeste Grant was a terrible liar. Nova could see how worried she was.

"Then I can go home?" Nova asked.

"Of course," answered her mom and dad at the same time.

Nova managed a weak smile. She could get through anything as long as her dad was alive. She couldn't stop staring at him. He looked exactly as she remembered. It was as if the last nine months hadn't happened. He was wearing jeans and a dark blue plaid shirt with a gray T-shirt underneath. Nova had always thought her mother was right, that he was more like a big kid than a grown man. Nova had inherited his passion for the mysterious and his love of books, but not his playful personality. Even now, with concern written all over his face, he still had that sparkle in his hazel eyes.

"I love you so much, Dad." Nova's voice broke.

"I love you too, firefly." He smiled when he used his pet name for her.

"I thought I'd never hear you say that again," Nova said, tears spilling down her cheeks.

He looked confused again for a moment, then he pulled her into his arms and held her. "You'll be all right. You've just had a rough day."

"But where have you been?"

"I've been right here. You were sleeping," he assured her, frowning again.

Why didn't he understand? Nova's head was still pounding. She tried to get her thoughts together. Why didn't anyone else think it was shocking that Dayton Grant was back from the dead? Why was she the only one freaking out? *Maybe it never happened. Maybe* that *was the dream and this is reality. Maybe I* am *insane.*

The afternoon ticked by slowly as Nova drifted in and out of consciousness. Her parents took turns at her bedside, offering her hospital juice cups, which tasted more like flavored water than any kind of juice she'd ever had. Still, Nova dutifully drank, which pleased her mother immensely. She hovered over her daughter, constantly fluffing her pillows and rearranging her covers. Nova smiled and thanked her each time, even though any movement made her head hurt even worse. At least her mother was the old Celeste again. Her natural deep brown hair was layered to frame her delicate face and her beautiful dark eyes. This was the mother she'd grown up with, before the accident that had taken both her parents – one to death and one to depression.

Celeste noticed Nova staring at her and smiled. "How are you feeling?" She pulled the covers up again.

"I'm okay, Mom. Just tired." The truth was, her head was pounding. She probably had a concussion from diving into the driveway.

"Try to rest, honey."

Nova closed her eyes and tried not to think about the

pain in her head. All she wanted to do was sleep. She'd found herself in a different reality, been told convincingly by Ethan that she was his girlfriend, split her head open on her driveway, and talked to her dead father. She was exhausted.

She heard her mother step away and whisper something to her dad. They sounded concerned, but Nova couldn't make out what they were saying except for an occasional word here and there. She tried to sleep, even after a nurse came in to check her temperature and left the light on over her bed. Between the glaring light, the splitting headache, and her parents whispering, sleep was nearly impossible. To make matters worse, her monitor was beeping again. Why didn't someone come in and shut it off? It took several minutes, but someone finally slipped in and turned it off before rushing out again.

"Can I get you anything, honey?" her mother asked.

"I'm okay." Nova just wanted to be left alone for now, so after a few minutes, she pretended again to sleep.

Probably thinking she couldn't hear them, Nova's parents stopped being as careful and talked in normal voices.

"Day, she cut school and passed out in our driveway. We need to let them run tests."

"I think we need to talk to her and find out what's going on first." Her dad's voice was strained.

"What kind of explanation could she possibly have for what happened? You don't think she's on drugs, do you?"

"No, I don't think so."

"Well, *something* is going on."

"I know. I'd just like to hear what she has to say before we let them start running tests on her."

"Let's see what the doctor says, okay?" Her mother came back to her bedside and pushed the hair out of her eyes. "I want her to be all right, Day."

"I know, sweetheart." His voice had softened. "We'll do whatever the doctor recommends."

That was the end of the conversation. Some time

later, after Nova had "woken up," her mom turned the TV on, but the noise bothered Nova's head, so she clicked it off again. Nova wondered what had become of Marshall, but for some reason, she didn't ask. A neighbor probably met him at the bus stop. She wanted to talk to him, to ask him about the past nine months. Maybe she could figure out a way to do that without freaking him out, but she would have to be careful. She couldn't let her parents know how messed up things really were.

Finally, at about three o'clock, a nurse who didn't look much older than Nova came in, flipping on the remaining lights in the room.

"I'm Katie. I'm here to take Nova downstairs for her MRI," she said cheerfully, as if having an MRI was good thing, like going for ice cream.

As she was unhooking the monitors, another nurse came in to help lift Nova onto a narrow rolling bed. She was a large, impressive woman wearing an expression that clearly said, "Don't mess with me."

"Only one parent is allowed to go with her," the new nurse announced firmly.

"I'll go, Day," her mother said quickly, taking Nova's hand.

Katie grabbed Nova's chart and IV bag as the other nurse barked orders.

"Just relax, honey," Celeste said softly, glancing at the new nurse, who was obviously in charge. "About how long will this take, uh...?"

"Ursula," offered the burly nurse.

"How long will this take, Ursula?" Celeste asked meekly.

"About an hour and a half. The dad can wait here." She shot Dayton a stern look.

There was clearly no arguing with her, so he dropped into his chair again and gave Nova the thumbs-up. As the nurses were getting the IV situated and tucking the sheet around Nova, he scooted his chair closer and whispered, "Wonder what time she has to be at her night job."

"What?" Nova whispered back, utterly confused.

He glanced at Ursula, then back at Nova. "Prison guard."

Celeste gave him a warning look. "Dayton, behave!" she whispered.

He leaned back in his chair and winked at Nova. She had the overpowering urge to jump off the gurney and hug him. If this was all in her head, she decided right there that she didn't want to get better. She'd just stay crazy.

The nurses finished their preparations and pushed the gurney out into the hallway, knocking over the IV stand and dropping the clipboard holding her chart in the process. After sorting that out, they were on their way. Katie seemed to be having a hard time controlling the bed, because every few feet, it bumped into the wall, making Nova's head hurt worse.

"I probably have a concussion you know," Nova grumbled when the gurney smacked into the wall for the fourth or fifth time.

"This one has a stuck wheel. We're trying to get it to behave, but it has a mind of its own," Katie said, trying unsuccessfully to push the bed in a straight line.

As they moved down the hallway, bumping into something every few feet, Ursula kept asking Nova questions like what day it was, what year it was, where she went to school, and so on. Each time Nova answered correctly, her mother looked relieved.

"I'm okay, Mom," Nova said, closing her eyes. "I just want to sleep."

"Why is she so tired?" Her mother's voice sounded far away.

It was Katie who answered. "It's typical with a concussion. She hit her head pretty hard."

Nova must have drifted off, because the next thing

she knew, the nurses were helping her onto a sliding bench attached to the MRI machine. She felt a brief moment of panic.

"Just keep your eyes closed," said Ursula in a much kinder voice than before.

Nova closed her eyes and tried to relax as the bench slid forward and the machine began making a series of noises. It wasn't as bad as she had imagined, so she used the time to plan her strategy. She had no idea what had happened to alter her reality, but it had changed and she had to deal with that. The first thing she wanted to do was get back to the house to see what else was different. She also had to come up with a story that would explain her "confusion" and fainting in the driveway since everyone but her seemed to think this life was normal. She needed to be cautious about what she said from this point on. The last thing she wanted was to be stuck in the hospital or worse, a psych ward.

They must have changed gurneys for the ride back, because she didn't smack into the wall even once. Katie made sure Nova was securely tucked into her hospital bed before leaving the room and closing the door behind her.

Almost immediately, Nova drifted off to sleep again and dreamed that she was at her dad's funeral, looking into his empty casket. Except now it wasn't empty. Dayton Grant lay there with his hands folded neatly over his chest. He looked artificial, like a wax figure. Her mother's gold pendant was peeking out from under the lapel of his suit. At the funeral, they had each put something in the casket before it was lowered into the ground. Her dad had given the pendant to her mother on their first anniversary. Nova had chosen a picture she'd drawn when she was five years old. For some reason, her dad had always cherished it, even framing it to display on his desk. Marshall's choice had been the most heartbreaking. It was a picture taken on their father-and-son camping trip just three weeks before the accident.

Nova tried to spot the other items inside the casket,

but they were nowhere to be seen. *Where's my drawing, Dad?* She reached out cautiously to touch his hand.

He opened his eyes and winked. "I guess the joke's on them, firefly."

CHAPTER 6

Nova was awakened, in a cold sweat, by a persistent knocking on the door. Her eyes searched the hospital room frantically. "Where's Dad?"

"Right here," he answered from the bench behind her hospital bed.

Her mother stood at the door, talking to someone. She stepped aside, and Dayton jumped up as an inappropriately cheerful gentleman in a suit came striding into the room. He shook hands with Nova's parents, introducing himself as Dr. Donovan, before turning his attention to her.

"Well, you must be Nova." He grabbed a chair and pulled it over to the side of the bed. It made an awful noise as he dragged it across the floor, and Nova winced.

Dr. Donovan sat in the chair and leaned forward. "We've had quite a busy day today, haven't we!"

It wasn't really a question, so Nova just looked at him.

"Would you like to tell me about it?"

Not really. She knew exactly who this guy was. Shrink. But she'd had time in the MRI to think about this. She was ready for him.

"I'm really sorry for worrying everybody," Nova said sweetly.

"Well, that's all right, young lady. Maybe you can explain what you and Evan were doing walking home from school this morning instead of going to class. Let's start there." Dr. Donovan leaned forward and waited.

"It's Ethan," Nova corrected.

Dr. Donovan looked slightly annoyed, then his false smile returned. "All right, *Ethan.*"

"Ethan and I just decided to cut class today. I'm sorry I caused so much trouble." Nova tried to seem sincere when what she wanted to say was, "My whole world is screwed up and my dad's back from the dead, so get out of my face."

"We aren't angry, Nova. We're just trying to figure out why you were confused before you fell." Dr. Donovan leaned in a little closer.

He had a stain on his tie that looked as though it had been there for a while. Maybe there wasn't a Mrs. Donovan around to point it out. Or maybe there *was* a Mrs. Donovan, and she was in a loony bin somewhere because being married to Dr. Cheerful had driven her over the edge.

"You can talk to me, Nova." His artificial smiled widened.

Nova felt a chill go up her spine. Her situation was scary enough without having to sit in a hospital gown being grilled by some shrink. She cleared her throat, still trying to sound contrite. "It was supposed to be a joke. Ethan didn't want to cut school and I did, so I made up a story. I didn't know he'd believe me."

"That was a mean thing to do, don't you think?"

Nova found his intense eye contact unnerving. Had he blinked even once since they started talking? She averted her eyes. "Yeah. Sorry."

"So how do you explain the fact that you passed out?"

"I didn't eat dinner last night or breakfast this morning." Nova tried to swallow the lump in her throat.

"So you think you were weak from hunger?" He still wasn't blinking.

"Yeah. I guess."

From the look on her mother's face, Nova's explanation was working, at least for her, but her dad was eyeing her suspiciously.

The doctor had finally wiped the smile off his face. "Why did you ask your boyfriend if your father was alive? You really scared him."

How did he know that? When had he talked to Ethan? Nova tried not to let him see that he had thrown her a little. "Like I said, it was a joke. Sorry." She attempted to look ashamed.

Dr. Donovan leaned in closer still and lowered his voice. His breath smelled like garlic, and Nova felt queasy again. "You seem to have an explanation for everything, don't you?" He was definitely suspicious. "Is there anything going on at school you'd like to talk about?"

Nova shook her head, which was a mistake since any movement made it ache even more. It was hard to focus on what he was saying when her head was throbbing and all she could think about was the fact that he still hadn't blinked. How could someone even do that – keep their eyes open indefinitely until they dried into a couple of raisins?

"How about that boyfriend of yours? What's his name? Evan?"

"Ethan," Nova corrected again. Was he doing that deliberately? She looked him straight in his dry eyes.

"Right, Ethan. Anything you'd like to tell me about Ethan?"

"No." Fortunately Nova remembered not to shake her head.

"All right, young lady." Dr. Donovan stood up and pushed his chair back. It made the awful screeching noise again. "Let's see what the MRI shows." He shook hands with Nova's parents. "I'll be back in a bit." He looked at Nova and said, "No more skipping meals, young lady. I hope you see how foolish that is. And no more *lying*." He looked at her pointedly, then turned and left the room.

After an awkward silence, Dayton cleared his throat and turned to his wife. "Maybe you should step outside and call Marshall at the Jameson's. He's probably scared."

"You're right. Poor guy's probably very worried. Back in a minute, honey." She kissed Nova on the forehead then left the room.

Dayton looked at his daughter and frowned. "I think we need to talk. What's going on with you? Is there something else you want to talk about?"

"Did you notice Dr. Donovan didn't blink the whole time he was here?"

"What?" He tried unsuccessfully to maintain his stern demeanor. "Really? Not once?"

"Not once," Nova said, smiling in spite of her head.

He chuckled. "Okay, that's not what I meant when I said we needed to talk."

Nova suddenly felt like crying. She wanted so badly to tell her dad everything, but she couldn't bring herself to do it. What could she say anyway? *Well, Dad, you've been dead for nine months. We never found your body, but we had a funeral anyway. I hope you liked the picture I put in your coffin.* There was no way to tell him the truth and make it sound believable. And falling apart would only make things worse. She'd have to figure it out on her own.

"I'm sorry I caused so much trouble. I didn't mean to. I just want to go home and forget about today. I don't know how this became such a big deal."

He frowned. "Well for one thing, you have five stitches in your head from passing out in our driveway. That's a pretty big deal. We could start with that." He wasn't going to let this go away.

Nova felt as if her head was about to burst. "Can we at least talk about it later? I'm so tired and my head hurts."

"Okay, later. But we *are* going to talk," he said firmly, plopping down in the chair next to her bed again.

Celeste returned carrying a prepackaged sandwich and apple juice. "Marshall's fine." She smiled, obviously relieved. "The Jamesons got a new puppy and that's all he could talk about." She pulled the rolling tray over to the bed and set the sandwich and juice on it for Nova.

"Thank God. I'm starving." Nova unwrapped the sandwich and shoved a corner into her mouth.

"Goodness, slow down." Her mom laughed.

Nova was eating the last of her sandwich when another doctor walked in carrying her chart. "Good news. The MRI was clear. No tumors or blood clots."

"So other than the cut on her head, she's fine?" her mother asked hopefully.

"She does have a mild concussion, so you'll need to keep an eye on her," answered the doctor. "As long as she takes it easy, I think it's okay for her to go home, especially since Dr. Donovan says he can't find a reason to keep her here. You'll have to bring her back in two weeks so we can see how she's doing and take the stitches out." He hesitated, looking at Dayton. "I'm a big fan, by the way. I've read all your books."

"Thanks." Her dad smiled politely, but Nova could tell he was uncomfortable. He never had been one to enjoy attention from adoring fans, especially when he met them on the street, or in this case, in the hospital.

The doctor was holding Nova's chart, a pen in his hand. Nova half expected him to ask her dad to autograph it, but after an awkward moment, he backed toward the door. "Well, take care of her. We don't want her overdoing it."

"We'll make sure she takes it easy," Dayton said, and Celeste nodded.

About thirty minutes later, they were on their way home. Nova leaned her head against the seat and mulled over her predicament. Her dad hadn't died in the accident. She could accept that. She could even accept that the car had somehow miraculously been put back together. But why didn't anyone else remember he'd been gone for the last nine months?

Nova closed her eyes, trying not to think anymore. The pain in her head was relentless, and the car ride disagreed with her stomach. She wasn't sure she'd make it home without throwing up. Her mom was chattering away in the front seat, oblivious to the fact that Nova was about to splatter a partially digested turkey-and-cheese sandwich all over the Volvo's leather seats.

"How much longer?" Nova asked weakly.

"Just about there," her mother assured her. "I'm going to call the school in the morning and let them know you won't be in this week."

Nova took several deep breaths to quell her growing nausea. *Thank God,* she thought when they finally turned into the driveway. Her dad opened her car door and helped her into the house and down the hall to her room.

She sat on the side of the bed and kicked off her shoes. "I'm okay, Dad. You don't have to hover. I just want to lie down." Nova started to tear up again but managed to fight it off. She needed to figure out a way to stop crying every time she looked at him.

He lingered at the door for a moment, then turned and walked up the hall to his office. Nova heard the door close behind him. She lay down on the bed, carefully pulled her pillow under her aching head, and stared at the ceiling. Wait…where was the spider? Ignoring the pain, Nova stood on the bed, straining to see the spot where the smudge had been. It wasn't there. Not even the runaway leg.

Her mother appeared at her door, carrying a glass of water. "Nova, what on earth are you doing?"

"I'm looking for my spider," she responded without thinking.

"You have a concussion! Get down from there right

now!"

"Sorry, Mom." Nova sat down, still gazing at the ceiling in case she'd missed it somehow.

Celeste walked to the side of the bed and looked at the ceiling. "I don't see a spider, honey."

"It's gone," Nova said, surprised at how disappointed she felt. She just wanted *something* to be the same, so she'd know for sure she wasn't crazy, that the other life had been real.

Her mom stood by the bed for a moment, watching her. "Maybe we should call the doctor."

"No, it's okay. I thought I saw a spider before. That's all." Nova lay back down and pulled the pillow under her head again. "I'm really tired."

Celeste put the water on the nightstand and sat on the edge of the bed. "Are you sure you're all right, honey?"

"I'm sure, Mom. Just sleepy."

She leaned over and kissed Nova's forehead. "Okay. Get some rest, but call me if you need anything."

After she left, the events of the day flew around Nova's mind like a nightmarish tornado. She needed to sleep but wouldn't have been surprised if she never did again. It really bothered her that the spider was gone. How could everything have changed so much? It was as if the past nine months had never happened. And how could she explain Ethan? In spite of the questions swirling around, her brain eventually shut down and she fell soundly asleep until Marshall shook her awake.

"Hey, Nova. I heard you tried to break the driveway with your head," he whispered, then giggled at his own joke.

"That's real funny, Marshall." Nova looked at the clock on the nightstand. It read ten o'clock. "Don't you have school tomorrow?"

"Yeah," he whispered again, his eyes darting to the doorway. "I just wanted to see how bad you got hurt." He looked genuinely concerned.

"I'm okay, kid. Go to bed."

Marshall didn't move. "Your bandage has a little bit of blood on it."

"I know. It's okay."

"I bet you're gonna have a wicked scar!"

Nova smiled. "You think so?"

"Yeah." Marshall turned to leave.

"Hey, kid." Nova pushed up on one elbow. "Do you know Ethan?"

He looked back at her. "Duh."

"I heard you two play video games sometimes. Was he over here yesterday?"

"You know he was." Marshall frowned. "I'm not playing with him anymore though. He cheats."

"What do you mean he cheats?"

"He lets me win. He thinks he's being nice, but that's still cheating. Tell him not to do that, okay?"

"Okay." She felt the hairs stand up on the back of her neck. So Ethan had been telling the truth.

CHAPTER 7

Nova slept for the rest of the night, waking only when her mother came in to check on her every two hours. By the next morning, she was feeling a little better. At about ten o'clock, her mom breezed in to announce that the principal had decided that, under the circumstances, Nova's presence was not required for the remaining week and a half until summer break.

"So you're officially on vacation, honey." She gingerly brushed Nova's hair back from her face. "My beautiful girl. I'm so glad you're okay. You really gave us a scare."

"I know, Mom," Nova responded groggily.

"It's okay. I want you to take it easy today. Doctor's orders." She leaned down and kissed Nova on the forehead. "I'll make you some breakfast when you're ready."

"Thanks. Where's Dad?"

"In his office. Where else?" She laughed.

Nova tried to sleep, but she couldn't relax. She wanted to talk to her dad, but he stayed in his office, only occasionally coming out briefly before retreating again. His behavior was strange, as though he was worried about something other than her episode the previous day. He stuck his head in her room each time he ventured out, but he seemed on edge and avoided eye contact. Coming back from the dead had apparently affected him.

For the rest of the day, her mother made sure she did nothing that would reopen her head wound or aggravate her concussion. No reading. No video games. She wasn't even allowed to watch TV while her brain healed. There was nothing to do but lie around thinking about her bizarre change in circumstances.

Ethan kept trying to reach her, but she managed to avoid talking to him by pretending to be asleep when he called. She wasn't sure if she could trust him not to run to her parents and report every word that came out of her mouth. He obviously had no idea what she was going through. He'd been humoring her, thinking she would snap back to normal any second. Either that or he thought she was nuts. As crazy as it sounded, she had decided that nothing was wrong with her mentally. Something real had happened to change her world. She didn't know why, but she was absolutely certain of it. She just couldn't figure out why she was the only one who'd noticed.

The rest of the Grant family treated Nova as if she was made of glass. They seemed to be going out of their way not to upset her. At dinner that evening, they talked about meaningless, ordinary things. No one mentioned her "breakdown," or the hospital, or school, or Ethan, or *anything* important. They apparently thought she was on the verge of falling apart at any given moment. Nova just wanted them to treat her normally, but the atmosphere around the table was anything but normal.

When they were nearly finished eating, the subject of Marshall's fourth grade orientation came up. The principal had decided that when school started in September, the rising fourth graders, or "juniors," at Samuel Clemens Elementary School would be allowed to choose an elective class to attend after lunch every day. The purpose, as he explained it, was to prepare them for middle school. The whole school – teachers, parents and students – was buzzing about it. Some weren't sure they liked the idea, but Marshall was over the moon. He had a list of possible electives, and they discussed the merits of each one at great length. The lively conversation finally felt like home, everyone laughing and talking at once. It reminded Nova of her old life, before the accident.

The playful Dayton Grant was suddenly back as well. She caught him smiling at her as he'd done a thousand times before. He was the dad she remembered. She hoped this turn of events would last, but after dinner, his mood changed and he retreated to his office again, shutting the door.

When she passed it on the way to her room a little while later, he was still in there. She listened at the door. No sound. Why was he spending so much time alone in his office? Was something going on in there that would explain his changed behavior and her new reality? Nova was anxious to find out, but she couldn't search his office effectively after he went to bed because her parents' bedroom was right next door. Any noise would travel easily into the next room and she would be caught. As difficult as it had been to explain passing out in the driveway, it would be even harder to explain searching her dad's office in the middle of the night. They would surely think she had lost it and would haul her back to see Dr. Cheerful at the hospital.

"No, thank you," Nova said under her breath. She would just have to be patient until an opportunity presented itself. She hoped when that time came, she'd find some answers.

On Friday, Nova would finally get her chance. Sometime after dinner Thursday night, her parents decided that they would both go to Marshall's school for his orientation the next morning. Nova had insisted that she'd be fine alone for those few hours, and it worked. The orientation was scheduled from nine thirty until noon, with lunch provided afterward. Nova would have the whole morning to herself, so she'd finally get the opportunity to look around her dad's office. The more she thought about it, the more certain she felt that he was hiding something in there.

Every time Nova let her mind go back to the time before this past week, back to her other life, she felt physically ill. She decided she had to embrace this new reality. After all, this new life was better. Her dad hadn't died in the river. He was alive and well. Her mother was the way she had been before his death, smiling and happy. She didn't dye her hair every few weeks and look in the paper for jobs she wasn't going to apply for. She was the old mom, the mom before the accident. But Nova still needed answers.

***

The next morning, the Grants left the house for Samuel Clemens Elementary School at eight thirty in the morning. It was much earlier than necessary, but Marshall was driving them crazy.

"I want to sign up for my elective before all the good ones are gone!" He must have said a dozen times that morning. Nova was still in bed, but Marshall was talking so loudly that she could hear every word. Her parents peeked in on her before they left, but she pretended to still be sleeping.

"Do you think it's okay to leave her, Day?" her mom whispered.

"She'll be fine. She'll probably sleep most of the time." he replied.

Nova heard footsteps down the hall but sensed that she was still being watched, so she continued to lie perfectly still, breathing evenly. After a minute or two, she heard someone gently close her door. Nova was sure it was her dad who had stayed to make sure she was really asleep. He'd picked up a tack in his shoe while they were at the hospital, and she heard it clicking as he walked back up the hall.

After she heard the Mustang fire up, Nova stayed in bed for a few minutes, listening intently for any sound that would indicate someone had stayed behind after all. The house was silent. Slowly, she got out of bed, tiptoed to her door, and opened it quietly. She stood there listening. Nothing.

Nova bolted up the hall to her dad's office, but when she grabbed the doorknob, it wouldn't budge. Locked! He rarely locked the office, except during the month before Christmas when her parents hid presents in there. Fortunately, she'd stashed a key away when she was nine years old so she could sneak in to check out her Christmas gifts. After a few years of no surprises, she'd quit looking. But the key was probably still where she'd hidden it. At least she hoped it was. It was possible that was one of the things that had changed in this reality.

Nova sprinted back to her room and got down on her hands and knees by her bed. Leaning over made her head throb a little, but she didn't care. She held her breath and reached underneath the bed, feeling carefully along the edge while praying it would be there. At first she felt nothing but rough wood, then her fingers encountered the cool metal key, taped securely to the frame. She let out a sigh of relief and yanked it free, glancing at the poster on her wall as she sat up. One-eyed George stared at her disapprovingly.

"Who asked you?" Nova muttered.

She trotted back up the hall to the office and inserted the key into the lock, turning until she heard it trip. Quietly, she opened the door, still nervous that her father might actually be in there, waiting for her. Maybe the new Dayton Grant could read her mind and knew what she was up to. Since he'd been able to change her reality, anything was possible. But the office was empty. She took a deep breath and stepped inside.

The shades were drawn, leaving only dim light and shadows in the room, but Nova was familiar with the layout and confidently closed the door. How many times had she come in here after her dad died, just wanting to be close to him in some way? She would sit at his desk and breathe in his smell. It was funny how the room could retain his essence – his favorite aftershave mixed with peppermints from the bowl on his desk. He must have eaten a dozen a day.

She'd spent hours in his office after he died, imagining that any minute he could walk through the door. "What are you doing in here, firefly?" he'd say. But he never came home. She shook her head. *Dad isn't dead*, she reminded herself. It was odd that she still missed him.

"Better get started," she said out loud.

CHAPTER 8

Nova surveyed her surroundings. Dark wood shelves, crammed with books and trinkets from all over the world, lined three of the walls from floor to ceiling. Her dad was always on the lookout for ideas, and much of his inspiration came from the volumes and trinkets he collected on his travels.

After a trip to Zurich, he had written his first best seller, *Other World*, about a team of young scientists who discovered a way to travel between universes in order to save their dying world.

An ornate eighteenth century bronze box that he'd found at a market in Kathmandu had inspired his second best seller, *The Tibetan Box*. In the story, the box had the ability to transport the owner, Sebastian Worthington, anywhere in time. All he had to do was to put an item from a specific time period into the box and fasten the clasp. He always kept a newly minted coin with him in order to return to the present time.

Dayton had always had a particular affinity for time travel and that was a recurring theme in his writing and the books he collected, but it wasn't the only subject that inspired him. He had collected books about parallel universes, alternate realities, and alien worlds as well. With his insatiable curiosity, all of it intrigued him.

Nova had loved spending time with her dad in his office, helping him sort through his piles of research. He took great pleasure in the fact that his daughter shared his passion for science fiction, especially since the rest of the family had no interest in the subject. He had promised that when she was older, he would take her along on one of his "fact-finding missions" as he called them. They had finally agreed that it would be the summer she turned sixteen.

How many hours had they sat across from each other at his desk, planning their trip? Too many to count. They had poured over maps and planned every step of their itinerary. She wondered if she'd still get to take that trip with him, since she would be turning sixteen in a month. Or had this Dayton Grant never made that promise?

Nova scanned the room again. She had no idea what she was looking for, but it seemed logical to start with the massive antique desk that dominated the middle of the room. A heavy brass lamp sat in the right hand corner. She reached under the shade and pulled the chain, instantly bathing the desktop in warm light.

"Okay, this isn't something you see every day," she said.

Her dad's desk was clean. There were no papers strewn about, no half-eaten sandwich or three-day-old cup of coffee. He was not the neatest person on the planet, so why was his desk spotless? Never in her life had she seen it like this.

"So Dad comes back from the grave a neat freak?" she muttered. A shiver ran up her spine.

Glancing at his bowl of mints, she noticed it was full of empty wrappers. At least that hadn't changed, which she found oddly comforting. If he didn't like mints anymore, there would be only one logical reason. He was some kind of imposter.

"I'm sorry, Mr. Grant. You failed the peppermint test and that's never wrong." Nova giggled in spite of herself.

She plopped down in her dad's chair and pulled on the middle drawer. Locked. Why couldn't anything just be easy? Nova tried all the drawers, but none of them would open. Like the office door, her dad never locked his desk. At least he hadn't before the accident. Apparently this Dayton Grant wasn't as trusting.

She tried her best to force the middle drawer open by grabbing the edges and jerking as hard as she could. Breaking it was probably not a good plan, but desperation was setting in. Who knew when she'd get another chance like this? Suddenly remembering the crowbar hanging on the wall in the garage, she dashed off to get it, nearly knocking off a piece of the doorframe on her return. She hoped no one would notice the deep scratch since it was above eye level, but there was nothing she could do about it.

"No turning back now," Nova muttered as she inserted the tip of the crowbar between the front of the drawer and top of the desk and slowly put her weight against it.

At first, nothing happened. The old desk was apparently going to put up a fight. She kept putting more and more pressure on the crowbar until finally the drawer popped open, accompanied by the slightly sickening sound of the lock breaking – another thing she hoped she wouldn't have to explain. Nova tried her best to replace the splintered piece, but it was no use. She'd just have to press on and deal with the consequences later.

The drawer contained mostly the normal odds and ends you would find in any office: pens, pencils, paper clips, business cards from people he had met somewhere, a stapler and extra staples. Nova didn't care about any of that because she'd found what she needed. Keys. Lots and lots of keys. The drawer was full of them, all shapes and sizes, old rusty ones and shiny new ones. There must have been at least thirty or forty. There weren't that many locks in the house, maybe not on their whole street, so what could he possibly need them all for?

One by one, she tried each key in the bottom right drawer, with no luck. Nova glanced up and noticed the plaque over the office door. She found it comforting that this Dayton Grant had chosen the same one, although she'd never paid much attention to it until now. It was a quote from *The Ancient Mariner*:

"Water, water everywhere and nary a drop to drink."

What a sick joke. *I guess that means none of these keys are gonna work.* She tried key number twenty-four. Surprisingly, it hesitated a little then produced a satisfying *click* as the drawer popped open.

"Ha!" she yelled, breaking the silence and startling herself.

She stood perfectly still for a moment, listening for any noise that would tell her she was no longer alone in the house. The only sound was a clock ticking. Nova looked around the room until she spotted an old and unfamiliar mantel clock on the shelf behind her. *One more little thing that's different, I guess.* She wondered how many subtle differences she would notice if she really paid attention. She shook her head and turned her attention to the open drawer.

Inside were two large file folders, so overstuffed that Nova couldn't figure out how her dad had managed to fit them into the drawer in the first place. Getting them out would be tough. The folders weren't labeled in any way, so she wrestled the closest one out of the drawer, careful not to spill its contents all over the floor. When she had successfully extracted it, she plopped the file on the desk and leafed through. Inside were pages and pages of notes in her father's familiar script. Nova recognized scenarios that had been used in several of her dad's elaborate science fiction stories, but some ideas were unfamiliar, maybe planned for a future novel. She wondered if her dad would eventually have used them to write another best seller.

Her brain kept going back to her other life, the one where her dad was dead. Holding the pages made her feel the pain of his loss all over again. And yet, he wasn't gone. He was at Samuel Clemens Elementary School right now, hobnobbing with other parents of rising fourth graders. For the hundredth time, she wondered how that was possible.

Nova continued to flip through the pages, realizing that she'd better hurry if she was going to see everything. She moved on to the second folder, which contained mostly sketches. Dayton Grant was not only an accomplished writer; he was also a talented artist. His sketches were used on the covers of his books and occasionally appeared in the actual text. Once again, Nova recognized some of them, but others were new to her. How could he bear to leave such wonderful drawings crammed in an overstuffed file folder under lock and key?

About halfway through the file, she came across a series of sketches of a young girl with shoulder-length golden-blond hair and hazel eyes. There were at least a dozen in a row, all of the same girl – her imaginary friend, Allie. Why had her dad drawn her over and over? Maybe he had intended to use her in one of his stories. Nova held up a sketch, examining it closely.

"Allie looks kind of like…Marshall…and Dad," she muttered, feeling an odd sense of déjà vu.

The little girl did look a lot like Marshall, but there were subtle differences. She had delicate features like Nova, but not Nova's dark hair and brown eyes. People had always said that Nova resembled her mother. "You two look more like sisters than mother and daughter." How many times had she heard that? Nova studied the girl in the picture. There was a hint of a dimple in her left cheek, and her mouth turned up slightly on the edges, just like Marshall's. Nova stared at the drawing, taking in every detail. *She could be my sister, a cross between Mom and Dad.* She shivered even though the room wasn't the least bit chilly.

She laid the drawing on the desk, intending to keep that one, and carefully replaced the other sketches and notes. Getting the bulging file folders back in the drawer was tricky, but she managed and heard the satisfying click as the drawer closed completely. Most likely her dad wouldn't notice anything amiss. Nova was feeling satisfied with herself until she remembered the broken lock on the middle drawer.

Oh well. If she got busted, it had better be for a good reason. She glanced at the clock behind the desk. *Ten forty!* How had so much time passed? She had barely seen anything. She'd spent too much time reading the notes and looking at the sketches. She'd have to hurry if she was going to get through the rest of the drawers before her parents returned with Marshall.

Nova grabbed the key and locked the drawer with the folders, then she turned her attention to the other side of the desk, once again choosing the large drawer on the bottom. When she inserted the key, it caught before it grudgingly turned. Inside were hanging files containing more folders. The first one was labeled "Dayton Samuels Grant." It contained her father's birth certificate and passport. Nova leafed through the pages of his passport, marveling at his extensive travels represented by dozens of stamps. After his passport was the letter he had received from his publisher when he sold his first book. There were also photos of him as a child and a handwritten story, obviously penned when he was a little boy.

The short story was called "The Adventures of Day Grant." It was about a boy who traveled from world to world. In each world, his family was the same, but they lived in different houses and had different lives. Nova marveled at the fact that, even as a child, her father had been a gifted writer. She also noticed with a chill that this story was eerily similar to her real life.

The next file was labeled, "Celeste Richardson Grant." Nova looked in her mom's file and found her birth certificate and passport as well. Other than those items, her file was empty. Nova wasn't surprised. Her mother kept most of her personal things in a box under her bed. She had remarked more than once that Dayton was to leave her things alone, since the unfortunate items that found their way into his office were rarely seen again. Sometimes her mother teased her dad, calling his office "the black hole."

The next folder in the drawer was labeled, "Nova Eleanor Grant." Inside were her birth certificate, hospital bracelet, school records, and several pictures she'd drawn for her dad when she was a little girl. He'd been sick for several months – she couldn't remember exactly what had been wrong with him – but he wouldn't leave the house or talk to anyone. Nova remembered him being very sad and that she was the only one he had wanted to spend time with. He would sit in his office all day, waiting for her to return from kindergarten. As soon as she came in the door, she'd hear him call, "Is that you, firefly?" Nova could remember it as if it were yesterday. That was when he'd started calling her firefly. She would run up the hall into his office, and he would scoop her up and hold her.

Nova had loved the office even then. She loved the smell of her dad and the books. It sounded funny to say she loved her dad's smell, but it was true. Those were some of the most vivid memories of her childhood. The desk in his office had a slide-out panel on the front, and she would sit on a pillow in a chair across from him and color for hours. She would draw picture after picture, trying so hard to make him happy.

One of her pictures was of their family standing under a tree. Floating above the figures that represented the four of them was another figure, an angel with crude wings and yellow hair. Her dad had loved that picture so much he'd framed it and displayed it on his desk. Nova didn't know why that drawing had pleased him so much more than all the others, but it had obviously been special to him. When the time had come to choose something for his empty coffin, that was what she had chosen – the picture from his desk. The picture that was now nowhere to be seen.

Again, Nova had to purposely turn her attention back to the task at hand. There were two files left in the drawer. She pulled out the first one and saw that it was labeled, "Marshall Sheldon Grant." The contents were very much like hers: a birth certificate, his hospital bracelet, school report cards, and a few other papers. She set it aside and pulled out the last folder. Suddenly, she felt as if all the air had been sucked out of her lungs. This couldn't be right! Nova's heart was in her throat. The label read, "Alana Marie Grant."

CHAPTER 9

Nova stared at the folder for at least two minutes, afraid to look inside. Finally she held her breath and opened it. There was a birth certificate just like hers, except it read: Alana Marie Grant. Nova grabbed her own folder again, her eyes darting back and forth between the two until her tears blurred the words to the point that she couldn't read any longer. She had a twin sister, born exactly sixteen minutes after her.

Nova could barely breathe. How could she have a twin and not know it? Why had no one ever even mentioned Alana? What had happened to her? The answer came on the next page in Alana's file – a death certificate stating that Alana Marie Grant died at 8:04 a.m. on July 12, just twenty-one minutes after she was born.

Tears streamed down Nova's cheeks. "Alana."

When she said the name out loud, a fleeting image jumped into her head. A little girl with golden hair was splashing in a pool and laughing. "Come on, Nova! Jump in!"

A chill went up her spine. It felt like a memory, not something she'd conjured in her head. She closed her eyes and waited.

"Nova, jump!" The little girl's voice was familiar, as though she'd heard it many times.

She tried to hang on to the image, but it was gone as suddenly as it had appeared. Nova stared at the folder for several minutes, trying hard to summon it again. Nothing.

Maybe there was something to the theory that said twins were eternally connected somehow, their spirits inseparable. She had heard of documentaries dedicated to that idea, featuring sets of twins who instinctively knew when something was wrong with the other, even if they were separated by thousands of miles. Was her sister's spirit following her around, still connected to her in some way? For some reason, she found that idea appealing, not scary at all.

Nova looked at Alana's birth certificate again. It would have been wonderful to have a twin sister to grow up with. She loved Marshall, but it wasn't the same. They were almost seven years apart. Why had her parents never told her about Alana? Why had they never taken her to see where her sister was buried or explained the circumstances of her death? And when Nova thought of her sister, why did she conjure up an image of a little girl with golden hair, a little girl who looked an awful lot like her imaginary friend?

"Alana," she whispered, hoping for another fleeting image. She closed her eyes and concentrated.

There she was again, in the water. "Nova, jump!"

Nova could see herself cautiously stepping into the water from the shallow end. Again, the scene faded until there was nothing there. But it had felt real, like a memory.

She was desperate for answers, but there were no details on the death certificate. Maybe something else in the file would explain what had happened to her sister. Nova leafed through and saw several hospital bills and a receipt from the company that had supplied Alana's headstone. On the receipt were details about the stone that had been ordered. It was to read, "Alana Marie Grant, beloved daughter and sister."

Beloved sister? And yet Nova's parents had never mentioned her. On their dresser was a photo of her mother when she was pregnant. Nova had always loved that picture because her mom had said, "That's when I was expecting you." But she had really been expecting Nova *and* Alana.

The last thing in Alana's folder was a sketch, drawn in her dad's familiar style. It was of a little girl with golden-blond hair and expressive hazel eyes. It was the same girl that her father had drawn over and over. Only at the bottom of this sketch were the words, "Alana, five years old. My angel."

Nova looked at the drawing she'd laid on the desk. It was definitely the same girl. How had her dad drawn pictures of a five-year-old Alana when she'd died as a baby? And why did she just happen to look like Nova's imaginary friend, Allie? Nova studied the sketch.

"How did I imagine you, sister?" Nova whispered, shuddering.

While she was shocked at discovering Alana, that fact did nothing to explain her own bizarre circumstances. She had to keep looking.

"What else are you hiding Dad?" she muttered.

Nova replaced the files, locked the drawer, and froze. Someone was knocking on the back door. She stayed perfectly still. The office window was open slightly, and any sound she made would surely travel the short distance to the unwelcome guest on the back porch.

A minute or so passed and she started to think that the intruder had given up and left. Then the knocking started again, more insistent this time. Nova crept to the window and tried to see who it was without moving the shade too much. Just as she looked, the person stepped closer to the door and out of sight. The knocking began again, much louder this time. It finally stopped, and the visitor stepped back into view. Ethan! What was he doing here?

Nova dropped the key on the desk and raced up the hall

into the kitchen. Her nerves were already frayed from the events of the week and the discovery in her father's office. The last thing she needed was to have to pretend everything was normal to Ethan.

Flinging the door open, she nearly screamed, "Ethan, what…why are you here?"

"Why haven't you returned my calls?" he demanded.

"I guess I just ha-haven't felt up to it," Nova stammered.

"I've been worried sick about you! Your dad was weird at the hospital and told me to go home. Then some doctor grabbed me in the hallway. You haven't called me. You haven't been at school. What's going on?"

"Nothing's going on. I'm fine. Go away!" Nova started to slam the door in his face.

"Wait! That's it? That's all I get from you after cutting school to help you and then being totally freaked out wondering what happened? That's the best you can do?"

"Okay, I'm sorry. It was just a joke to get out of school. It went too far." Nova's head throbbed.

"A joke? Are you serious?" Ethan's wounded expression was almost too much to bear.

But what if she told him the truth? Would he repeat every word to her parents…or, God forbid, Dr. Cheerful? "Just go home. I don't want to hurt you."

He put his arms around her and held her. Nova could hear his heart beating furiously. "I know something's wrong. Please let me help you. I promise, whatever it is, you can trust me."

Nova felt herself starting to crumble. She needed someone to talk to so badly. She pulled back and looked into his face. "If any of this gets back to my parents, we're through. I'll say you lied and never talk to you again. Do you understand? You have to promise me. Just between us, okay?"

Ethan nodded, still wearing a grave expression. Nova

didn't know how much she should tell him, but once she started talking, it all gushed out. She told him about waking up and finding that her world had changed and her dad was alive. She told him about her time in the hospital and her plan to find out what had happened. She told him about searching her dad's office and finding Alana's file. Nova had to take a second to catch her breath several times before she was through, but it was a tremendous relief to say it all out loud.

Ethan listened intently without saying a word. When she was through, he just stood there looking at her with an expression that was impossible to read. Moments passed, and still he didn't speak. The silence was crushing. She shouldn't have trusted him, she thought frantically. He thought she was crazy, and who could blame him? It sounded crazy. She had a dead twin sister no one had ever mentioned. Her dad was also dead, but now he wasn't anymore. None of her friends were the same, and she had a boyfriend she barely knew. Who would believe all of that?

Nova knew she was about to become hysterical again, but she could do nothing to stop it. She burst into tears, snapping Ethan out of his trance.

He grabbed her by the shoulders and shook her gently. " Look at me. I'm here. We're gonna figure this out." Ethan wrapped his arms around her again and held her while she sobbed into his chest. "It's gonna be okay. I don't know exactly what's going on, but I believe you. I'm in."

Nova felt a tremendous sense of relief. "Ethan, what's happened to me?"

"I don't know, but we'll find out." He sounded so reassuring.

She relaxed and let him hold her. How had she never seen this side of him before? Why had they never been friends in her other life? Maybe she really hadn't had another life. Even if she had, it didn't matter now. She didn't want to go back to it. In that life, her dad was dead and she didn't have Ethan. No, if she had a choice she would stay here, safe in Ethan's arms.

After a few minutes, Nova collected herself enough to ask, "How did you get to the hospital? You weren't in the ambulance." She wiped her eyes on his shirt but he didn't seem to mind.

"Your mom showed up at your house right after you left. She actually passed the ambulance on your street. I rode with her."

"But how did you get home?'

"My mom picked me up. She blew a fuse when I called her and told her where I was." Ethan chuckled. "Nothing compared to your mom though. Talk about freaking out! I was worried she was gonna wreck the car before we got there."

Nova looked up at him and smiled. "So you risked your life for me, huh?"

"Any time, hot girl." He held on to her another moment before stepping back and asking, "Shouldn't we check out the rest of the desk before your parents get home?"

Nova threw her arms around his neck and hugged him hard. Then she grabbed his hand and nearly dragged him through the hallway into her dad's office. They only had a short time before her parents returned.

"So what was in your file?" Ethan asked breathlessly.

"Just normal stuff, birth certificate, you know," she answered, snatching the key from the top of the desk. She unlocked the drawer she'd just been through and retrieved her sister's folder. "This is Alana's file."

Ethan took the folder from Nova's trembling hands and read the contents. "Wow, that sucks," he muttered before handing it back. "Sorry."

"What about the drawing? How could my dad have drawn a picture of Alana when she was five? She died the day she was born." *And the even weirder part is that she looks like my imaginary friend...* Nova decided to leave that out. No reason to say one more thing that made her sound crazy.

Ethan frowned. "Maybe he was imagining what she could have looked like. She looks kind of like Marshall, doesn't she?"

Nova thought about that. It made sense. Her dad had a great imagination. She could see him at his desk, thinking about his other daughter and wondering what she would have been like, then deciding to sketch her, the Alana in his head. It sounded like something her dad would do. Maybe Nova had seen one of the sketches and sort of attached that face to Allie.

"You're pretty smart, Ethan. That's probably exactly what happened. He drew her the way he imagined her, kind of like Marshall but also a little like me." Nova smiled at Ethan, and he looked pleased. "I want to look in the other drawers too. That's what I was starting to do when you showed up. Maybe I'll find something that explains—"

The sound of a heavy car door closing, like one on a vintage Mustang, made them freeze in place.

"Is that—"

"Yes!" Nova gasped as she ran around the desk, frantically trying to put everything back in its place. She couldn't do anything about the broken lock on the first drawer, but she was able to shut it and managed to lock all the others.

"Nova, come on!" Ethan whispered.

She nearly tripped on the crowbar. "Crap! I don't have time to put it back in the garage!"

Ethan used his foot to shove it under the bookcase beside the door. "He won't see it. Let's go!"

Nova grabbed the sketch of Allie that she'd kept from the file, folded it quickly, and stuck it in her pocket along with the desk key. Ethan stood in the doorway waving frantically for her to hurry up. She dashed into the hall, jammed the office key in the lock and turned until it clicked. Nearly tripping over each other, they shot up the hall and into the kitchen. Nova yanked open the refrigerator door and was reaching for the water pitcher when her parents walked in.

"Look who came to visit me!" she exclaimed, trying desperately to catch her breath.

Ethan just stood there with a silly grin on his face. She wasn't sure what her parents thought, but it was probably something normal like, "I bet they've been making out," and not "I bet they've been slinking around the office, trying to figure out why Dayton isn't dead anymore." Ethan, apparently thinking the same thing, laughed out loud, and everybody stared. Nova gave him a withering look.

Her dad frowned. "Ethan, shouldn't you be in school?"

"Ye-yes, sir," Ethan said.

Sir? Nova tried not to laugh herself.

"I wanted to see how Nova was doing," Ethan answered sincerely.

"That's not something you could have done after school?"

Ethan looked at his shoes. "Sorry, Mr. Grant. I should've waited."

Nova glanced at her dad and opened her mouth to say something but stopped when she saw his expression. He was staring at her with the same look on his face that she had seen many times since the hospital.

Her mom gave her dad a nudge. "It was sweet of you to be worried, Ethan. No more cutting school though, okay? I'd hate to have to call your parents." She didn't really sound mad.

"There's only one more week anyway," Ethan mumbled. "It's just exams now, and I only have one." He looked at Nova for help.

"I'll walk him out," Nova said.

"Tell Marshall to come in and change. He jumped out of the car and grabbed his skateboard the minute we got home."

"Sure, Mom," Nova said, relieved to get out of there without having to answer any more questions. She had the uncomfortable feeling that she was capable of blurting out the truth without thinking. Better to avoid unnecessary conversation with her parents for now.

When they were outside, Ethan leaned in and whispered, "I have an idea. When can you get back in your dad's office?"

"I don't know," Nova replied. "Did you see the look on his face?"

"I was kind of busy checking out my shoes," Ethan said jokingly.

"Not funny." Nova jabbed him in the ribs with her elbow. "Seriously, didn't you think he was acting weird?"

Ethan shrugged. "Just acting like a dad who thinks his daughter's been making out with her boyfriend under his own roof."

"Yeah, maybe. Anyway, what's your idea?"

"I think we need to get back into your dad's office to check out the bookshelves. You didn't look there, did you?"

"I didn't have time to."

"There could be something in one of his books that would help us figure out what's going on. My parents have a copy machine at the store. If we find something important, we can copy it and put it back before your dad notices."

Nova raised her eyebrows. "We?"

"Yes, we." Ethan smiled. "Like I said, I'm in."

Nova looked back at the kitchen window to see if her parents were watching, but they were nowhere in sight. So she wrapped her arms around Ethan's waist and laid her head on his chest. He put his arms around her and pulled her in closer, gently kissing the top of her head.

"You guys are gross!" Marshall yelled, coming up the street on his skateboard.

"Marshall, go away!" Nova yelled back.

"I wanna tell you about my elective!" He grinned,

hopping off his skateboard and walking across the yard.

"I guess that's my cue," Ethan said, giving her one more squeeze. "Call me tonight after your parents go to bed."

Nova stood in the yard and watched Ethan jog down the street. It was funny that she hadn't really known him in her other life, but maybe they would have eventually gotten together. She pictured Delilah's reaction to that scenario. "I'm dating Ethan now, Dee. Hope you don't mind." *Yeah, right. I definitely would've limped away from that conversation.*

Marshall rolled up on his skateboard, grinning from ear to ear. "I'm gonna be an astronaut! That's my elective. Space!"

Nova put her arm around his shoulders and smiled. "Perfect."

CHAPTER 10

At ten after midnight, Nova crept up the hall to her parents' bedroom. A floorboard creaked loudly when she leaned in to put her ear against the door. She held her breath, waiting. There was no sound from inside. Relieved, she glanced at the closed door to the office right next to their room. It was tempting to sneak in again, but she couldn't risk waking her parents as she rummaged around her dad's things. Careful to avoid the creaky board, she made her way back to her room at the end of the hallway and quietly closed the door.

Grabbing her phone from the nightstand, she climbed into bed and under the covers, only realizing then that she didn't know Ethan's number. Her address book was in the nightstand drawer. Flipping through, she found that Ethan was the first one listed under "E." She'd drawn a heart around his name.

"I guess it's official now. I have a boyfriend." Nova chuckled to herself.

He answered on the first ring. "What's up, hot girl?"

"Really? You have to come up with another nickname."

"Nah, I like hot girl."

Nova could picture him lying in bed, talking to her on the phone with a smug grin on his face. Maybe he was imagining her the same way.

"Are you in bed?" she asked as nonchalantly as she could manage.

"On the back porch," He chuckled. "Sorry to disappoint."

Nova felt her cheeks redden. "Oh my God, get over yourself. Let's hear this fabulous idea of yours."

"Way to break the mood." He laughed. "Okay, here goes. This might sound a little crazy, but hear me out. You know your dad is into all this science fiction stuff, right?"

"Right."

What if what happened to you has something to do with that? What if he stumbled across something, or did something that caused your memories to change?"

"How?" Nova sat up, anxious to see where he was going with this.

"I don't know, but maybe he discovered something when he was doing research for one of his books – some sort of mind control or hypnosis. That sounds like something from one of his books, doesn't it? How else would you explain what's happened to you? Why do you have so many memories that have nothing to do with your real life? He has to have done something to you. Or you could have stumbled onto something that you weren't supposed to see that caused all of this. You just can't remember."

Nova frowned. She also thought her dad's involvement in science fiction was the key to figuring out this whole situation. "Okay. Keep going."

"We need to get back in his office. But that's an obvious place to look. If he's really trying to make sure something is hidden, is there any place he thinks you'd never go? Someplace he'd feel safe hiding something dangerous?"

"Like what?" she asked.

"I don't know. Maybe the other Nova in suspended animation? Who knows?" Ethan laughed, but it sounded strained.

"Real funny." The idea of finding another version of herself gave her chills. She thought for a moment. "The attic."

Ethan was skeptical. "Are you sure? That seems like an obvious place to stash something to me."

"Not really," Nova said. "First of all, you have to use a ladder to get up in there and it's a really tight space. Plus, we had mice a few years ago, and the exterminators said they were living in the attic. Dad knows there's no way on earth any of us would want to go up there now."

"Okay. I guess we should start there then."

Nova made a face. "If we see mice…"

"Don't worry. I'll protect you, hot girl."

Nova rolled her eyes. "Fine. We'll look in the attic."

"Okay, when can we do this?" Ethan asked excitedly.

"I'm not sure."

Her dad hardly ever left the house when he was writing. The problem was that she had no idea if he was writing right now or not. She'd been dropped into this reality without a frame of reference. For all she knew, he could be in the middle of something or in a dry spell. Based on the condition of his desk, she guessed he was in a dry spell. There was no way to be absolutely sure though, because he spent a lot of time in his office for someone who wasn't working. What was he doing in there for hours at a time if he wasn't writing?

"I'm just gonna have to wait. Sooner or later, my dad will leave the house. I feel like he's watching me though, so I have to be careful."

"I want in on this," Ethan declared. "Call me the second he leaves, and I'll get to your house as soon as I can."

"Okay." Nova thought she heard someone in the hall. "I have to go. Call me tomorrow," she whispered, quickly hanging up and pretending to be asleep.

Someone cracked open her door. Nova lay perfectly still, breathing evenly. After a minute or two, the door clicked shut again and she took a deep breath.

Her head was throbbing. She gingerly touched the spot where the stitches were, and her fingers came away slightly damp. Turning on her lamp was out of the question. She'd just have to assume it was blood. Nova lay on her side with the wound facing up, trying to relax. With her throbbing and apparently bleeding head, it took her hours to finally fall asleep.

The only good thing that came out of her restless night was that she had plenty of time to think, and she had a revelation. Maybe her dad was hanging around all the time because she was acting strange, not like herself. Her plan was to try to act as normal as possible, or what she assumed would be normal. Maybe all she had to do was act happy. As long as he believed nothing was *wrong*, that might be enough to get him to leave.

Nova got up around seven thirty in the morning and rooted through the bag from the hospital that contained fresh gauze and tape. The stain on her current bandage wasn't as large as she'd feared it would be, but her parents would most likely freak out if they saw it. In the bathroom, she carefully peeled the bloody gauze away, grimacing when she saw the stitches holding the gash in her head together. The wound was about three inches long, with caked-on blood in some spots. No wonder it was still painful. She stashed the old bandage in her bathroom trash can, making sure to push it to the bottom so it wouldn't be noticed, and set to work covering the wound with fresh gauze. The new bandage looked as close to the original as she could manage. Hopefully no one would even notice the change.

By eight o'clock, she had cinnamon buns, one of the few things she knew how to make, in the oven. It wasn't long before the aroma filled the house and Marshall came bouncing in.

"You're cooking?" he asked. "It smells good!"

"They'll be ready soon, Marsh. Do you want milk?" Nova asked cheerfully.

Marshall looked suspicious. "What's with you?"

"Nothing. I just felt like cinnamon buns. And I know you like them too." She smiled at her little brother. Out of everyone, he seemed the most like himself. It was nice to have someone who hadn't changed.

"Can I have two?" Marshall asked hopefully.

"Sure, kiddo!" Nova laughed.

Marshall broke into a grin. "You haven't called me kiddo in a long time."

"Really?" *So much for acting normal.* "What do I usually call you?"

"Hmm. Mostly nothing, I guess. Just Marshall. Or Marsh."

Nova felt a wave of guilt. He obviously missed the time she used to spend playing with him when he was younger. Once she'd started high school, she had stopped paying much attention to him, a fact that was apparently also true in this reality.

"Well, it's kiddo again." She gave him a warm smile as she grabbed glasses and poured milk. "I think they're ready."

They were sitting at the table munching on warm cinnamon buns when Dayton strolled in. "I thought I smelled something delicious."

"I made a dozen, but we're doing our best to eat them all."

"You can't make something that smells this good and not share." He pulled up a chair. "How are you feeling today, firefly?"

"I feel good." She smiled at him.

"That's what I like to hear!" He seemed relieved. "I thought I'd go get gas for the mower. Want to tag along?"

Nova tried to keep her voice nonchalant. "I think I'm gonna hang out with Marshall this morning. Next time okay?"

"Sure." He smiled approvingly. "I like it when you two hang out." He picked out a second cinnamon bun before pushing back his chair and grabbing his keys. "Save some of those for when your mom gets up. She'll be upset if she comes in to that aroma and there aren't any left."

"Sure thing, Dad."

Five minutes after he pulled out of the driveway in his Mustang, Celeste came in dressed for a run. "You had to make my favorite? You know I'm trying to stay in shape!" She reached over Marshall and grabbed a sticky cinnamon bun from the plate. "What the heck. It's energy food." She laughed. "You kids clean up while I'm gone, okay?"

"No problem. We're gonna take care of it."

Marshall didn't look thrilled about that. "I knew there was a catch."

"Come on, kiddo. This won't take long." Nova had already started loading the few dishes into the dishwasher. Marshall made a big show of wiping the table by knocking the crumbs off onto the floor.

"Marshall, that's not cleaning. That's relocating." Nova laughed, handing him a broom and dustpan.

"You just said clean the table. You didn't say anything about the floor."

"Just sweep it up, kid," Nova said, trying to keep her voice light.

Marshall grumbled but did a fair job of getting the crumbs up, and before long, they were finished.

"What now?" he asked. "You wanna play video games?"

"Uh...sure. How about this? You play, and I'll watch. You're much better at it than I am."

Marshall looked skeptical. "That doesn't sound like much fun for you. What do you wanna do?"

Nova smiled, giving him a quick hug. "You're a good brother." She pretended to think for a minute then said excitedly, "Would you like to go on a treasure hunt?"

"I'm not four, you know. There isn't any real treasure around here." Marshall was clearly insulted. "If you don't wanna do anything with me, just say so."

"I'm sorry, Marsh. I really do like hanging out with you. I was just thinking that I'd like to look up in the attic. It could be fun, and no telling what we might find. I know Mom and Dad put some of our old toys up there. And Grandma Kate left some things here years ago, old pictures and dishes and things."

"Pictures and dishes? Are you serious? You want me to go up in the attic for pictures and dishes? What if the mice are back? Can't you think of anything else to do?" Marshall whined.

"Not just pictures and dishes, Marshall. There were all sorts of things. There's an old trunk that used to belong to Grandma Kate. You know what's usually in old trunks? Treasure, like jewelry and old coins."

Now Marshall was interested. "That could be okay, I guess. But what about the mice?"

"I'll go up first and check, but I'm sure the mice are gone."

Marshall gave in. "How do we get up there?"

The access door was in the ceiling in the hallway.

"We'll have to get the ladder from the garage," Nova replied.

"Maybe we should wait for Dad."

"You know Dad will go right to the shed to gas up the mower and then he'll be cutting the grass for at least an hour. I can handle the ladder if you help me."

Marshall reluctantly agreed, dragging his feet and mumbling about getting in trouble all the way to the garage. The ladder was surprisingly lightweight, and they easily carried it inside and positioned it under the attic access. Nova climbed up and pushed against the door. It was heavy but not impossible to handle. Soon she was scrambling up through the ceiling, into the attic.

As she reached around for the chain to turn on the light, her hand brushed a spider web and she shuddered. There were probably all kinds of undesirable creatures crawling around the attic. Maybe this wasn't such a good idea. It dawned on her that she had promised to call Ethan before looking up there anyway.

"Nova, hurry up!" Marshall yelled.

He had apparently decided he wanted to look in the attic after all.

"Give me a second, Marsh!" Nova called down to him, deciding at that moment to forget about calling Ethan. She'd explain later. Who knew when another chance like this would present itself?

She reached again and felt the cool metal of the chain dangling from a single bulb. Nova gave it a tug, bathing the cramped space in warm light. Looking around, she couldn't spot any organization. Boxes were stacked along the edge of the floored area and halfway into the middle. Only some appeared to be labeled. Nova's and Marshall's baby clothes, Marshall's Legos, miscellaneous school records, and Grandma Kate's dishes. The other boxes appeared to be stuffed with everything from old clothes to discarded kitchen items. There were stacks of board games and old books, even a set of encyclopedias from 1969. There didn't appear to be any order to the mess. *This is definitely the work of Dayton Grant.* If Mom had been up here, everything would have been labeled and placed in neat rows. She spotted Grandma Kate's trunk behind several mystery boxes and a stack of books.

"I'm coming up," yelled Marshall. "Are there spiders?"

"Just a few."

"Really?" Now Marshall wasn't sure.

"It's okay, Marshall. I found the trunk." She knew that would get him up there.

Marshall poked his head into the attic cautiously. "Are you sure it's okay?"

"It's okay, kiddo." Nova helped him up.

"You don't think we should've asked Mom and Dad about this, do you?" asked Marshall.

"I'm sure it's okay. Dad let me come up here last summer to look around. That's when I found the old wooden horse that's on our mantel." Nova hoped the horse was actually on the mantel. It was entirely possible that it had been there in the old life, but not in this one. Relieved that Marshall didn't question her statement, she made a mental note to be more careful in the future.

"Let's look in there first," she said, pointing at the trunk.

Marshall pushed a box aside and climbed over a stack of books, knocking them in all directions. Dust drifted up from the pile that now took up even more space on the attic floor.

"Nice," said Nova.

"Sorry," Marshall groaned.

They each grabbed a side of the trunk lid and pulled. Nothing happened.

"Are you pulling, Marshall?"

"Yeah. Look. It's locked." He pointed at the front panel where, sure enough, a rusty padlock dangled from the clasp.

Nova's heart sank. Why was everything locked now? She didn't remember anything being locked in her old life.

"What are we gonna do now?" Marshall asked, disappointed.

"I don't know. Let me think."

Nova wondered if one of the keys in her dad's office would fit it. She could go down the ladder, retrieve the keys, and get back before her dad got home, but then she'd have to worry about getting them back in the desk without being caught. She was mulling the scenario over when Marshall spoke up cheerfully.

"Hey, look!" He plucked the lock right off the latch. "It wasn't closed." Marshall seemed to be very proud of himself.

Nova put her arm around him and squeezed his shoulder. "Good going, kiddo! I guess you're a lot more observant than I am."

They each grabbed a corner of the lid and shoved until it creaked open.

"Man, that stinks!" Marshall pinched his nose. "It smells like something died."

"How would you know what something dead smells like?" Nova replied.

"I know 'cause Andy and me found a dead squirrel in his basement and it smelled just like this."

Marshall sat back on his heels, content to let Nova rummage through the contents of the trunk while he held his nose shut. Kate's trunk looked as if it hadn't been disturbed in years, which probably meant there wouldn't be anything in there pertaining to Nova's changed reality. If her dad had hidden something, the contents wouldn't be so neatly arranged and covered in dust.

"What's in there?" Marshall finally asked in a nasally voice.

"Marshall, cut it out. You sound like you have a cold. Man up, okay? It's not that bad."

"It's gross," Marshall replied.

Nova ignored him. She was mesmerized by Grandma Kate's trunk. In it were old letters, lace doilies that had obviously been crocheted by hand, a gold locket with a broken chain, a pair of delicate white gloves, an old church hymnal, and many photos of people who were long gone, people she would never know. Some of the pictures had been taken in front of an old farmhouse. The photos were yellowed and cracked with age. Nova had no idea where they had been taken or who the people were, but they had been lovingly bundled in delicate paper and tied with ribbon. She almost felt guilty disturbing them, but curiosity won out. Those people could be her great-grandparents, aunts and uncles, but not one face looked familiar. Then she thought to look on the backs of the photographs and found one with writing.

It said, "Dayton and Evelyn Grant with children at Old Fort." Nova flipped the picture back over and looked at the people again. The man and woman looked older than they must have been, because their children were all young. There were two girls and a boy. The older girl looked about three or four years old. The other girl was sitting on her mother's lap. She appeared to be the youngest, no more than two years old. *That must be Grandma Kate.* She was the only one smiling. The boy looked about five or six years old. Nova studied the man in the picture.

"So you're the one my dad is named for," she said softly. She couldn't see any resemblance between this serious-looking gentleman and her boyish dad.

Marshall was getting restless. "Let's look at some other stuff. This is boring."

"Don't you want to see what your grandmother and great-grandparents looked like?" Nova handed the picture to her little brother.

He gave it a quick glance then handed it back. "That was thrilling. Now what?"

"Okay, you're hopeless. Go look over there." Nova pointed at the other side of the attic door. "I think that's where I saw some interesting things."

Marshall eyed her suspiciously. "You didn't see anything over there because you've been glued to this trunk the whole time."

"Okay. Whatever. Just go look, okay?"

Marshall climbed back over the books, making an

even bigger mess. Nova figured he'd last another five minutes, then he'd be out of there. Sure enough, he descended the ladder a few minutes later, grumbling about their supposedly fun time together. She felt a twinge of guilt and decided she'd find a way to make it up to him later. She knew she'd have to explain why she'd dragged him into the attic to look around in the first place, but figured she could come up with something. She was getting to be a skillful liar.

Nova took out a bundle of letters, also carefully tied with a ribbon, and gently opened the first one. It was a letter from her grandmother to her grandfather. He was obviously away from her, and she told him how much she missed him and longed for his return. Apparently they had only been married a short while when he had to leave.

Nova refolded the letter and was putting it back with the others when she heard movement downstairs.

Her dad's voice called out, "Nova, are you up there?"

"Yes. I'm coming down," she answered, quickly closing the trunk and descending the ladder.

He was waiting for her at the bottom. "What were you doing in the attic?"

"Just looking around. I've been so bored being cooped up here. Marshall and I thought it would be fun," she said casually.

He frowned. "I don't want you up there. It's not safe. You have a concussion and shouldn't be climbing around in the attic. Do you understand?"

Nova shifted her weight uncomfortably. "Sure, Dad. I won't go back up there. I'm sorry."

His tone softened a little. "Why don't you sit on the porch for a while? You look like you need some fresh air."

"Maybe later. I think I'll lie down for a while."

"Okay, but no more exploring. The doctor said you should take it easy for a couple of weeks."

"Sure thing. No more exploring."

He hugged her suddenly. "I didn't mean to sound

mad, honey. I just have a lot on my mind. Do you forgive your old man?"

"It's okay, Dad." Nova put her arms around him. How many times had she wished she could do that during those nine months when he was gone? She vowed to make a greater effort not to worry him. Whatever was going on with her couldn't be something he'd done intentionally, but that didn't mean he wasn't involved in some way.

When Nova was back in her room with the door closed, she reached under her shirt and pulled out the small bundle of letters that she had tucked into the waist of her jeans. She pulled up on her mattress and gently inserted them between it and the box spring, careful not to tear the delicate paper. She was about to crawl under the quilt when she remembered the sketch she'd taken from the office. Rooting through her dirty clothes basket, she found the jeans with the drawing and desk key in the pocket and slid them under the mattress next to the letters.

The bed felt heavenly when she finally lay down, and it didn't take long for her to fall asleep.

CHAPTER 11

Nova had no idea how long she'd been sleeping when she was awakened by the noise of the lawnmower. She sat up slowly, so as not to aggravate her head, and tiptoed into the hallway. Marshall was playing a video game in the den, and she could hear the shower running in her parents' room. Deciding to take advantage of the rare opportunity for a little privacy, she closed the door to her room, crawled back onto her bed, and called Ethan.

He picked up on the first ring. "You must be psychic! I was just getting ready to call you."

"Can you come over and ask me to go to your house?"

He laughed. "Why don't I ask you now?"

"I want you to ask me in front of my mom. She really seems to like you, and I want her to let me go. She might not unless she's put on the spot. Mom and Dad still act like I'm gonna break."

"Okay. Where are we really going?"

Nova could tell he was smiling – expecting something outrageous from her, no doubt.

"Umm…to your house?" Nova replied. "We need to

do some research, and I have no privacy here."

"Okay. I'm on my way."

Nova pulled on a clean pair of jeans and a short-sleeved blue pullover. As an afterthought, she grabbed the tube of mascara from her dresser and added a little substance to her already abundant lashes. She knew she was blessed with her mother's dark, expressive eyes, but she rarely took the time to show them off. She quickly stepped into sandals, grabbed her book bag, and darted up the hall to the office. This time it was unlocked. She slipped in and closed the door behind her.

She scanned the shelves, finally choosing two of the books her dad had collected on parallel universes. Next she chose one of her dad's older novels about a man living in two worlds at once. Out of all of his books, it seemed the closest to her own situation, except that in the book, he was able to go back and forth freely. It was just as well that she didn't possess the ability to visit her old life. Why go back to such a dismal existence? She shoved both books into her bag.

Nova was sitting at the table when her mom came into the kitchen wearing a terry cloth robe, her hair in a towel.

"Where are you headed, Nova? I thought you were resting."

Nova opened her mouth to answer just as Ethan knocked on the back door.

"Ethan! Come in!" her mother said cheerfully as she opened the door, seemingly forgetting that she was only partially dressed.

Nova wanted to laugh out loud.

"I just came by to get Nova. My mom's been dying to see her since her, uh, accident. We'll just hang out at my house for a while if that's okay, Mrs. Grant. I promise to make her take it easy. No heavy lifting or anything." He gave her his most charming smile.

Nova looked over at her mom and again had to stifle a

laugh. Celeste Grant was completely smitten. Ethan could probably talk her into just about anything.

"I guess it's all right. Just for a little while though, okay?" Her mother smiled, even holding the door for them.

"That was smooth," Nova said when she heard the door close behind them.

"What's in the bag?" Ethan asked.

"Books." Nova wasn't going to tell him anything else until they were someplace private. They had started across the backyard when something dawned on her. She stopped suddenly and looked back at the house as she felt her face go completely white.

"What?" Ethan stared at her. "Nova, what?"

It had hit her that her dad must have been in the house when she'd gotten up the morning she passed out in the driveway. When she came to breakfast and there was no chip in the table and her mom was making waffles, he had been there somewhere, in his office or in their bedroom. Somewhere. She had left the house the same way she and Ethan were leaving now – across the backyard.

"You can't see our driveway from here," Nova said, fighting back tears. "My dad was in the house Wednesday morning, before I left for school, and I didn't know it. I couldn't see his car."

Ethan took her hand and pulled her along until they reached the street, out of sight of her house. Tears were spilling down her cheeks.

"Oh my God, Ethan. He was there, and I didn't know it. I could have seen him then."

"Nova," Ethan said gently, "nothing's changed. It doesn't matter. You see him now all the time."

"I know. It's just…none of this makes any sense. I almost forget how crazy this whole situation is sometimes. Then it hits me again like a brick wall. I still have no idea why I'm here."

"Well you *are* here, and that's all I care about."

They were standing in the street having an emotional discussion, but Nova couldn't help it. Sometimes reality smacked her in the face so hard, there was no keeping it from showing.

Ethan looked around and spotted Mrs. Wilson or Willard walking her dog. "Why is it always her?" He turned his attention back to Nova and lowered his voice. "We need to focus on things that are in our control. Everything else just has to wait. We'll figure it out sometime, or if we don't, who cares really? You're here. You said yourself that this is better. So let's just be happy about that okay?"

Ethan made a lot of sense, but Nova wasn't sure she'd ever be able to let it go. Always wondering would drive her crazy. She grabbed the bottom of his shirt and wiped her face with it.

"Really?" he demanded playfully. "Gross."

Mrs. Wilson or Willard had stopped walking and was watching them.

Nova leaned toward Ethan and whispered, "What's her name? Wilson? Willard? Williams?"

"Who knows?" Ethan whispered back.

"Hi, Mrs. W!" Nova called.

Ethan grinned.

"Hello, kids," Mrs. W responded sternly. "Everything all right?"

"Sure!" Nova tried to sound cheerful as she and Ethan started walking again. "How far is your house from here?"

This time it was Ethan who slammed on the brakes. "Seriously?"

"Yeah. What's the big deal? How far?" Nova was baffled by his response.

"You've been there a hundred times." Ethan's voice carried a little too much, and Mrs. W stopped and stared again.

"Let's just go. Maybe we need to stop talking until we get there."

"Yeah," he replied, but she could tell his mind was reeling.

So maybe he didn't really believe she was from another reality. He was just being supportive. Nova decided she could live with that. After all, if she were in his shoes, she'd probably have trouble believing something as crazy as this too. She gave him points for going along with her.

Ethan's house, it turned out, was exactly two blocks down from the bus stop. His parents obviously spent a lot of time working in the yard. The grass was lush and green, and there were blooming bushes and flowers bordering a brick walkway to the front porch and up against the house. More flowers adorned the windowsills and hung in pots around the porch. It looked like something in a magazine.

"This is incredible!" Nova exclaimed.

Ethan opened his mouth to say something but appeared to change his mind. She knew what he was probably thinking though. If she had been to his house a hundred times, then she'd seen the yard a hundred times. But for her, this was the first time.

They made their way up the walk and stepped onto the porch. Nova wasn't prepared for what happened next.

Ethan's mother – at least, she hoped it was his mother – burst out of the front door and threw her arms around Nova, giving her a huge hug. "Nova, honey, I'm so glad you're all right! Look at you, just as pretty as ever. I've been so worried!"

Nova had tried to look as normal as possible, removing the bandage now that her wound had dried up and covering the stitches in her scalp by pulling her hair to the side with a clip.

Apparently she hadn't been successful though, because Ethan's mother noticed immediately and grimaced. "That must hurt."

"I'm fine, M-Mrs....uh..." Nova racked her brain for Ethan's last name. Had she ever known?

Reacting to the neon HELP sign she must have been wearing, Ethan began coughing uncontrollably.

"Ethan, for heaven's sake!" His mother patted him hard on the back.

Nova caught Ethan's eye. "Thank you," she mouthed.

"Sorry, Mom." Ethan grinned. "Swallowed some spit the wrong way."

"Good heavens! You're not in a locker room. Do you have to be gross in front of Nova?"

Mrs. Whatever was still shaking her head as they followed her inside to a veritable showroom of blooming plants. In the sunroom to their right, flowers adorned every corner, some in wrought-iron stands and others on the side tables that flanked two love seats, unsurprisingly covered in floral fabric. More fresh flowers graced the dining room table and sprung from ornate ceramic pots at the bay window.

"You have a lot of flowers," Nova said.

Ethan chuckled. "Tell me about it. My parents own a nursery, so we have them all year."

"That's nice." Nova smiled.

"Yeah. Lucky me." Ethan clearly wasn't into it.

His mother had gone into the kitchen to put some cookies in to bake, so he took the opportunity to secretly give Nova a tour.

"Mom will wonder what's up if you don't know your way around. She'll think you have brain damage or something. Oh, and our last name is MacGrady. You call my mom Mrs. Mac," he whispered.

"Thanks," Nova whispered back. "Seriously though, you live in a fairy-tale house – beautiful yard, big front porch, flowers everywhere, mom in the kitchen baking cookies..."

Ethan rolled his eyes. "Can it." He took her arm and steered her down a hallway to the left. "My parents' room is down here." He pointed at a bedroom at the end of the hallway. "The other one's a guest room that we only use a couple times a year when my aunt and uncle come from Ohio. They have three little kids, all mutants."

"What?" Nova giggled. "They can't be that bad."

"The oldest claims she's from another planet. And frankly, I believe her."

"Oh my God." Nova couldn't stop laughing. "So what's wrong with the other two?"

"We're not sure. But last time they were here, the dog went missing."

"You have a dog?"

"Well…we did."

"Oh my God! Are you serious?"

He smiled. "Nah, I'm just kidding. He came back after a couple of days. He's around here somewhere."

Nova jabbed him in the side. Hard. "Don't do that to me!"

Ethan whistled, and a golden retriever came bounding down the hall from the kitchen.

"This is Jack," Ethan said, rubbing his head.

"He's beautiful! You're so lucky. I'd love to have a dog like this."

"I'll tell you what. Next time the little alien and her mutant siblings come for a visit, Jack can stay at your house." Ethan laughed.

"Deal!" Nova wrapped her arms around the dog and giggled while he licked her face.

"You know, I had plans to do that later." Ethan winked.

"Forget it. I'm covered in dog saliva."

They could smell the cookies baking, and Mrs. Mac called for the dog. That was all it took to send Jack bounding off in the direction of the kitchen.

"Mom always lets Jack have cookies when my dad's not home. He grew up with dogs and says they shouldn't have stuff like that."

"Where's your dad?" she asked.

"He's at a flower festival in Florida."

Nova started to open her mouth.

"Don't," Ethan said quickly.

Nova giggled. "I was just going to ask what the point was. You have enough flowers *here* for a festival."

"This is nothing. Trust me. We usually go every year, and when we get home, Mom goes crazy with the flowers. Believe it or not, this is pretty subdued. She even tried to stick a bunch of daisies in my room when we got back last year."

"Ouch!" Nova laughed.

"Yeah."

"So why didn't you and your mom go with him this year?"

"The nursery manager just quit, so Mom needed to stay here to run things."

"Why didn't you go with your dad?"

"It's not much fun. Mostly it's a lot of work. Besides, I'm getting Sam's truck soon, so I wanted to be here."

"Who's Sam?" she asked.

"My brother. He's about to start college in Texas. He wasn't supposed to leave until August, but he got a part-time job at the bookstore and they wanted him to go ahead and start now. He left a week ago."

"So I guess I know him," Nova said matter-of-factly.

"Yeah. He really likes you."

"Well, that's good." Nova smiled, but there seemed to be something Ethan wasn't telling her. "Is that the only reason you didn't go?"

"You asked me not to," he replied.

"Oh." She tried to think of something else to say in that awkward moment, but she couldn't come up with anything.

Ethan finally spoke up instead. "Come on. I'll show you my room."

He led her to the other side of the house and down a

shorter hallway, where there were two more bedrooms. Ethan's was the one on the right. It was a stark contrast to the rest of the house. Clothes were strewn about, the bed was unmade, and there was a plate of something that looked as though it used to be cake on his desk.

"Wow, Ethan. Nice of you to clean up."

"Hey, only for you, hot girl." He grinned. "And this *is* clean."

"I'm surprised your mom lets you keep it like this."

"We have an understanding. She doesn't mess with my room, and I don't contaminate the rest of the house."

"Yuck. What's that on your desk? Petrified cake?" Nova asked sweetly.

Ethan shot her a scathing look. "That's not cake."

"Please don't tell me what it is then."

Ethan grabbed her book bag and sat on the floor with his bed as a backrest. Nova plopped down beside him, impatient to get started.

"So what are we looking for?" Ethan asked.

"Good question. I don't know what to call this thing that happened to me, but I thought these were a good place to start." She pulled the books out of the bag and set them on the floor between them.

Ethan picked up one, read the title, and shook his head in disbelief . "Yeah, right. You seriously think you're in a parallel universe? C'mon! You're not being rational. It's impossible."

"All right, what would you call it? I woke up and my life had changed overnight. My dad, who'd been dead for nine months, isn't dead anymore. I have a boyfriend that I didn't have before, and my best friend is practically a stranger. Not to mention all the other little things I've noticed. And that's another thing. I'm the *only* one who notices any of this. To you and everyone else, *nothing* has changed. So either I'm insane or I just got here. I guarantee you I'm not insane. So that leaves door number two. I just got here. And here's the big question. Where was I before?" Nova caught her breath before continuing. "Seriously, Ethan, if I'm here now, is another Nova in my old world, freaking out because her dad is dead, her mom is depressed, her boyfriend doesn't know her, and she can't stand her new best friend? If I think about it for long, I feel like my brain is gonna explode. So do me a favor and be supportive, even if you can't believe any of this."

Ethan's mouth dropped open. "Jeez, Nova, sorry. Okay, you're from a parallel universe. The good news is that I usually like this version of you as much as the old Nova. Not right now of course, but usually." He grinned.

Nova giggled and jabbed him in the ribs. "I think you're the crazy one."

"Add mood swings to your list of complaints," Ethan teased.

Nova took the book and started leafing through it. There was a whole chapter devoted to interviews with scientists from all over the country who had strong opinions regarding the existence of parallel universes. Some treated the subject as mere speculation, and others claimed that we already possessed the ability to accomplish travel between our universe and others. Some referred to the other worlds as alternate realities. One scientist even suggested that anyone could learn how to travel to other dimensions. That one was the most promising, but while he believed it was possible, he gave no information on exactly how to do it. The more Nova read, the more frustrated and confused she felt. If the theories were correct, travel between universes would take a tremendous amount of energy. Someone wouldn't just go to bed one night and wake up somewhere else.

"This is depressing." Nova sighed, dropping the book on the floor. "None of this explains what happened to me."

They looked through the other books, but they were no more help.

"Let's give it a rest for now," Ethan suggested. "I feel

like my brain's melting, and I don't think you're gonna get answers from any book. It's too bad we haven't been able to look any more around your house."

Nova cleared her throat. "Actually…I did look in the attic."

"Without me? I thought you were gonna call." Ethan looked wounded.

"I'm sorry. It just kind of happened. Mom and Dad left Marshall and me alone in the house."

"Marshall didn't wonder why you were up in the attic?"

"He went with me."

"You took *Marshall* and didn't call me? I could've been there in five minutes."

"I'm sorry. I didn't know how long we'd have to look. Besides, you should be glad I didn't call you because Dad came home and got mad that I was up there. If you'd been with me, it would've been even worse."

"Okay, maybe you're right. But next time you go snooping around, promise me you'll call me."

"I promise." Nova smiled, relieved he didn't seem mad anymore. "The only place I really looked was in my grandmother's trunk, but I only found old letters and photos in there. Nothing stood out as important."

"Old letters?" Ethan asked. "What did they say?"

Nova hadn't really thought about the letters since she hid them under her mattress, but she told Ethan about the one she'd read.

"Maybe we should take another look at them," he said.

"That'll be tricky. I think my dad's determined to never leave me in the house alone again, especially since he caught me in the attic. It's really weird."

"We'll think of a way," Ethan assured her.

Mrs. MacGrady called from the kitchen, "Would you kids like a warm cookie?"

Nova poked Ethan in the ribs again. "I told you." She giggled. "Fairy tale."

"Yeah, I know. Don't rub it in." Ethan sighed.

Nova grinned. "Your mom's sweet."

When they stepped into the kitchen, the aroma was heavenly. They sat at the table eating cookies for a half an hour before Nova finally said she needed to get home.

"Okay, you come back soon, Nova." Mrs. Mac gave her another big hug.

Nova assured her that she'd be over again later in the week, and Mrs. Mac seemed satisfied.

"Now I see how you turned out so perfect. Well, except for the disastrous room," Nova teased as they walked to her house.

"Funny. So what do we do now?" Ethan asked.

"I don't know. Can I call you later?"

Ethan's face fell in disappointment. "I guess so. Are you sure you don't want me to stick around?"

"I really need to lie down. Sorry."

She wasn't lying. She hadn't had a decent night's sleep since she landed in this reality. As they approached her house, Ethan stopped and kissed her gently on the lips, making her heart race a little.

"Call me later, hot girl." He turned and headed home.

Nova went inside and straight to her room. She tried to think about what she'd read in her dad's books, but she couldn't seem to focus on anything but the kiss. His lips had felt warm and familiar. Nova had often imagined what her first kiss would be like, and this one exceeded her expectations. She didn't count Mason Phillips's clumsy peanut-butter-and-jelly kiss in kindergarten. Ethan's kiss was amazing. It felt natural.

She collapsed onto her bed, smiling. This life was definitely better. She kicked off her shoes and cradled her pillow, looking at the spot where the spider used to be. It didn't matter. That was the old life, and she never wanted to go back. She closed her eyes and soon fell asleep.

Nova stood at the edge of the river, watching what was left of her dad's Mustang float along with the current. The car was upside down, and two of the wheels were spinning. Somewhere off in the distance, she heard her dad calling out to her, saying her name over and over.

"I'm here, Dad!" she called back, but he didn't seem to hear her.

His voice faded and finally trailed off.

She stepped into the water, feeling the cold seeping into her shoes and up her legs. "Dad! Where are you?"

But there was no response.

CHAPTER 12

Nova jolted awake, her face wet with perspiration. She could hear her dad calling her and thought for a moment that she was still in the dream. Then her bedroom door cracked open.

"Are you sleeping, firefly?" A cheerful Dayton Grant, alive and well, came striding in. He immediately lost the playful smile when he saw her. "What's wrong?" He sat down beside her and felt her forehead.

"Nothing, Dad. Just a bad dream."

"What was it about?" He was trying to sound comforting, but Nova could hear the sudden strain in his voice.

"Just stupid things. I don't really remember. I'm okay now."

He studied his daughter's face, frowning. "Are you sure?"

Once again she thought, *He knows something.* "I'm fine. Hungry actually. I didn't have lunch, just cookies."

"How's your head?" He was still looking at her, studying her expression.

"It's not hurting that much now," she said, relieved

that was true.

"Okay, good." He seemed hesitant to leave. "Did you take a couple of books from my office?"

Nova's throat went dry. "Uh…yeah. I felt like reading."

He frowned. "I don't think that's good for your head. You have a concussion, you know."

"You're probably right. It's on my sheet of instructions from the hospital, I think. No reading. Sorry."

"That's okay, honey. I just want you to take care of yourself."

"I know."

"Okay, then…so you're hungry?" he asked.

"I'm starving. Is dinner ready?" Nova tried her best to sound cheerful.

He smiled. "Yeah. Your mom made lasagna."

"Okay, I'm up," Nova said.

He looked like he wanted to say something else, but after an awkward pause, he got up and left the room.

When Nova strolled into the kitchen ten minutes later, her face was freshly washed and she was wearing sweatpants and a white T-shirt. She had pulled her hair up into a high ponytail.

Dayton was already sitting in his chair at the table. He smiled when he saw her. "There's my little girl."

Her mother seemed to be in a cheerful mood as she bustled around the kitchen. "Did you have fun at Ethan's?"

"Yeah. It was great." Nova chuckled. "Mrs. Mac made cookies."

Her mom rolled her eyes. "I can't compete with that woman."

Nova laughed. "It's okay. It's almost too perfect over there. I like it here better."

She gave her daughter a grateful look and took the lasagna out of the oven as Marshall walked in the back door carrying his skateboard. "You can set the table, Marshall."

"What? I just got here!"

"Wash your hands first," she said, ignoring his outburst. "And leave that skateboard outside."

"Aww, man!" Marshall turned to head out the back door again, and the end of his skateboard smacked the edge of the kitchen table, knocking off a chip.

Nova froze. She stared at the broken spot with her mouth hanging open until her mother's voice startled her.

"Marshall Grant! Look what you did!"

"Sorry, Mom," Marshall whined.

"So I guess you were always meant to chip the table," Nova muttered without thinking.

Everyone looked at her. Nova couldn't think of anything to say that would make her careless comment less weird, so she grabbed the plates off of the counter and started setting the table while her little brother headed outside with his skateboard.

After a moment, her mother said, "I told Marshall to do that."

"I know. I just thought I'd help." Nova turned around to grab a handful of utensils from the drawer in the cabinet next to the table. When she turned back, her eyes met her dad's. He was staring at her, an odd expression on his face. She quickly looked away and focused on setting the table, pretending to take great care with the arrangement of each place setting.

She managed to make it through dinner but she'd lost her appetite and could barely eat a thing. Her brain was in overdrive. The broken edge of the table was in the exact same spot as before, as if it had been there all along. If Marshall was meant to chip the table, were the other things – like her dad dying – meant to happen too? Was there some cosmic force just waiting for an opportunity to push him into the river?

Nova looked up. Her mom was staring at her, a concerned look on her face.

"Did you hear me? I asked if you were finished with your lasagna."

"Yeah, sorry, Mom."

"You didn't eat very much."

"I'm not that hungry."

Her mother jumped up and came around the table to put her arms around Nova. "That's all right. I can make you something later if you get hungry. Why don't you go lie down? Marshall can clear the table."

Marshall groaned and Celeste shot him a stern look. "Anything you want to say mister?"

Marshall glanced at the jagged chip in the table. "No," he answered sheepishly.

Relieved to return to the peace and quiet of her bedroom, Nova allowed herself some time to ponder the ramifications of the chip in the table. She tried not to let her mind go down the "what's meant to be is meant to be" road. If that were true, her dad was destined to die too. She flatly refused to accept that possibility. It had to be a coincidence that Marshall had broken the table. It was an accident waiting to happen. Not because of destiny, but because there wasn't enough room in the kitchen to turn around with a skateboard.

Nova shoved the incident out of her mind and trudged down the hall to the bathroom. After showering and changing into a T-shirt and boxers, she crawled into bed. She seemed to be tired all the time now. Nova closed her eyes and dozed off almost immediately.

***

The sound of her dad's Mustang firing up in the driveway woke her the next morning. Nova looked at the clock on her nightstand and groaned. Seven twenty. Her bed was so comfortable that she was tempted to roll over and sleep some more. Then the realization hit her that her dad had actually left the house. She jumped out of bed and grabbed a pair of sweatpants out of her dresser, pulling them on as she practically ran up the hall to the kitchen. Her mother was unloading the dishwasher.

"Mom!" she said breathlessly.

"Nova, good grief! You scared me half to death!"

"Oh, sorry. Uh, where did Dad go?"

"To meet Jason about his new book," her mother responded, still frowning.

Jason Channing was her dad's agent. He was also one of his biggest fans. Nova liked him because he treated her like an adult. Even when she was little, he had always asked for her opinion as if he was genuinely interested. He also liked to talk...and talk. If her dad was meeting him about a book, he'd most likely be gone for hours.

"So I guess he's working," Nova mused.

"Of course he's working," her mom answered irritably. "You know he's been doing research for the book."

"Oh, yeah." Nova had known no such thing, but that wasn't something she could tell her mom. "I'm sorry I scared you."

Celeste finally smiled. "That's all right, honey. Just don't give me a heart attack so early in the morning."

Nova poured a bowl of cereal and scarfed it down before she realized that her mom was watching her, grinning.

"What?" Nova asked.

"It's just good to see you acting like yourself."

"Gee thanks. I guess pigging out is my usual thing, huh?" Nova laughed.

"Well, sort of." She smiled.

"Why is Dad meeting Jason this morning? Don't we have church?"

Her mom shook her head. "Don't you remember? Last weekend they said there'd be no service this week because Pastor Greg is on vacation and there's no one to fill in."

Nova, of course, didn't remember that because this

time last week, she had been trudging through her other life. She couldn't very well use that excuse though, so she said, "Oh yeah, I forgot. Maybe we should join a bigger church that actually has more than one minister." She winked.

Her mother loved the little church they attended because it was so small and intimate. She had said so many times, even though Nova and Marshall complained about it. Dayton didn't seem to care one way or the other.

"Very funny, Nova. That's why I like it. I know everybody."

"Sure, Mom. So what are you gonna do today?"

"I'm going to get coffee with a couple of the other moms from Marshall's class, then going to the grocery store. And I have to pick Marshall up at Tucker's house around three."

"Marshall's at Tucker's?" Nova asked.

"He slept over. He came in to tell you good-bye last night, but you were already asleep."

Nova could hardly contain her excitement. Her dad was probably going to be gone for hours. Marshall was out of the house, and now her mom was leaving. Nova tried to sound casual when she said, "Okay. I think I'll just work on my closet while you're gone. It's a mess."

She took her bowl to the sink, rinsed it, and put it in the dishwasher, forcing herself to act like nothing was up.

"Don't overdo it," her mom called as she closed the back door.

Nova waited a moment, just to be sure she was gone, then tore down the hallway to the office. This time, the door was unlocked. She decided to give the top of the desk a once-over and then concentrate on the bookshelves. Her dad had a flip calendar on top of the desk turned to today's date. It read "Meet Jason – 7:30 – Anna's Café." Nova flipped the calendar back to yesterday. There was only one notation, written in pencil. It read, "Find letters."

Could he mean her grandmother's letters? Were they

important in some way? Had he gone into the attic, looked in the trunk, and found they were missing?

Nova raced down the hallway to her room and dropped to her knees beside her bed. She reached between the mattress and box spring until she felt the edge of the delicate bundle. Pushing up on the mattress, she extracted them from their hiding place. After untying the ribbon, she bypassed the letter she'd already read and chose the next envelope, carefully pulling out the paper and unfolding it. She immediately felt a lump in her throat as she read.

Dearest Day,

I received your sad letter and I must tell you no. I will not help you do what you want to do. It's a dangerous game you want to play and you must not do it. I know how upset you are and I understand. I went through something very similar and it still haunts me. I tried to undo what happened with no success, only more pain. You can't go back, no matter how many times you try. I have generations of changing paths to back up what I say. My own mother and my grandfather changed over and over in their lifetimes. It never works out the way you hope it will. This gift is not a gift at all. It is a curse.

You have a beautiful daughter who needs you to be her father. She is here now. You must only think of her. The other one is gone forever. Your family will endure, as we all have. I know your heart is broken. Mine is broken for you. Please don't think me heartless, because the opposite is true. It is because of my great love for you that I have said these things. I want only what's best for you.

With much love and concern,
Mother

Nova's head was spinning. She read the letter over and over until finally she sat on the floor next to her bed and leaned her head against the mattress, unable to focus anymore. It was as she'd suspected. Her dad had done something that caused her life to change. And maybe it wasn't the first time. It was obvious from the letter that if she wanted any real answers, he would have to provide them. What had he asked his mother to help him with that was so dangerous? And what was this family *curse?* And why was he so different now?

Just then the phone rang, and Nova jumped up, jerking it off the base. "Hello?"

"Hey, hot girl."

"Ethan!" Nova was trying not to lose control. "He knows! He knows what happened to me. I'm sure of it!"

"Whoa, slow down. Who are you talking about?" Ethan sounded taken aback.

"My dad. He knows what's going on. I went back to the office and on his calendar yesterday, it said to find the letters. So I figured he could be talking about the letters I found in Grandma Kate's trunk. I decided to look at them again. There's a letter from her to my dad, talking about her not helping him do something dangerous. And about him being brokenhearted and having a daughter who needs him. She was telling him not to do something back then, and I think it has to do with what happened to me now."

Ethan hesitated a moment before responding. "Nova, it sounds like she was comforting him. Maybe she wrote the letter after your sister died."

"No, I'm telling you, the whole letter is strange. I'll read it to you." She read it, and when she finished, Ethan said nothing. "Well?"

"Okay, I admit it's weird. What kind of game do you think she was talking about?"

"I don't know for sure, but I think maybe he wanted to change what had happened to Alana. And maybe he knew how to do that, but it was dangerous. Obviously the gift being a curse was a warning from my grandmother. I have to ask him about this. Something's been up with my dad ever since I got here. I've felt like he knew something all this time, but I wasn't sure. Now I'm sure."

"You have to be careful. If you start asking him about the letter, he's gonna want to know why you're so curious. You'll have to tell him what you told me, and then who knows what'll happen to you? You could end up back in the hospital or worse."

Nova's hands were shaking so that she could barely hold the phone. "I'm telling you he *already* knows what happened to me. I know he does. There has to be some kind of explanation for why I'm here, however crazy it is. I think my dad can tell me what that is. I *have* to ask him. He's not going to put me in the hospital. I'm going to get answers."

"Please, let me come over. Let's look through the other letters first, okay?" Ethan pleaded. "Maybe we'll find out more."

"We'll look through the other letters, but I'm still talking to my dad." Nova was determined. "This is the first clue I've found, and I'm not waiting."

"Okay. I'm on my way," Ethan said.

CHAPTER 13

Nova paced in the kitchen, waiting for Ethan. He seemed to be taking a lot longer than usual. If her dad walked in instead, she knew she would pounce on him, demanding answers. What had he done that had caused her world to change? And if he wanted to do whatever it was after Alana died, why had he waited until now, years later?

Nova was so deep in her own thoughts that she didn't even notice Ethan come in. She turned around and he was standing there, staring at her with his mouth open.

"What!" Nova yelled.

"Whoa!" Ethan held up his hands. "Take a step back. You look nuts."

"Nuts?" Nova nearly screamed.

"Yeah, nuts." Ethan grinned.

Nova lowered her voice. "Okay, fine. Maybe I have a reason."

"I know you feel like you've made an incredible discovery, and maybe you have. But you need to stay calm. If you jump on your dad the second he gets home, you're not gonna get the answers you want. So how about calming down a little and showing me the letter?"

Ethan was making a lot of sense, but it still irritated Nova. It wasn't his life that had been turned upside down. No one thought *he* was crazy. He had no idea what she was going through. Nova stood there fuming for a minute, then she took a deep breath.

"The letter's in my room." She turned and stomped down the hallway.

Ethan followed at what he probably figured was a safe distance. When they got to Nova's room, she retrieved the letter from under her pillow and handed it to him.

"There. Read it," she demanded.

Ethan read the letter twice. "Nova, I don't blame you for thinking this means something. Have you read any of the other letters? I mean, besides the one that your grandmother wrote to your grandfather?"

"Not yet," she replied. "I've kind of been stuck on this one."

"Maybe we should read them." Ethan sat down and patted the floor beside him. "Looks like we have time." He smiled.

Nova retrieved the hidden bundle of letters from her bed and sat on the floor next to Ethan. Being next to him, she relaxed a little. Ethan was right. She needed to be calm and focused. She couldn't attack her dad and accuse him of yanking her into another reality. That sounded crazy. Even if he had done exactly that, he would deny it if she seemed hysterical.

Nova chose another envelope and pulled out the delicate paper. This one was also a letter to her grandfather. It was more cheerful than the first one. Apparently Grandma Kate was expecting him home soon and had some happy news for him. Nova wondered if the happy news had been that she was expecting a baby – a baby that would grow up to be Dayton Grant.

They looked through all of the letters, but none were to her dad. Most were to Nova's grandfather. A few letters were in envelopes with no address on the outside. They were to someone named Jeannie and had apparently never been mailed.

The letters to Jeannie were kind of sad. Grandma Kate told her about things that were going on: a bake sale at the church, squirrels living in her attic, a neighbor falling and breaking his leg, a new recipe for canned peaches. She always ended with how much she missed Jeannie and would like to see her. One letter mentioned an argument and how sorry she was. Nova wondered what had happened between them and why her grandmother had never mailed the letters.

"I remember my dad talking about an aunt Jean," Nova said. "I think she lives somewhere in North Carolina."

"Why don't we just talk to your grandmother?" Ethan suggested.

"We can't," Nova said sadly. "She died years ago, right after Marshall was born."

"She couldn't have been that old. Was she sick?"

"It was an accident. She was walking early in the morning, and a car swerved or something. There was a big drop-off by the road, and she fell. My mom told me. Dad never talks about her. I barely remember her, but I do remember she hardly ever smiled."

"Sorry…okay then, what about tracking down your aunt Jean? If this is some family curse, she would probably know about it too."

"That's not a bad idea," Nova agreed. "I just have to figure out how to bring it up. Maybe I can talk my parents into visiting her."

"Well, if you do, ask your mom if you can bring your boyfriend along." Ethan grinned. "I think she likes me."

Nova giggled. "I'm not sure she likes you *that* much."

Ethan pretended to be wounded. "Well ask her anyway."

"Will do." Nova patted him on the arm.

Ethan leaned over and surprised her with a tender kiss.

This one actually gave her goose bumps. Nova reminded herself that she needed to stay focused on figuring things out, but she couldn't keep her mind on that with Ethan so close to her. They were sitting on the floor in her bedroom, and no one else was home. She wondered if, in this reality, she and Ethan had done more than kiss. She wanted to ask him but wasn't really sure she wanted to know. For now, things with Ethan were perfect. Better not rock the boat.

"You're a good kisser." Nova gave him an awkward smile.

"Right back at you, hot girl," Ethan said softly, then he kissed her again.

This one lasted much longer, and Nova was breathless afterward. "Ethan...I'm sorry. I really like you, and I don't know how I'd get through this if you weren't here. But we need to take things slowly, okay?" Nova was embarrassed.

Ethan put his arms around her and held her. "Slowly is fine, hot girl. And in case you were wondering, the answer is no, we haven't gone much further than this. I wouldn't do anything to hurt you."

Nova wrapped her arms around Ethan and laid her head on his shoulder. He really was wonderful. No matter what else happened, she never wanted to go back to her old life. She could have stayed there, cradled in Ethan's arms, but time was ticking away. Her dad had already been gone over two hours, so he could be home soon.

Nova reluctantly pulled away from Ethan. "Let's take a look around the office again. My dad might be home soon, so we need to hurry."

Ethan jumped up. "Sure thing."

Nova laughed as he sprinted down the hall and into the office. "Wait up!"

"Come on! Get the lead out!" Ethan called.

She dashed after him, still laughing.

"Like I said before – mood swings," Ethan teased.

"Shut up, I think you're the one with mood swings."

They settled into the task of reading the title of every book in the office. Ethan started with the top shelf closest to the door, and Nova started on the bottom. They took turns reading them off. Nothing stood out as particularly important until Ethan stopped about halfway through the second shelf. There was a large book with nothing written on the spine. When Ethan pulled it out to read the title, he found another book behind it.

"This is interesting."

"What?"

"This isn't a book at all. It's a journal. It was hidden behind the others."

Nova grabbed it from Ethan. "Let me see."

She immediately recognized her dad's handwriting on the first page. The book was dusty, so it apparently hadn't been disturbed in a long time. With trembling hands, she opened the cover. The first entry had been written right after Nova was born. Actually, after Nova *and Alana* were born.

I don't know how I'm going to live with myself after this. It's all my fault. I've robbed her of five years! Why did this happen? I need help. Mother has to help me. The pain is more than I can stand. I have to convince her. Nothing matters anymore if I can't fix this. I know it can be fixed. Please, God, help me convince her. I don't think I can do it on my own. I've been trying for weeks and nothing is happening. Why can't I do this?

Nova turned to the next page.

She isn't going to help me. I can hardly bear to look at Nova. She just reminds me of what I've lost. I know it's wrong to feel this way.

Nova felt sick to her stomach.

Ethan put his arm around her. "Maybe we shouldn't read any more," he said gently.

Nova shook her head. "No. I'm fine. I want to know."

She turned to the next page. The entry on that page had been written several months after the first two.

When Nova smiled at me today it was like a light shining in the darkness. My little firefly.

Then on the next page –

She sits across from me and draws pictures, trying to cheer me up. She drew one today with an angel watching over the four of us. I have to let go. I still have a daughter who needs me.

There were no more entries after that. He had apparently decided not to continue the journal that had started so painfully.

"Are you okay?" Ethan asked carefully.

"Yeah. I guess I know now why my dad calls me firefly, and why he loved that picture so much."

"Do you want to keep looking? We still haven't found anything that explains *your* situation."

"Let's keep going."

Nova put the journal back in its spot and carefully replaced the book that hid it. It broke her heart that there'd been a time when it had been hard for her dad to even look at her, but one thing she'd learned over the nine months after the accident was how to shove her pain down deep inside. She'd gotten pretty good at it, but that probably wasn't a good thing. She took a deep breath and started reading titles again as Ethan did the same. Soon they were halfway down the wall behind the desk and had still found nothing useful.

Nearly an hour later, they heard Dayton's Mustang pull into the driveway. They'd been careful to put every book back in its place as they went along, so it was easy to leave the office quickly. They were sitting on the couch in the den, sipping cans of soda, when he came strolling in. He was obviously in a great mood.

"Hey, you two!" he said cheerfully. "What have you been up to?"

Some of Nova's drink went down the wrong way and she coughed uncontrollably. Ethan pounded on her back.

"I'm okay," she managed to sputter.

"Hmm. Anything you want to confess?" Her dad raised an eyebrow, clearly amused. "I was a teenager once, you know."

"Actually, Dad, Ethan and I had a big party while you were gone. It got a little out of hand and the police showed up and hauled everyone off. We were making out in the closet, so they missed us."

He chuckled. "Just don't tell your mother."

They could hear him still laughing as he closed his office door.

"Well he's back in the office again," Nova whispered. "I don't know what he does in there. Supposedly he's in the middle of a book, but his desk is way too clean. No papers, no notes, nothing. I'm telling you, I've seen him when he's writing. His desk should be a mess. His whole office looks like a bomb went off when he's really into a book. Mom says he's writing, but it's weird. I don't see how he could be that different in this reality."

"I don't know. Maybe you could burst in and see what he's up to," Ethan suggested. "If you still plan to talk to him, you could catch him off guard."

Nova thought for a moment. Then she stood and grabbed Ethan's hand, pulling him to his feet. "You need to leave. I don't know what's gonna happen, but you shouldn't be here."

"Are you sure? I can stay if you want me to."

"No, I need to do this alone. This is the perfect time.

Mom isn't here, and neither is Marshall. I promise I'll call you. Just go now, okay?"

"Okay." Ethan hugged her, apparently reluctant to leave.

Nova could tell he was worried and probably hurt as well, but this was something she had to do on her own. She heard the back door close as he left.

Nova stood in the den for a couple of minutes. She couldn't seem to get her feet to move. Now that she had the opportunity to confront her dad, she couldn't figure out how to do it. Her stomach felt as if it were full of knots and her throat was so dry she wasn't sure she could get a sound out. She silently prayed for the strength to find out the truth. The alternative was never knowing, and she didn't think she could live with that. No. It had to be now.

Here goes. She walked down the hall and stopped at the office. Her hands were trembling when she reached for the knob.

CHAPTER 14

Nova grasped the doorknob and tried to turn it. Locked, of course. She stood silently for a moment while all of her resolve melted away. Just a couple of hours ago she'd been ready to scream at her dad, to make him tell her the truth. Now, she felt like she couldn't do it. What if he told her something awful? What if he somehow managed to send her back to the old life? She was about to turn and run when she heard her dad call out to her.

"Is that you, firefly?"

"Yeah, Dad. Are you busy?"

She heard his footsteps, then the door opened.

"I'm working. Can it wait?"

"Sure. I g-guess so." Nova suddenly felt as if she was going to pass out from nerves.

"Are you sure? I can make some time."

Nova's heart was pounding out of her chest as she looked up at her dad. Dayton Grant. It had to be him. This couldn't just be another *version* of him. He was her dad, the same one who let her color pictures at his desk while he worked. The same one who called her firefly.

"Dad...I..." Nova couldn't get the words out before

bursting into tears. Somehow she ended up in his arms while he stroked her hair and tried to comfort her.

"What is it, firefly? You can talk to me about anything."

"Can I? Because you don't seem the same," she sobbed.

"The same as what? What are you saying?" His voice was strained. "Is this about Ethan? Has he done something?"

Nova pulled away. "No…I mean, yes. It's about Ethan, and you and me and Mom and Marshall. It's about everything!"

"Nova, what—"

"I know about Alana! How could you never tell me about her? Why didn't you or Mom ever tell me I had a twin sister?" Nova felt herself losing control but couldn't stop it. "You never said a word. Nothing!"

"Oh my God." His face was white as a sheet. "How?"

"It doesn't matter!" Nova yelled. "That's not all, and you know it! What happened to *me?* I know you can tell me. Why am I here? How did you come back? Why is everything different?"

He retreated into his office and somehow managed to collapse into his chair. He leaned over and put his head in his hands. "Oh my God." He kept saying it over and over. When he finally looked up, he had an anguished look on his face. "I'm so sorry honey. I never meant to hurt you. I didn't know it had affected you. I would have talked to you about it if I had known."

Nova felt numb. "Are you my dad?"

"Yes, of course I am."

"Then why are you so different?"

His tortured expression was almost too much to bear. He hesitated a moment then seemed to pull himself together. "What do you remember?"

"I remember another life. In that life, you were dead. You had a wreck on the bridge the first day of school. I forgot my class schedule, and you went back to get it. It was my fault. You were killed when your car went into the river."

"I'm so sorry. That must have been awful for you." He shook his head.

"It was terrible for all of us," she answered solemnly. "They never found your body. It was horrible. We buried a casket, but you weren't in it. Everything changed after that. Mom was depressed. Marshall and I stopped getting along. No one was happy anymore. It's like we all died a little with you." Nova tried to catch her breath. "Then last Wednesday, I got up and everything was different. The first thing I noticed was the missing chip in the table."

"What chip?" he asked, confused.

"Marshall broke a chunk out of the kitchen table with his skateboard after you died. That's why I froze when he broke it again in the same spot last night."

"Interesting…" he frowned.

"Yeah. But that's not all that was different. Mom's hair was back to normal, instead of the red-orange it was the night before. And Delilah and Ethan. They weren't the same either. So many things were wrong, or at least different. Then I came home and you were here…like nothing ever happened."

Nova tried to collect her thoughts so she'd make sense, but her brain was racing. She decided to skip ahead to the letter.

"Dad, I found Grandma Kate's letters when I was in the attic. I pulled them out again this morning, and there was a letter to you about how she wouldn't help you."

"So the letter was there, in Mother's trunk." He wasn't really asking her. "I was so angry when I read it that I sent it back to her. I wondered if she kept it. He shook his head. "I was mad at her for so long, but she was right. Changing is dangerous."

"I don't understand. What happened? What did you do?"

"It's a long story, but the gist of it is that the Grant family has a...gift. Not all of us have it. But most do. Like me, and my mother, your grandma Kate. My aunt Jean and uncle Bill also had the ability. So did my grandmother, Evelyn. She was a Grant by birth too. She and my grandfather were second cousins. Many others in the family also had the gift, going back as far as anyone can remember."

"So what is this gift?" Nova held her breath, not entirely sure she wanted to know.

"You'd better sit down." He offered her his chair.

She shook her head, climbed onto the desk, and crossed her legs under her.

He sat in his chair again and gave her a sort of half smile. "We can sometimes change things. I mean... change our past. I don't know how to explain it, except that we have the ability to travel back in time to a specific event in order to take a different path. It's very hard to do. At least for me it is. I've only managed twice. Once when your sister, Alana, passed away." His eyes misted over. "And once, on the day of the car accident. In both cases, I switched instantly during a moment of intense emotion. I don't know how to describe it, except to say it's like reaching out with your mind and grabbing hold of a memory."

Nova struggled to accept what he was saying. "Time travel? That's the gift?"

"That's the gift," he said solemnly.

"How? I mean...can I do it too?"

"I don't know. And I can't tell you exactly how to do it. It's not that simple. You have to be taught if you want to control it. But your grandmother never wanted me to travel, so she refused to talk to me about it and wouldn't allow anyone else to either. Her stance on the matter broke us off from the rest of the family."

"So that's why we don't see them?"

"Right. When I was a kid, they all talked about traveling around me when Mother wasn't around. But your grandma Kate got mad and made them stop. She and her sister, Aunt Jean, had a big fight. Mother didn't want me to learn how to use the ability because something bad had happened when she traveled. I think it had to do with a child, too. She never talked about it."

"Why didn't you ask her?"

"My mother was pretty closed off. You know, hard to talk to. I know her life wasn't easy, and I'm sure what happened when she traveled had a lot to do with it. My dad died before I was born."

"I know. I'm really sorry." Nova didn't know what else to say. She wanted him to keep talking, to keep telling her about traveling but he sat in his chair, staring out the window. "Dad?"

He looked back at her. "Sorry. I was just thinking. Anyway, when I was about ten years old, we went to visit Aunt Jean at Willow Hill. We were sitting on the porch one afternoon, and the subject of time travel came up again. Mother and Aunt Jean had a knock-down-drag-out about it, and Aunt Jean stormed into the house. We packed up the car and started to leave, but I'd forgotten something in the guest room and had to go back inside. When I was coming down the stairs to leave again, Aunt Jean was waiting at the bottom. She stopped me and said to come see her when I got older and she would tell me some things I needed to know. That was the last time I ever saw her."

"And you never talked to her again?"

"No. When Mother died, I thought about trying to get in touch with Aunt Jean and the rest of the family, but I never did. It was just easier to leave things alone, I guess."

Nova's head felt as if it were going to explode. The Grant family had a gift, which meant she most likely had it too. But what her dad was describing defied belief. He was talking about the ability to time travel. It was too incredible to be real, yet it was the only explanation that made sense. Nova's mind turned back to her sister.

"What happened to Alana?"

His eyes misted over again. "It was her heart. She had a defect that went undetected for almost five years. You both started swimming lessons the summer before kindergarten. You were afraid of the water, but Alana loved it. She was so excited that she jumped in the first day and the instructor had to grab her." He smiled.

"Oh my God…the pool! She was telling me to jump in too. I remember. How can that be possible?"

"I don't know. I have so many questions myself," he said quietly. "Like I said, she jumped right in. I hollered for her to wait, but she was so confident. She came out sputtering but smiling and yelled, 'Did you see me Daddy?'" He wiped his eyes with his shirtsleeve. "It happened during your third lesson. You were practicing holding on to floats and kicking. She made it halfway across the pool and suddenly just let go and went under. The instructor was only a couple of feet away and pulled her up instantly, but something was wrong. When he lifted her out of the pool, Alana's lips were blue. Someone called 9-1-1 while the instructor performed CPR. It felt like an eternity waiting for the paramedics to get there. They did everything they possibly could to bring her back, but she was gone."

"Oh my God." She closed her eyes and tried to block out the image of her sister lying by the pool, not breathing. "Was I there when it happened?"

"You were sitting across the pool, waiting for your turn. One of the other instructors grabbed you and took you out."

"I'm glad I don't remember that."

He squeezed her arm. "Me too, firefly."

"What did you do after she died. I mean, how did you get through it?"

"We had you. We had to keep going. It was even harder after the autopsy revealed a heart defect that could have been corrected with surgery if we had only known about it. That's when I decided to go back. I would insist she be checked out as an infant, and she would live a long healthy life. That was my plan."

"So what happened? Why didn't it work?"

"In the first life, your mom had a wreck and broke her leg two weeks before you were due. She was in a lot of pain and refused medication because of the babies. Her blood pressure shot up from the stress, and her doctor ordered a Cesarean section. Your mom never even went into labor. They took Alana out first."

"So technically I had a big sister." Nova smiled wistfully.

"Yes, you did. You were both beautiful babies...perfect. We never knew anything was wrong with Alana. The second time around, I was able to prevent the accident and you girls were born naturally. I wasn't worried about the birth because I was preoccupied with making sure Alana was checked for a heart condition.

"Your mom went into labor, but she didn't progress very quickly. This time, you were born first and your mother was exhausted. The monitor showed that Alana's heartbeat had dropped, and everyone in the delivery room went into overdrive. She was already in the birth canal, so the doctor had to use every method to get her out. When she was finally born, she looked gray and she wasn't breathing. All of a sudden, it seemed there were twice as many people in the room, working on her frantically. They did everything they could. I couldn't believe I had come back to save her and instead I'd lost five years with her. It was more than I thought I could bear."

"So you and Mom decided to never talk about her?" Nova asked.

"We talked about her. Just not around you and Marshall. I know we should've told you both about your sister, but for some reason, we could never get it out. It was even harder for me than it was for your mother. She was

140

devastated to lose her baby, but I lost a child that I'd loved for five years. I had memories of Alana that your mom would never have."

"What do you mean? Mom didn't know?"

"No. She thinks she lost her baby the day she was born."

"So no one knows but you?" Nova asked incredulously.

"No one. It was awful. In my mind, I could hear Alana's beautiful little voice calling me Daddy, saying she loved me. I had thousands of memories to be tortured by. And the worst part was not being able to talk about her that way. I felt completely alone. Your mother had no idea what I'd done. I couldn't tell her." He was staring out the window again. "Then when you were about two years old, you started talking to 'Allie.' The first time I heard you in your room I actually thought I might have changed timelines again. I went rushing in there, but you were alone. I asked you where she was, and you pointed to the rocking horse. You said, 'There she is, Daddy.' For a minute, I almost thought I could see her too."

He studied Nova for a moment, then continued. "It was hard on your mom, you talking about Allie. She was still grieving over losing her other baby girl. I didn't think she'd ever get over it completely, but for me...I don't know. It was almost comforting to hear you playing with your imaginary friend. I could pretend she was real too." He seemed to be far away again. "That's what you called your sister, you know. Allie."

"Why didn't you try again?"

His face clouded over. "I started to...many times. But then I'd think about what Mother said, about traveling causing more pain. I was afraid I'd screw things up even worse."

Nova didn't know what to say. She felt so sorry for her parents, especially her dad, but so many thoughts were swirling around her head. As sad as she was about Alana, she was also exhilarated. Her family could travel through time! Most likely, *she* could travel through time!

"I wish you'd told me about this family *gift*. But I guess I wouldn't have believed you before I changed myself."

"I'm sorry." He brushed her hair out of her face. "This must have been so scary for you, not understanding. The ironic thing is that I had planned to tell you before the accident on the bridge. You were getting older and I thought you needed to know, that it would be dangerous not to tell you. I even wrote it on my calendar. But then, I traveled and, well…everything was different. I couldn't deal with it, I guess."

"I saw the note on your calendar. It drove me crazy, wondering what you were going to tell me. I thought it was probably about our trip though."

"When did you see it?" He looked confused.

"After you died."

"Oh, right. I'm sorry I put you through so much – the accident, then the switch to this timeline. You must have been so confused."

"It's been awful. It's not that I want to go back. I don't. This life is so much better. In the old life, Mom was really depressed. She complained all the time and kept dying her hair. She was lost without you. She was worried about money and kept looking for jobs. But as far as I know, she never applied for any. We never laughed. In that life, Delilah was my best friend. Ethan was her boyfriend. I barely knew him."

"You and Delilah were pretty close."

"Yeah."

Neither of them said anything for a few minutes, each lost in their own thoughts.

Finally Nova asked, "Do you remember the accident?"

"I remember," he answered, his voice strained. "I drove home to get your schedule on the first day of school. On the way back across the bridge, a city sanitation truck crossed the line and hit me. I tried to avoid it, but there was nowhere to go. The Mustang went through the guardrail and into the river."

"You remember dying?"

"Not exactly. I remember *almost* dying."

"But they didn't find your body. They said it was washed downriver."

"I guess in that timeline, it was."

"I don't understand! How could you die and still travel back to change it?"

"I couldn't. I traveled before I died. It wasn't on purpose; it just happened. Not that I'm complaining." He shook his head. "When the car hit the water, all I could think of was you and me, sitting in my office and planning our trip. It was like everything happened in slow motion. I wanted to be home, not in the water. The next thing I knew, I was sitting in my office, in this chair. It happened in an instant, like flipping a switch. I wasn't wet. I wasn't even wearing the same clothes. I sat there for a long time, at least a couple of hours, sick to my stomach, not moving. Then all of a sudden, this strange kid was banging on the door, yelling that you'd fainted in the driveway. I didn't even know who he was, but he obviously knew me. I ran outside to you, and the rest you should remember. Well most of it anyway, since you had a concussion."

Nova had been listening intently to everything her dad said. The whole thing sounded incredible, and impossible. But then, so did her circumstance. She would have to suspend her disbelief if she wanted to truly understand. One thing didn't add up though.

"Dad, you said the Grants can go *back* in time, but that's not what happened. You went forward. I just woke up and everything was different, as if I'd been in this reality all along. I can remember the other life, but to everyone else, it's like it never happened."

He shrugged. "I don't have any answers for you. When I was a kid, I never heard anyone in the family talk about going forward. It was always going back. The Grant family has used this power for generations to change their lives. They've changed events like deaths, marriages, crop failures. Once they even changed the outcome of a war by altering the results of a key battle. Hindsight is a frustrating thing for most people, unless you can actually use the information to change your life. The Grants have done that for generations. But like I said, no one ever mentioned going forward. And that's apparently what I did. There was no control on my part. I was flung forward nine months."

"So you're saying that you were suddenly here, in your office, the morning I fainted in the driveway?"

"That's right."

"Okay...then where were you the nine months before that?"

"What do you mean?"

Nova leaned forward, frowning. "Well, I know where I was. I was here, dealing with a crappy life without you. So if I came forward too, why did I have to go through that?"

He leaned back in his chair, and sighed. "I don't know. I wish I did, but I don't. This whole thing is almost as much a mystery to me as it is to you."

"Okay, here's another thing. If you didn't go back, why are so many things different? If you only changed the past nine months, why isn't everything before that the same?"

He frowned. "Like I said before, I don't know. I know that's not what you want to hear, but it's the truth. I've spent hours and hours in here since the accident, reading everything I have on time travel, trying to figure out how this happened. I have no idea what the repercussions of traveling forward are. For the most part, everything *is* the same. Only a

144

few things are different. Speaking of which, where did this Ethan kid come from? Your mother clearly knows him, but I don't remember ever seeing him before the accident."

"He's my boyfriend. Apparently he's been my boyfriend since the eighth grade. I'd say that qualifies as something that's definitely different. And Delilah can't stand me. We've never been friends."

"Really?"

"Yeah," Nova sighed.

"Bummer." He grinned. "I always thought she was kind of silly anyway."

"She was okay. She got me through some bad times. You don't know what it was like after you died. It was awful. Delilah kept things in perspective, I guess. If it wasn't about her, it wasn't important." Nova managed a wry smile. "I guess she was pretty self-absorbed, but I still miss her."

"I'm sorry."

Neither of them said anything for few moments.

"So you really missed your old man, huh? Guess it's pretty dull around here without me." He smiled, giving her shoulder a nudge.

Nova would have laughed, but she couldn't get a nagging question out of her mind. "Dad, why didn't you talk to me about all of this right away? Why did you let me suffer when you knew how confused and freaked out I must be?"

He seemed taken aback. "I didn't know you had awakened into a world that was different. Since everything was normal to everyone else, I thought it was normal to you too. I knew you were acting strange, but I thought it was my fault, that you could tell something was wrong with me."

"You *have* been different. But I guess I can understand why. You've been going through the same thing I have."

"Except that I knew about the ability and you didn't. I'm so sorry, firefly. I should've realized something had happened to you too, but I couldn't wrap my head around *my* situation. One minute I was plunging into the river, and the next I was dry as a bone, sitting at my desk. I don't think I could've figured anything out right then."

Nova was having trouble wrapping her head around things too. Apparently at some point during the same morning, she and her dad had been yanked into this reality.

"Do you know what time the, uh, *switch* happened?"

He nodded. "Seven fifteen, according to the clock on the shelf."

"I guess I slept through it," Nova mused. What would that have been like if she'd been awake? Would she have been able to see her dad appear out of thin air? Or the Mustang suddenly materialize in the driveway? Or even her mom's hair change back to its natural color? The whole thing was mind-blowing.

Then she thought of something else. "Wait, if the accident happened after you dropped me off and went back home, why didn't you get here at that same time, just nine months in the future? That should have been about eight thirty. And why nine months? Why not the next day? Or even the same day?"

"I don't know. I don't understand how the whole thing works, but I guess you can travel to any time on any day. I just remember that when I realized I was sitting at my desk that morning, the clock said seven fifteen."

Nova looked at the clock perched conspicuously on the shelf behind the desk. "Where did that come from? I don't recognize it."

"No idea." He looked at Nova, and they both chuckled, quickly advancing to that uncontrollable laughter that makes your stomach hurt.

Tears ran down Nova's face. "This is insane."

They laughed until they heard Marshall and Celeste talking in the kitchen.

"What's so funny, you two?" her mother called.

"Nothing!" Nova choked out.

She looked at her dad. He stopped laughing and put his finger to his lips.

"We can't share any of this with anyone. That includes Mom, Marshall, and Ethan," he whispered.

Nova felt a lump in her throat. "Dad..."

"What?" he asked warily.

"I've sort of been talking to Ethan about...well, not about this exactly of course, but about something being wrong...about my old life and this one. He knows."

Dayton frowned. "I don't really know this kid. Can we trust him?"

"Yes. He's been incredible. Trust me, it'll be okay if Ethan knows. Please let me talk to him. He's gonna ask me anyway."

Her dad was still frowning. "Use your own judgment, firefly, but remember, no one outside of my family has ever known about this gift. No one. That's why I never told your mom."

"I understand. I'll be careful." Nova hesitated. Something had just dawned on her. "Dad?"

"Hmm?"

"If you're the one who came forward in time, why do I remember the old life? Shouldn't I be like everyone else, remembering only this life? Shouldn't the old me just be gone?"

He thought about it for a moment. "Maybe it means you also have the gift, and when I jumped forward into this new reality, you changed too. If I can remember the old life, I guess it makes sense you would too, if you're like me. You know, a time traveler."

"Oh my God. I'm like a character in one of your books. Except for real." Nova felt as if her world had shifted again. If she had the gift, then she had the ability to travel in time as well. And maybe she could learn to control it. That opened up so many possibilities.

"We'll find a way to talk about it later." He wrapped

his arms around her and gave her a reassuring hug.

"I love you, Dad," Nova said softly.

"I love you too, firefly."

Celeste stuck her head in the office door and grinned. "Well, I see you two are having a good afternoon! Marshall wants pizza. How about trying out the new place on Hilltop Road? It's supposed to be good."

"That sounds awesome!" Nova jumped up.

"I didn't mean right now! It's only four." She laughed.

"I keep forgetting to have lunch. Can we go now?"

"Nova Grant, how do you *forget* to have lunch?" she exclaimed as she walked away.

Nova started to follow her, but Dayton put his hand on her arm and motioned for her to wait. When her mom was out of earshot, he asked, "How did you get into my desk? I'm sure it was locked. It doesn't matter now. I'm just curious."

"I broke the middle drawer – the one with the keys," she answered sheepishly. She reached under the bookcase by the door and pulled out the crowbar.

He shook his head and laughed. "I hadn't even noticed. Did you scratch the door frame too?"

"Yeah that was me," she admitted sheepishly.

"Shouldn't be too hard to fix. I guess the drawer doesn't matter since there's nothing to hide anymore." He smiled.

"What are you doing with so many keys? There must be thirty or forty in there."

"Most of them were in Grandma Kate's house, in a box under the sink in the kitchen. I didn't know what they were for, but I kept them anyway, just in case. I still have her house and thought maybe one day I'd find out what each one opened. You know me and mysteries."

"You still own her house?" Nova asked incredulously. "Why haven't you ever told me?"

"I don't know. After she died, I guess I just didn't

feel like talking about it. It's been a while since I've been there. Bad memories. We argued right before her accident."

"I'm sorry, Dad. I'm sure she forgave you."

"I hope so."

"Is there anything else I should know? Any more revelations?" Nova grinned.

He chuckled. "Not that I can think of. Look, can we talk again later? I think I've had all the drama I can handle for now."

"Agreed. Let's go eat pizza." Nova smiled.

Dayton grabbed his keys from the desktop and dashed out the door. "Let's take the Mustang. Come on, Marshall!"

As the Grant family piled into the Mustang, laughing, Nova let her newfound knowledge sink in. Nova Grant – time traveler. This life was getting better and better.

CHAPTER 15

Nova lay in bed that night, thinking about the events of the day. Having her dad to talk to made everything seem normal again, even though their lives were anything *but* normal. Ethan had been calling all evening. He'd already left five messages for her to call him back. *I have to tell him,* she thought. Once again, the phone next to her bed rang. She pulled the pillow over her head and waited for it to stop. Right now, she just wanted to sleep. She wasn't up for talking about her conversation with her dad, especially since she was still processing the information herself. How could she begin to explain it to Ethan? She closed her eyes and let her brain shut down, slipping slowly toward unconsciousness until something jolted her awake again. Someone was in her room. She lay perfectly still, hardly breathing, and listened. The floorboard by the window creaked.

"Nova? Are you awake?" Ethan whispered softly.

"Ethan! You scared me to death!" Nova whispered a little too loudly, her heart pounding.

Ethan knelt beside her bed and put his hand on her mouth. "Shh! Don't wake up your parents."

"How'd you get in?" Nova demanded.

"Crawled in through the window. You really shouldn't keep it open."

She laughed. "I didn't think I had to worry about a creeper like you stalking me in the middle of the night."

"Well, now you know. Let's make this quick. I have lots of other houses to break into."

Nova could see Ethan's shape by the light streaming in the window from the lamppost next door, but she couldn't make out the expression on his face. He was trying to sound light, but his voice had an underlying anxious tone. He was probably worried because she hadn't called him yet to tell him what had happened with her dad. She really would rather have talked to him tomorrow. Her thoughts were jumbled, especially since he had awakened her from the first sound sleep she'd had in over a week.

"Ethan, I was gonna call you tomorrow."

"Tomorrow? You were waiting until tomorrow? I guess that's fine. I wasn't worried or anything. I wasn't even thinking about it." Now he sounded genuinely irritated.

"You don't have to be sarcastic. It was a confusing afternoon. I was exhausted, and my brain felt like it was gonna explode. This isn't about you, you know. It's *my* life that's screwed up." As soon as she got the words out, she regretted them. Ethan had been great to her without expecting anything in return. How could she be so mean?

Ethan stood. "Okay. We'll talk later." He turned back toward the open window.

"Wait…"

He hesitated then vaulted over the windowsill and out into the yard. She jumped up in time to see him jogging away.

Nova sat on her bed, thinking about everything her dad had said. She wondered if she also had the Grant gift. "Maybe I can go back in time to just before Ethan woke me up."

She lay down and closed her eyes, trying to will

herself back to sleep, but after thirty minutes or so, she gave up and got out of bed. Nova pulled on shorts, a T-shirt, and sneakers. Carefully, she arranged the pillows and quilt on her bed to make it look occupied, then she stood back to survey her handiwork. Her parents would certainly be able to tell she was gone if they stepped into her room rather than peeking in from the doorway, but they most likely wouldn't do that.

The clock on Nova's nightstand read 2:20 a.m. Her mom was usually up by six, so Nova figured she had about three and a half hours before she had to be back. She climbed out of the window and sprinted across the yard and down the street toward Ethan's house.

When she got there, she had to stop and think about which window was his. It wouldn't go very well if she accidently woke his parents. She remembered that Ethan's room was to the right and on the backside of the house, so she made her way through the dense shrubbery and circled around to the backyard. There she encountered a problem. The lot sloped from front to back, so the bedroom window that should be Ethan's was a good eight feet off the ground.

"What now?" she whispered to herself.

"You could always go in through the door like a normal person."

Nova nearly jumped out of her skin and barely managed to stifle a scream. "Oh my God! Are you trying to literally scare me to death?"

"Nah. What's up, hot girl?" Ethan sounded very pleased with himself.

Nova was still trying to breathe through the adrenaline rush he had given her. "Why are you out here?"

"I've been sitting on the deck trying to decide whether or not to forgive you and go back to your house." He laughed.

"Can we go inside?" she whispered.

"Sure thing. Right this way."

Ethan grabbed her hand and led her up the steps to the

deck. He quietly unlocked the back door with a key he'd extracted from his pocket. They silently made their way through the mudroom, the kitchen, and down the hall to his room, carefully closing the door behind them.

"We'll be okay now," he said, a split second before stumbling over a pile of discarded clothes on the floor and knocking over his desk chair. They both held their breath, but there wasn't a sound from anywhere else in the house.

"My mom is an insanely light sleeper," he whispered. "We'll have to be really quiet."

Ethan flicked on the desk lamp, and Nova shook her head.

"I figured your room couldn't possibly be as bad as I remembered, and I was right. It's worse. Is that the same piece of cake on your desk?"

"I told you before. It's not cake."

"You're a pig." Nova giggled. "I pity the person who marries you."

"Ouch." Ethan pretended to be crushed.

In addition to the clothes on the floor, there were clothes and potato chips strewn across his bed. He did his best to scoop them up and deposit them in the trashcan beside his desk.

"You're throwing the clothes away too?" Nova asked.

"Nah. I'll get them out later."

"I'm serious, Ethan. You need an intervention. This isn't normal."

"Well, my mom used to make me clean it up, but she got tired of nagging me all the time, so she'd sneak in here when I was at school and I'd come home to a miraculously clean room. Then one day she had a meltdown about it and said if I wanted to live in a sty, that was my choice but she was through with it. So it's kind of been like this ever since. Honestly, once it got this bad, it sort of quit getting worse. So I'm good with it."

"Can you at least get rid of the cake?"

Ethan gave her a withering look. "I told you, it's not cake."

Nova rolled her eyes. "Whatever it is, get rid of it. There's something growing on it."

"Okay, hot girl. Just for you." Ethan pulled her into a hug. "You're forgiven for not calling me, by the way."

Nova pulled away and sat on the floor next to Ethan's bed. From her point of view, it was the only clear spot. Ethan dropped down beside her and took her hand.

"What happened?" he asked carefully, brushing a strand of dark hair away from her face.

The tender gesture made Nova's heart race a little. She took a deep breath. "I talked to my dad. You know when we were talking about the possibilities of something…um…supernatural causing what happened to me?"

"Yeah," Ethan responded cautiously.

"Well, we were right. Not about mind control or the whole parallel universe thing, but it *is* something in that category. Kind of like science fiction, except it's not fiction."

"So tell me." Ethan sat completely still, waiting.

"Okay. Here goes. Just listen and don't say anything until I'm through."

Ethan nodded without speaking.

Nova cleared her throat. "My family – that is, my dad's family – has a gift. Some of us have the ability to time travel. Apparently the Grants have been doing it for generations. I don't know when it started or how it's done. Neither does my dad. But it happens. Dad time traveled the first time when my sister, Alana, died."

"When you were born?" Ethan asked.

"No. Alana had a heart condition that no one knew about. She died from it during a swimming lesson just after our fifth birthday."

"But the death certificate said she died right after she was born," Ethan pointed out.

"I know. In another timeline, she lived for five years. When she died, my dad was crushed. He knew about the ability that ran in his family and tried to go back to when she was born so he could fix it. He wanted to make them test her heart as an infant so she could have surgery and live. That was his plan. But when he traveled back to right before our birth, it caused a change in what happened. Instead of being born by Cesarean, my mom went into labor. It lasted a long time and the strain caused Alana's heart to stop. That's when she died at birth."

Ethan stared at Nova, frowning. "That just isn't possible."

"I know how crazy it sounds, but it's the truth. And that's not all of it. He remembers the accident. I forgot my class schedule that morning, so he went back home to get it. On his way back, he was crossing the bridge and a city sanitation truck hit him. He remembers going through the rail and into the water. At the time, all he could think about was being back home. It happened instantly, like flipping a switch. He came forward to the morning we cut school and I passed out in the driveway. He sort of *woke up* sitting at his desk in his office. Instead of going back in time, he went *forward*. And when his reality changed, mine did too. What doesn't make sense to me though is that if he went forward, why did some of the past change too?"

"That's the only thing that doesn't make sense to you?" Ethan asked incredulously.

"Yeah, pretty much. I guess I've accepted everything else." Nova marveled at how true that statement was.

"So let me get this straight. Your dad went ahead in time, and that caused some of the things in the past to change, like me for instance."

"Yes! And Delilah." Then she remembered the chip in the kitchen table. "And the chip! Except now it's back. Marshall smacked it with his skateboard and broke it again."

"What chip?"

"There was a broken spot in our kitchen table. I used to snag all my clothes on it. In this life, it wasn't there. But then Marshall came in and hit the table and it broke in exactly the same spot. What does that mean?"

"I have no idea. You're melting my brain. I mean seriously, I can actually *feel* my brain. That can't be a good thing. I can't process all of this." Ethan leaned over and put his head in his hands. "Okay, so your dad remembers the accident. But instead of dying, he time traveled into the future, and that's where we are now."

"Yeah." Nova tried to read Ethan's expression.

All of a sudden, Ethan's face lit up. "Nova! It can't have happened like you said, because your dad wouldn't have gone back to school! You didn't forget your schedule. I had dinner at your house the night before. Your dad grilled steaks, I noticed your schedule lying on the counter, and your mom made you put it in your backpack. I saw you the next morning at school, and you had it. So you see, he wouldn't have had any reason to bring it."

Nova thought about that for a minute. Then it started to make sense. "That must be why some things in the past changed. They had to change in order for my dad to be alive. When he came forward, it had to make sense. Maybe if you hadn't been there, I *would have* forgotten my schedule. Then my dad would have had the wreck. And maybe if you had to be there to prevent the wreck, then other things had to happen differently too. There must be a reason for every change in my past. I just don't know what all of those reasons are."

Ethan groaned. "Maybe you were right. We need to talk about this tomorrow. I don't think I can hear any more tonight."

"I have to get back anyway." Nova was suddenly exhausted. "My mom gets up at the crack of dawn, and you have school. Call me later." She got up to leave, but Ethan stopped her.

"Wait. I'll walk you home."

Neither of them said a word all the way back to Nova's house. She climbed in through her window then watched him jog across her yard, then between the houses where the bus stop was. As soon as he was out of sight, she crawled into bed and fell asleep almost instantly.

CHAPTER 16

Marshall came bursting in at seven forty-five.

"Nova! We're going to North Carolina on Saturday, and we're staying at a horse farm! It's gonna be awesome! Maybe we'll get to ride some of the horses! Do you think they'll let us?"

Marshall's voice seemed to be coming from far away. Nova tried to shake off the layer of fog in her brain.

"Marshall, good grief. I was still sleeping," she managed to get out.

"Oh, sorry. I forgot you don't have to go to school," he said sheepishly. "Wow, Nova, you look awful!"

"Thanks." Nova pulled the pillow over her head. "Now get lost."

Marshall started to leave but stopped at the door. "It's great about going to North Carolina though, don't you think?"

"Yes, Marshall. It's great. Now go eat breakfast or something."

Marshall bounded out of her room and accidently slammed her door. She tried to will herself back to sleep, but she could still hear him yelling, "I can't wait to go! It'll be awesome!"

"What's so awesome about it?" Nova groaned.

She definitely wasn't excited about a road trip to North Carolina. She'd have to think of a way out of it. Maybe she could stay at Ethan's. Considering the state of his room, she could be in there a week and no one would even notice. She'd talk to him later and come up with a good excuse for not going. Why would her dad agree to take a trip right now anyway, just when they were trying to sort things out? What would make him want to go to…North Carolina!

Nova sat bolt upright. That was where her dad had lived as a child. They were going to see Aunt Jean! Nova shot out of bed. Still wearing the T-shirt and shorts from last night, she flung open her door and sprinted to the office.

Her dad was sitting at his desk, leaning back in his chair and smiling. "Well, look who's up!"

"Is it true? Are we going to Aunt Jean's?"

"You bet." He grinned and motioned for her to close the door. Then he leaned across his desk and whispered, "I think it's time we talked to someone in the family who knows more about our *gift* than we do."

"This is incredible!" replied Nova. "How did you manage it?"

"All I had to do was agree, actually. Your mom's been after me to reconnect with my family in North Carolina, so this morning, I brought it up and she insisted we go. Since she doesn't have any family left, she feels like you and Marshall have really missed out. I've already called Aunt Jean, and she was ecstatic."

"When do we leave?"

"Saturday morning, bright and early."

"What about Mom and Marshall? How will we get rid of them?"

"Oh come on, Nova, they're not that bad." He laughed.

"Very funny. You know what I mean. How will we be able to talk to Aunt Jean with them there?"

"Let me worry about that. Aunt Jean knows we want to talk. She sounded pretty sharp on the phone, so I'm sure she'll find a way for us to be alone." He put his hand on Nova's shoulder. "Are you ready for this, firefly?"

"I'm ready." Nova hesitated, then decided to tell him about her talk with Ethan.

When she was through, his face had lost all traces of humor. "I'm not sure it was such a good idea to tell him everything. What if he talks about it to someone else?"

"Even if he did, which he won't, who'd believe him?"

"Good point," he agreed. "Still, I wish you hadn't told him. It's going to make things awkward when he's around."

Nova hadn't thought of that. "Maybe we should take him with us on the trip. You know, rip off the Band-Aid and get it over with."

Her dad's stern expression remained in spite of her attempt to lighten the mood. "Absolutely not. This isn't just a vacation, Nova. I want to get some real answers from Aunt Jean. I've known my whole life that I have this ability. You can't imagine how frustrating it's been not understanding it, not having anyone to talk to about it."

Nova impulsively hugged her dad. He smiled and kissed her on the forehead. "At least now we have each other to talk to. I'm thankful for that, firefly."

Celeste opened the office door and stuck her head in. "Hey, you two. I made waffles, but Marshall is about to finish them off."

Nova turned to follow her mom then hesitated. Turning back to her dad, she whispered, "Are you planning to… *do something* at Aunt Jean's?"

His eyes shifted to his desktop. "What do you mean?"

"You know what I mean. Are you thinking about going back again?"

He looked directly at Nova. "No, I'm not." Then he

stood and bounded for the door. "Let's go eat some of those waffles before they're all gone!"

Nova didn't entirely believe him, but she couldn't help but laugh at her boyish dad. She followed him into the kitchen just as Marshall was stuffing the last waffle, wrapped in a napkin, into his backpack.

"Seriously? You're actually gonna eat that later?" Nova exclaimed.

"I do it all the time," Marshall admitted. "The lunch at school sucks."

"Marshall!" Celeste pretended to be shocked. "Language, Mister!"

"*Sucks* is not a bad word, Mom. Ask Nova. She says it all the time."

"Marshall Grant! I do not. And by the way, *you* suck!" Nova laughed.

"Nova!" Celeste looked at her husband. "Dayton, help me out here."

He shrugged his shoulders. "Sometimes 'sucks' just works, honey."

She threw her hands in the air. "I give up. You all suck."

Marshall took off for the bus stop amid peals of laughter.

Nova could see Marshall through the kitchen window. He was running across the back yard, his overstuffed backpack dragging behind him. She turned away just in time to see her mom snap her dad with a kitchen towel. He grabbed her and waltzed her around the kitchen, ending with a flourish in an elaborate dip. Her mother was beaming, her cheeks flushed.

He looked over at Nova and winked. "I guess your old man's still got it."

Laughing, her mom snapped him with the towel again. "You've got it all right. I'm just not sure what *it* is."

Nova grinned as she watched her parents behaving

like a couple of teenagers. *I really love this crazy family. No matter what happens at Aunt Jean's, I don't want anything to change.*

Since Marshall had scarfed down all of the waffles, Nova and her dad shared a banana and two bowls of cereal for breakfast. As usual, her mom got ready for her run.

As soon as they were alone, he grinned and leaned toward Nova. "You know, maybe we'll figure out how to time travel well enough from Aunt Jean to take a few quick trips. Nothing big, just going to the Ice House for hot fudge sundaes over and over. Or that Saturday we rented jet skis at Candlewood Lake. I'd like to do that a few more times. And my first book signing. That'd be cool to do again."

"Sure! We can't tell Mom though."

At that moment, Celeste came striding in, dressed in her running shorts and T-shirt. "Tell Mom what?"

Nova choked on her cereal. "Uh…uh…."

Her dad saved the moment. "Celeste, we're bound to have a few secrets, especially with a certain day coming up."

She beamed. "Oh yes! Well, don't let me interrupt." She pulled on her running shoes and nearly danced out the back door.

"Good save, Dad." Nova patted him on the back.

"She's still a kid about her birthday. At least we have a couple of weeks to come up with something to surprise her with. I have some work to do this morning. Why don't you start packing for Aunt Jean's. I'll bring your suitcase in from the garage."

"Okay. I'll do that this morning, but I need to see Ethan later. I want to tell him we're going."

"Just as long as you remember that he's *not* going. You understand that, right? We'll be gone less than two weeks. You can see him when you get back."

"Okay, Dad."

Nova spent the next hour going through her drawers and closet, feeling as though she was snooping through a stranger's belongings. The clothes were definitely her taste, but many items she'd never seen before. After basically living out of one drawer all week, it hadn't occurred to her that so much of her clothing would be unfamiliar. No matter. It was hard to keep her mind on a trivial activity like packing when all she could think of was meeting Aunt Jean.

Dayton's aunt was the one who had wanted to teach him how to use his gift all those years ago. Would she be willing to teach them both now? Nova wondered if Aunt Jean had managed to patch things up with Grandma Kate before she died. It was sad that the two sisters had fallen out of touch. They must have missed each other terribly.

Nova thought of Alana. She wished that she and Alana had been able to know each other. Having a sister would have been wonderful. She couldn't imagine throwing a relationship like that away over a quarrel. *If I had a chance to have my sister back, I'd never let anything like that happen.* She froze. *If I had a chance to have my sister back...* Nova's heartbeat quickened. *Dad has to try again. I know that's what he's thinking too. That's really why we're going. He thinks Aunt Jean will be able to help him get her back this time!*

Nova thought of the sketch that was still under her mattress – little Alana with golden hair and hazel eyes. Her expression had been playful. She'd probably had their dad's personality, always ready to laugh. What would Alana be like now? A chill ran up Nova's spine. Maybe they really could get her back, with Aunt Jean's help. But what else would change because of it? That was the big question. Would they lose someone else instead? Nova's head was starting to hurt a little. She lay down on her bed and closed her eyes, trying to will herself asleep again. She wanted to stop thinking for a while. Everything was so complicated.

After thirty minutes or so, she gave up and returned to packing. There was no real hurry since they weren't leaving until Saturday, but it was something to occupy her mind that didn't make her feel as though her brain were going to explode.

She couldn't wait to see Ethan. Somehow, everything seemed more normal when he was around. She picked up her phone to call him, but glanced at the time and realized he was at school, taking his one and only exam. He'd call her when he got home, she was sure. Until then, she'd try to stay busy getting ready for the trip.

It was almost noon when Nova finally heard from Ethan. She was so keyed up she nearly jumped out of her skin when her phone rang.

"Hi, hot girl! Man, am I glad that's over with. I hope I didn't just fail biology."

"Well if you did, there's always summer school," Nova said sweetly.

"You're hilarious."

"Are you coming over?"

"I have to go by my parents' store first to pick up some more flowers." Ethan didn't sound very enthused.

"*More* flowers?" Nova laughed. "How are you gonna get there?"

"In my truck." Ethan waited for a moment. "Hello? Did you hear me? I said *my truck.*"

He couldn't see that Nova's mouth was hanging open. "What…when…?"

"This morning. It's Sam's, but freshmen can't have cars. It's been sitting at the store since he left. So for now at least, it's mine."

"But, do you have a license?" Nova was completely flabbergasted.

"Yeah. I got it after my exam. Today's my birthday. Hello? I told you all of this two weeks ago."

"Two weeks ago? I wasn't here two weeks ago. So I guess you told the other me."

"Oh yeah. Sorry."

"No, I'm sorry. I forgot today was your birthday.

Well, that's not exactly true. I didn't *know* today was your birthday. Happy birthday, Ethan."

"Thanks."

There was an awkward silence while Nova tried to think of something else to say.

She took a deep breath. "Ethan! You have a truck now! That's incredible! It's amazing! I can't believe it!"

Ethan laughed. "Okay, don't overdo it. I forgive you."

"Well, that's a relief. Can you come over? I have to see this new mode of transportation. I hope it has airbags…and a roll bar…and maybe a parachute," she teased.

"Funny. I can come get you. You know, let you be seen with me in my manly truck."

"I can't wait." Nova giggled.

"On my way." Ethan was obviously excited. "You can go with me to get the flowers."

"Wait! Give me about thirty minutes, okay? I need to get ready."

"Okay, I'll be there in thirty."

Nova could tell he was grinning.

As soon as they hung up, she showered quickly, relieved to be able to wash her hair now that her head wound had healed over somewhat. She couldn't wait to get the stitches out, but that would have to wait until after they came back from Aunt Jean's. She blew her hair dry and pulled on fresh clothes.

Talking her mom into letting her ride with Ethan to his parents' nursery wasn't hard, so Nova was standing on the front porch when he drove up.

"I can't believe we have wheels!" Nova exclaimed before he could open the door.

"*We?*" Ethan grinned.

She reached through the driver's window and smacked him lightly in the jaw.

"Okay, okay…we." Ethan pulled back and shielded his face, then he jumped out and ran around to the passenger side and opened her door. "Climb in, hot girl!"

Nova slid onto the seat, and Ethan closed the door with a flourish.

"Dramatic!" Nova laughed.

"Well, you know. It's who I am." Ethan jumped in the other side and slowly backed out of the driveway.

They drove to the MacGradys' nursery to get the flowers, and it wasn't until they pulled into the parking lot that Nova realized what had just happened. That was the first time in over nine months that she had crossed the bridge without thinking about the accident. Before she could say anything about it, Ethan jumped out of the car. A few minutes later, he came back carrying a large pot spilling over with yellow and purple flowers. He put them in the back of the truck and leaned in Nova's window, giving her a tender kiss on the cheek.

"Where to, my lady?"

Nova blushed. "Anywhere that sells food. I'm starving."

"Burger Barn?"

"Definitely!" Nova hadn't been out of the house enough lately, and Burger Barn sounded like heaven to her. She had a lot to tell Ethan, but right now, she just wanted to be a teenage girl out with her boyfriend on his birthday. She could talk to him later.

Ethan jumped in the truck, and Nova slid over next to him, laying her head on his shoulder.

"Put your seat belt on, hot girl. I don't want to have to peel you off the windshield if we hit something."

Nova fastened the middle seat belt. "Are you planning to crash this manly truck?"

"No, but I'm feeling kind of reckless, so you never know." He laughed, putting his arm around her.

"I trust you," Nova said sincerely.

Ethan pulled her closer and kissed the top of her head. She looked up and he kissed her again, on the lips. Nova closed her eyes and let the kiss linger until they heard a car pull in beside them. They were still in the parking lot of the MacGradys' nursery and customers were coming and going. Ethan reluctantly started the truck.

CHAPTER 17

Nova's plan to talk later came to an abrupt halt the second they pulled out of the parking lot.

"Okay, hot girl. Spill it. What are you so excited about?"

"What? I'm excited to be out!" Nova poked him in the ribs.

"Yeah, but what else? Don't try to get out of it. I know you." He gave her a charming smile, exposing a dimple in his right cheek.

How had she not noticed that before? Smiling back, she pushed his chestnut hair away from his eyes. She had to admit that she had fallen hard for Ethan MacGrady. "Okay, but don't get all happy on me because the answer is no, you can't come too."

Nova proceeded to tell him about her family's upcoming trip to Aunt Jean's and her dad's plan to get answers about their ability to time travel. In spite of her enthusiasm, Ethan wasn't smiling anymore.

"Nova, it's great that you're gonna talk to your aunt. I just…well, do you think it's…uh." He was obviously worried about something.

"What?"

"I don't know. What if something goes wrong?"

Nova was baffled by his question. "What could go wrong? We're just talking to her."

"I know. But what if you find out how to do this...*thing,* and you decide to try it? Everything could change again and where would that leave us? You might be somewhere else and not even know me. Or even worse, I could be stuck with *Delilah.*" Ethan's attempt at humor didn't hide the fact that he was genuinely worried.

Nova put her hand on his arm. "I won't let that happen."

Ethan let his guard drop when she said that. "How can you say that? You wouldn't have any control."

"Maybe I *can* have control. Maybe Aunt Jean can explain how to use the power without it being so random. Dad said that people in our family went back and changed marriages, fortunes, even the outcome of war, so obviously there must be a way to control it."

Ethan clinched his jaw. "So you *are* planning to try it. Do you think you're gonna be able to bring your sister back? Is that what this is all about? Because I seem to recall you saying that you wanted to stay here, in this life...with me."

"I do want to stay with you! But what if there's a way to change my sister's fate and still have you? Wouldn't you do it if we were talking about Sam instead of Alana? What would you do if you were in my place?"

"I don't know. I guess I'd probably do the same thing." Ethan had pulled the truck into the parking lot at Burger Barn. He turned to look at her. "I don't want to lose you."

"I don't want to lose you either," she answered softly.

Why did it have to be so complicated? She didn't want to lose Ethan, but she'd go back for Alana if given the chance. How could she turn her back on her own sister? Nova felt a wave of sadness.

They sat in the truck outside the Burger Barn, neither of them saying a word. Finally, Ethan opened his door and got out. He walked around to Nova's side and tapped on the window, then he opened her door.

"C'mon, hot girl. It's my birthday. Let's have some fun." His cheerful tone sounded forced.

Nova hopped out of the truck and smiled at him. "Happy birthday, Ethan. I promise I won't do anything dangerous, okay?"

"Okay." But he didn't sound convinced, and honestly, she couldn't really keep that promise.

They made it through hamburgers, chili cheese fries, and chocolate milkshakes without mentioning the trip. Nova felt as though she'd never eaten so much in her life, but it was easier to avoid talking if she was stuffing her face. She was considering ordering more food when some kids from school showed up and came over to their table. Nova recognized Amanda, the same Amanda who'd been in the lunchroom with Ethan in her other life. The same one Delilah had ranted about.

"Oh my God, it's Nova Grant! We thought you were dead or something! You don't look like you were in an accident!"

Nova gave Ethan a questioning look.

"Uh, yeah. I told everyone about your *car accident*," he said, glancing at Amanda.

Two boys had joined her. Nova didn't know either one of them.

Amanda stood there glaring at Nova. "Thanks a lot for leaving me with the whole presentation to do *by myself*. I about had a heart attack!"

"Presentation?" Nova realized as soon as she asked that she should have kept her mouth shut. Now Amanda would really think she was nuts. If they'd been doing a project together, Nova should have known what it was. But of course she didn't.

Amanda's mouth hung open. Nova had to do something to save face, so she laughed. That didn't work. Amanda's mouth was still hanging open, which was pretty unattractive since Nova could see a wad of gum stuck in her cheek.

"Sorry, Amanda, I was just kidding! I really do feel bad about leaving you with the presentation. How did it go?"

Amanda closed her mouth, finally, and sat down beside Ethan, shoving him over so one of the boys could sit down too. The other guy sat next to Nova. Amanda was plastered against Ethan, and the buttons on her shirt were undone halfway down. Ethan was probably getting quite the view.

"Ethan, did I hear you got a new truck?" Amanda asked, completely ignoring Nova's question and flipping her obviously bleached hair behind her shoulder. "I'd love to ride in it some time. Maybe this afternoon? I'm not busy."

Nova looked at Ethan and rolled her eyes. At least he had the decency to look uncomfortable with Amanda practically in his lap.

"I'm…uh…not really sure I have time. I have to take Nova home."

The boy sitting across from Nova was tapping his finger on the table, obviously unhappy with Amanda's open flirting. He stood and said, "I'm leaving. If you want a ride, Amanda, come on."

"Oh my God, Bryan! Relax!" She smiled sweetly at Ethan. "Call me about that ride." Amanda stood to leave. "Come on, David. Before Bryan has a fit."

The boy sitting next to Nova slid out of the seat and looked back, though he couldn't seem to make eye contact. "Sorry about that, Nova."

When they were gone, Ethan gave Nova a sheepish grin. "Sorry. I just have that effect on women."

Nova kicked him under the table. "'I have to get Nova home'? That's the best you could do? How about, 'I don't want to give you a ride because I'm desperately in love with Nova and you make me sick'?"

Ethan laughed. "Next time. She caught me off guard."

As awkward as the situation with Amanda had been, it had at least lightened the mood. She decided not to tell Ethan that he had actually dated Amanda in her other life. Instead, she sat there for another half an hour, listening as Ethan filled her in on Amanda's group and some other kids they had known at school. Nova knew several of them in her other life, but she had no idea who some of the others were. It was a little unnerving to think that she could run into more strangers who knew her. Burger Barn was getting crowded, so they decided to go back to Ethan's house.

"Oh, man. I'm so full," Nova complained in the parking lot.

"Stop griping. I ate half of your burger!" When they were back in the truck, Ethan gently kissed her. "What now, hot girl?"

Nova moved closer and placed her hand on his cheek. She closed her eyes and kissed him, carefully at first, then with more urgency. Ethan pulled her into his arms, and Nova felt almost lightheaded. She let herself melt into his embrace. Finally, Nova pulled away and blushed.

"Wow. That was incredible," Ethan said breathlessly.

Nova looked down at her hands and nodded. She was embarrassed but exhilarated at the same time. Ethan was obviously waiting for her to say something, but she couldn't seem to get anything out. When she looked up, Ethan was grinning at her, and she relaxed a little.

She giggled. "What's so funny?"

"Nothing." Ethan was still grinning.

Nova poked him in the side. "Start this thing and let's get out of here. People are staring."

Several people in the parking lot had actually stopped to watch them. Ethan started the truck, put it in reverse, and backed out. They drove to Ethan's house in silence. There was really nothing else to say. Nova was going to do what she had to do.

Mrs. Mac met them as they pulled into the driveway. She looked frazzled. "Where have you been? I expected you home with those flowers an hour ago!"

"Sorry, Mom. Nova was hungry, so we stopped at Burger Barn."

Mrs. Mac seemed to notice Nova for the first time. "Oh, Nova! You must think I'm terrible. Of course it was all right for Ethan to take you to get something to eat. Are you still hungry? I have some spaghetti on the stove."

"She's fine, Mom. We're stuffed." Ethan grabbed Nova's hand and pulled her up the driveway. "We're going to my room," he called over his shoulder.

"What's the big hurry?" Nova exclaimed when they were in his room with the door shut.

Before she could say anything else, Ethan pulled her to him and kissed her. "I don't want you to go see your aunt. Please don't go."

"Ethan…what…?"

"I'm serious. I have a bad feeling. What if something terrible happens? Don't go."

Nova pulled away from Ethan. "I'm sorry, but I have to. I can't tell you how important this is to me. I need it."

"Well then, can't you convince your dad to let me come with you? Then at least I'd be there and maybe that would make a difference."

"What kind of difference would it make? If I travel back and it changes my history, it won't matter where you were when it happened. So there's no point to you coming along. It won't change anything."

Ethan looked miserable. He shoved his hands in his pockets and stared at the floor. After a few awkward minutes, he walked over and opened his door.

"Do you mind if I walk you home?" he asked solemnly.

Nova was taken aback. "Now? It's your birthday."

"Yeah. I think my parents have something planned. I'll tell them you couldn't stay."

"You don't want me to stay?" Nova was hurt. Why was he acting like this? Why couldn't he believe that she would do everything she could to keep him? "Ethan, I really want to stay."

"Not everything is about what *you* want," he said bitterly. "I'm sorry. I know you've been through a lot and you need answers. I guess I'd feel the same way. It's not because I don't understand. I just don't think I can be around you if I'm thinking the whole time that I might lose you in a few days."

"You're not going to lose me! Why can't you believe that?" Nova was close to breaking down.

"You don't know what's gonna happen if you try to go back, so stop pretending you do. Anything could change. *Everything* could be different. I guess the one bright spot is that at least I won't know I've been dumped."

Nova felt tears roll down her cheeks. "You don't have to walk me home."

She turned and walked out of his room, down the hall, and out the front door without looking back.

The rest of the week crept by at a snail's pace. Marshall's enthusiasm waned a little during the week but found new life on Friday night. Nova thought he would never stop bursting into her room with some fresh bit of news about Aunt Jean's place in Willow, North Carolina. Apparently she owned about a hundred and fifty acres, which included riding trails and a large pond for fishing and even an old cemetery dating back to the 1800s. Marshall planned to explore every inch of the place. Nova had never seen him so excited. She envied his innocent take on the world and wondered if he also had the family gift. If he did, it would be better not to tell him until he was older and had some of that impulsive personality under control. It would be fun to see his reaction though – "I can WHAT?" Nova chuckled just thinking about it.

She started to call Ethan before she went to bed on Friday night but decided against it. He hadn't called even once since their argument at his house. If she called him to say good-bye, it would just start over again. Better to leave things as they were.

Her suitcase was packed and her clothes were laid out for the morning. There was nothing left to do but get some sleep. Nova crawled into bed and closed her eyes.

Her dad cracked open her door and stuck his head in. "You asleep, firefly?"

"Almost," she answered.

He stepped into her room and sat on the edge of her bed. "What happened with you and Ethan? We haven't seen him all week."

Nova sat up. "He thinks I'm gonna ruin everything. He thinks I'll find out how to go back in time to save Alana and he'll lose me. He won't remember." She sighed. "Do you believe that'll happen?"

"I don't know what will happen." His voice sounded weary. Was he worried too? "Right now, all we're doing is going to talk to Aunt Jean. I'm beginning to think my mother had a point. Traveling's dangerous and anything can happen. I agree with Ethan. I don't want to lose you either. I tried to prevent Alana's death, and she just died earlier instead. What if I try again and lose you too?"

"This sucks." Nova was suddenly exhausted.

He didn't say anything for a moment, then he kissed her forehead. "Get some sleep, firefly."

"I won't try anything unless you agree, okay?"

"Okay," he answered. "I promise the same thing."

Nova hugged her dad. She felt better already. Safe.

"See you in the morning, bright and early." He stood and started to leave.

"How early?" Nova yawned.

"Five o'clock. Our flight leaves at seven thirty."

"If we oversleep, we can just take the Mustang."

"It's thirteen hours to Aunt Jean's."

"Never mind," she groaned.

Nova lay down and pulled her covers around her. She heard her door gently close, and slowly she drifted off and dreamed about the accident. This time, as she stood at the water's edge calling for her dad, she saw him walking up from the water.

"I'm here, firefly."

She threw her arms around him. A loose piece of metal from the Mustang was banging against the bridge railing, making a clinking sound. As she stood there with her dad, she tried to focus on his breathing and the rush of the river, but the noise became more pronounced until all she could hear was the metal tapping against the bridge.

Nova jerked awake, her heart pounding. She felt disoriented. Why could she still hear the tapping? As she came fully awake, she realized that the noise was coming from her window. In the dim light of the street lamp, she could make out a silhouette on the other side of the glass. She jumped up and tiptoed across the room. *Ethan!* She raised the window, whispering for him to come in.

But he shook his head. "I just wanted to see you before you left."

"I'm glad. Ethan—"

"Nova, you don't have to say anything, but there's something I need you to know. I love you. I'll never love anyone else the way I love you. I know I'd fall in love with you no matter when we met. If you go back and save Alana, you'll remember all of this, even if I don't. I want you to promise me one thing. Promise you'll do whatever it takes to get me back."

Nova felt tears rolling down her cheeks. "I promise."

He leaned in through the window and kissed her tenderly on the lips. When he started to pulled away, he hesitated a moment, his face just inches from hers. He seemed to be studying her in the dim light from the street lamp, taking in every detail. "Remember, you promised," he whispered. Then he jogged toward the road and out of sight.

CHAPTER 18

Marshall burst into Nova's room at one minute after five, hollering for her to get up.

"Marshall, get out of my room!" Nova yelled.

She'd hardly slept since talking to Ethan and was in no mood to interact with her exuberant little brother. There seemed to be no quelling his excitement though, and he bounded in and out for the next fifteen minutes while Nova tried to get dressed and fix her unruly hair.

"Seriously, kid, go away or you won't make it to Aunt Jean's," she said when he almost caught her without pants.

"We're leaving in five minutes!" Celeste called from the kitchen. "Marshall! Leave Nova alone and bring your suitcase in here. Nova, Dad needs yours too."

"Coming," Nova answered.

She grabbed her suitcase and shoulder bag as Marshall came out of his room, dragging his luggage. He was also wearing a camping backpack that appeared to be stuffed with everything he owned that wouldn't fit into the suitcase.

"Marshall, I don't think that qualifies as a carry-on!" Celeste exclaimed when he dropped it on the kitchen floor with a loud thud.

"It's all stuff I need for the trip!" he whined.

"Oh never mind," she answered. "Let's just get it in the car."

Dayton walked in from the garage, where the Volvo was already running. "Marshall, that backpack's too full, buddy. You won't be able to take it on the plane."

Marshall proceeded to pitch a fit, but he grudgingly pulled out his baseball bat, glove, baseballs, rollerblades, and helmet. He ran back to his room with the items and reappeared with a smaller pack that he proceeded to shove everything else into while Celeste stood over him, directing. After much arguing, and whining from Marshall, the smaller pack was ready for transport.

"That's more like it!" Dayton laughed.

Celeste produced chocolate chip muffins for the ride to the airport, and Marshall crammed a whole one in his mouth before stepping into the van. They hit the road at five thirty. With a forty-minute drive to the East Haven airport, they should make it with plenty of time to check their bags and get through security.

Nova had to admit that she was just as excited as Marshall. This could be the most amazing experience of her life. She wished she could call Ethan, but she had already decided not to contact him until she returned. It was better this way. When the trip was over, she'd figure out what needed to be done as far as he was concerned. Right now, she just wanted to think about finally meeting Aunt Jean and learning about the incredible family she came from. Nova looked at Marshall and wondered again if he also had the ability. While it was an awesome gift, it was also a burden. She wasn't sure she could wish that on her carefree little brother.

Once they arrived at the airport, they checked the bags, breezed through security, and made their way to the gate. Marshall's excitement dimmed a little when he stepped foot onto the fifty-passenger plane to Philadelphia.

"Wow. It's small," he said nervously.

"It's okay, Marshall," Nova assured him. "We'll be in Philadelphia in about an hour."

"You take the window seat," he said timidly.

"Sure thing." Nova smiled.

About halfway through the flight, Marshall's apprehension evaporated and he began asking non-stop questions about the Philadelphia airport, the plane to Charlotte, and Aunt Jean's house. Nova enjoyed the distraction at first. It kept her from thinking about Ethan. After a while though, she'd had enough.

"Marshall, you know I've never flown to Charlotte or been to Aunt Jean's. It's all new to me too, so stop asking so many questions!" She pulled out the safety instructions and began studying them.

"Why are you reading the safety instructions?" he asked anxiously.

"In case you don't shut up and I decide to jump out." Nova shoved the pamphlet into the pocket on the back of the seat in front of her and tapped him lightly on the chin.

Marshall giggled and pretended to punch her back.

Nova was relieved when the plane touched down in Philadelphia. Fortunately their gate for the next flight wasn't too far away and they easily made the connection with time to spare. Marshall wanted to buy a comic book in the shop next to the gate, so Celeste went with him to pay for it.

"How are you holding up?" Dayton asked as soon as they were out of earshot.

"Okay, I guess. I'm nervous but excited at the same time. Do you know what I mean?"

"I do," he answered. "Did you ever straighten things out with Ethan?"

"Not really."

"Maybe you should call him."

"I think I should wait until after we talk to Aunt Jean.

You know, in case we…I mean if we decide to try to—"

"Stop right there. We need to get one thing straight. No matter what Aunt Jean tells us, *you* are not going to do anything. I'm not going to go along with any scenario that involves you taking a risk."

"Are you trying to tell me that you're not thinking of doing the same thing? Dad, I know you're planning something! Why can't I be part of it?"

"I'm not planning anything. I'm just going to talk. That's it. If there's something to be done, we'll discuss that when we're back at home."

"When did you decide this?" Nova demanded. "Don't I get a say?"

"It's what I've been thinking all along. I just wasn't sure until this morning."

Neither of them said anything for a few minutes, then Nova spoke up again. "What if Aunt Jean can help us? Wouldn't it be better to do it while we're there?"

"I want to be sure it's worth it."

"Worth it? Why would that even be a question? Okay, so it didn't work out the first time you traveled, but I seem to recall it working out pretty well the second time. I'd call *not being dead anymore* working out! Wouldn't you?"

Celeste and Marshall reappeared on the concourse carrying a couple of comic books and some candy bars.

Her dad leaned toward her and whispered, "We'll continue this later."

"So what are you two talking about that's so serious?" her mother asked.

"Nothing, Mom," Nova replied. "I was talking about Ethan, that's all. I miss him."

She put her arm around Nova. "You'll be back soon, honey."

Nova smiled at her mom. *I hope so.* She appreciated her mother's concern. Marshall, however, couldn't have cared less. He was busy scarfing down a chocolate bar.

"When do we get on the plane?" he mumbled through a mouthful of candy.

Dayton laughed. "Soon, Marsh. You might want to pace yourself on the candy."

Marshall grinned, exposing a mouthful of brown teeth. "You have to try one of these, Nova!"

"You're gross," she responded.

Celeste was still watching Nova. "Seriously, what's up with you two? I feel like you're keeping something from me."

Nova looked at her dad, who shot her a warning look. "It's nothing, Mom. Ethan wanted to come with us and Dad said no. That's all. I was kind of mad about it and brought it up again, but it's okay now. I'm over it." Nova managed a weak smile.

"Maybe I should call Ethan's mother if he's putting this kind of pressure on you." She frowned.

"No, please don't!" Nova cried. "It's really okay now. We both understand. This is a family trip. Please don't say anything to his parents."

"Okay." She put her arm around her daughter again. "Are you all right?"

"I'm great," Nova lied, looking at her dad for help.

He took the hint and jumped in. "She's fine, Celeste. And it looks like we'd better get going." He pointed to the line forming to board their flight.

Marshall grabbed Nova's arm and practically dragged her down the ramp and onto the plane. "I want the window seat this time," he announced.

The flight to Charlotte lasted about two hours, but it seemed longer to Nova because Marshall didn't stop talking the whole way. She was considering barricading herself in the bathroom when the pilot announced that they were descending into Charlotte.

As soon as they landed, Dayton took off to secure the rental car while the others retrieved the luggage from baggage claim. Before long, they were on the road to Aunt Jean's.

Celeste admired the stately homes they passed shortly after leaving the airport. "This is a beautiful area. Don't you all think so?"

"It doesn't seem like the country to me," Marshall complained.

"Don't worry, big guy," Dayton said. "We still have a long way to go."

After about thirty minutes, the new development suddenly gave way to more rural dwellings and open land, as if they had crossed an invisible line between the city and the country. Planted fields bordered the road on the right, and Nova could just make out a barn and house far beyond that. On the left, a small home with a covered porch sat back off the road. A giant tree hovered protectively over the house, and as they passed, Nova noticed a tire swing hanging from one of its massive branches. It looked like something from a postcard. She wondered how long it would stay like this before civilization swallowed it up.

"Are we almost there?" Marshall asked impatiently.

"Not yet, Marshall," Dayton said.

After another ten miles or so, they came upon a sign that read: *Welcome to Historic Willow, North Carolina.* Immediately before them was the most quaint little town that Nova had ever seen. Train tracks divided the main street, called Old Willow Avenue, right down the middle. An ornate pedestrian bridge crossed from one side of the road to the other. Nova could imagine standing on the bridge and looking down as a train sped by. Hundred-year-old buildings lined both sides of the road, housing shops selling everything from antiques to groceries. A cute little café called Cora's Kitchen was bordered by a bookstore on one side and an old movie theater on the other.

"Can we stop here to eat?" Marshall asked hopefully.

Nova would have liked to explore the little town, but

that could wait. Right now, she was anxious to get to Aunt Jean's.

"Marshall, you're always hungry!" Celeste chuckled. "Your aunt is planning to feed us when we get there."

They continued down the main street and passed the Museum of the Willows, which was housed in what appeared to be an old church. The main part of town only took up about two city blocks, but it was apparently the place to be in Willow. Families strolled along the main drag, some pushing strollers or hanging on to little hands. Several of the shops had set up tables on the sidewalk, and small groups of people huddled around them, admiring the items displayed. At the end of the street was a farmers' market where local growers sold fresh vegetables and neighbors displayed homemade crafts. The whole atmosphere was very Norman Rockwell.

As they passed the farmers' market, the road split and they took the right fork. Almost immediately, the landscape changed. Dense forests hugged the country road on both sides for at least three or four miles, finally opening up to cow pastures on one side and rows of planted farmland on the other.

"How much farther, Dad?" whined Marshall.

"We'll be there soon, buddy. It's been years since I was here, but I think it's another five miles or so. Her place is called Willow Hill."

"Her house has a name?" Nova found that amusing.

"It's not just a house," he answered.

"Okay, her house and barn."

"You'll see," he said.

"Well, does she have a sign or something?" Nova pressed.

He chuckled. "You'll see."

"Good grief." Nova sighed.

After another five miles, there was still no Willow Hill in sight.

"Day, are you sure this is the right way?" Celeste

asked. "Maybe we should have turned back there."

Just then, they came up over a hill and before them was a beautiful estate – rolling pastures, groves of trees, and a long tree-lined drive. At least a dozen horses dotted the landscape, grazing in small groups. Under a stand of trees close to the road, a mare stood peacefully dozing while her foal frolicked around her.

"This can't be it!" Celeste exclaimed, looking at Dayton. "Is this your aunt's home?"

He laughed and turned into the elaborate entrance. On a large brass plaque embedded in one of the stone columns was the name of the farm, Willow Hill.

CHAPTER 19

Celeste gasped. "You didn't tell me it was like this!"

"Like I said, it's been years since I was here. It's changed a little. I remember this entrance though."

Marshall was literally bouncing up and down in his seat. "This place is amazing! I didn't know we had rich relatives!" he practically screamed.

"What do you think, Nova?" Dayton glanced over his shoulder. "Are you okay back there?"

"Yeah, I'm just shocked, I guess. I didn't expect a plantation." Nova strained to see up the long driveway to the house. It was an imposing two-story brick structure with a deep porch across the front and a balcony above it.

Nova saw someone standing on the steps, ready to greet them. She was wearing jeans, tall boots, and a yellow cotton blouse. Her partially gray hair was pulled back in a low bun. Even though she wasn't what Nova had expected, she figured this must be Aunt Jean. As they pulled to a stop in the circular drive, the woman came forward with a beaming smile.

"Dayton! I'm so glad you came!" she cried as she threw her arms around him in a bear hug.

"Aunt Jean," was all he managed to get out before having the air squeezed out of his lungs. When she finally released him, he took a deep breath and introduced the rest of the family.

"Celeste, honey, you don't know how glad I am to finally meet you!" Aunt Jean exclaimed as she dished out another bear hug. "I wasn't sure this day would ever come. And oh my goodness, I'm so glad to meet you kids too." She hugged Nova and exclaimed, "You're the prettiest thing I ever saw!"

Nova grinned awkwardly and managed a feeble thank you before Aunt Jean turned her attention to Marshall. He took a step back but was unable to avoid his great-aunt's enthusiastic embrace.

"I think the last time I saw your dad, he was about your age," she said. "But that's water under the bridge. Come inside. I have food on the table. You must be starving after such a long trip."

They all followed Aunt Jean up the steps and through the double doors into the house. The inside was even more impressive than the outside. The two-story foyer had a polished wood floor and a dual staircase leading up to a second-floor balcony that appeared to be furnished as a sitting area. To the right was a large living room with a grand piano, several overstuffed chairs, and bookcases filled with books and framed photos. On the left was a dining room with an ornately carved table surrounded by ten chairs.

"Aunt Jean, your house is beautiful!" Celeste exclaimed.

"Oh, thank you, dear. It's a little over the top for my liking, but my sister-in-law had extravagant taste. She decorated most of the house, but the kitchen was mine. She hardly ever went in there anyway." Aunt Jean lowered her voice to a whisper, "Couldn't even boil water."

Dayton glanced around. "So who else lives here?"

"Oh, just me now."

Nova and her dad exchanged a look that said, *So why is she whispering?* Nova laughed and then felt her face turn red.

Aunt Jean just babbled on. "Georgia, Bill's wife, died of cancer eleven years ago, and Bill died last year of a heart attack. Their son comes to visit a few times a year and brings his wife and four kids. It's a mad house when they're here, but I love it! My husband, Matthew Huckaby, passed away almost fourteen years ago. He loved this place. Of course it's changed since he was alive. We thought we'd all be growing old together here – Bill, Georgia, Matthew, and me." Aunt Jean's eyes misted over as she looked at Dayton. She seemed to be far away for a moment. "It's been so long since you were here, Day."

"I know. I'm sorry, Aunt Jean." He put his hand on his aunt's arm and gave it a squeeze. "But I'm here now."

Aunt Jean collected herself and announced, "Lunch is served in the kitchen. The dining room is for company. You're family, and family eats in the kitchen!"

They all trooped down the hall and into the enormous kitchen. There was a large double oven, a gas stove with six burners, two generous sinks, and rich wood cabinets. But the most impressive thing was the mammoth roughhewn wooden table with benches down both sides and an armchair at each end. On the table were bowls of fried chicken, corn on the cob, potato salad, rolls, and fresh strawberries. In the center were two apple pies and a plate of chocolate chip cookies. Nova figured that they could easily sit twenty people around that table, and it looked as if that was how many Aunt Jean had been expecting.

"Sit everyone. I'm pouring drinks. We have lemonade and tea, so what's your preference?"

"Do you have sugar for the tea?" Marshall asked.

It dawned on Nova that those were the first words out of his mouth since they had arrived.

"Are you kidding me?" Aunt Jean pretended to be

insulted. "This is the South. We only serve sweet tea."

Marshall grinned. "I'll have that then."

"That's my boy." Aunt Jean laughed.

The meal was delicious and the company jovial. Aunt Jean knew how to make them feel right at home. Nova wondered if Grandma Kate had been the same way. She didn't remember feeling all that comfortable around her, but Nova had been young when her grandmother died. She couldn't imagine anyone being able to stay mad at Aunt Jean. She thought about the letters that Grandma Kate had written to her older sister and how sad it was that she'd never mailed them.

Everyone at the table was laughing about something, but Nova's mind was a million miles away and she had no idea what the joke was. While the others finished eating and talking, Nova turned her attention to her surroundings. This room was equally as impressive as the other parts of the house that they had seen so far, but it felt completely different. This was a room you could be comfortable in. On the other side of the table was a sitting area with a rustic fireplace and cozy chairs.

"You could live in here if you added a bed," Nova said admiringly.

"A sweet girl after my own heart." Aunt Jean laughed. "Do you like to cook, Nova?"

"I guess. I can make cinnamon buns." Nova smiled sheepishly.

"Well, I'll have to teach you how make a few more things while you're here."

"God help us!" Marshall shook his head. "Get Nova to tell you about the time she tried to make ravioli."

Nova gave him a scathing look. Besides, she could hardly be blamed for a meal she had no memory of making.

"Cut it out, Marshall," Celeste warned halfheartedly. "You know her taco casserole was much worse."

"Very funny," Nova retorted.

Aunt Jean had come around with a tea pitcher, and she put her arm around Nova's shoulders. "Don't you worry, honey. We'll have them eating their words in a few days."

After lunch, Dayton and Marshall brought the luggage in from the car and hauled it upstairs, dividing it among three guest rooms. Marshall was thrilled with his room, which looked out over the barn and paddocks. It had a double bed with a rough wood headboard and a barrel made into a nightstand. In the corner sat a wooden trunk with a lamp shaped like an old-timey lantern. Next to the trunk was a huge armchair and ottoman covered in deep burgundy corduroy.

Marshall flopped into the chair and put his feet up. "This is the life!"

Their parents' room was on the front of the house, overlooking the tree-lined drive. French doors opened onto a balcony with rocking chairs. The room was furnished with a king-size sleigh bed, marble-topped nightstands, a chaise lounge, and a towering armoire. Celeste was delighted.

In Nova's opinion, however, she had the best room. The walls were painted a tranquil blue, and there was a four-poster bed with a night table and lamp on either side, a beautiful antique dresser, and a floral armchair and ottoman. But best of all, it had a window seat overlooking a beautiful garden and, beyond that, dense woods. It looked like something an artist had imagined and painted from the picture in his mind.

"This is perfect," Nova said, not realizing that her aunt was just outside the door.

"I'm glad you like it, honey. I knew this had to be your room." Aunt Jean smiled. "This is the most peaceful room in the house. You need a relaxing place to go when you want to get in touch with your thoughts. Don't you think?" Aunt Jean was studying Nova's face. "You have something you want to talk to me about, don't you, Nova?"

Nova didn't know what to say. Now that she was here

and had the opportunity to talk to her aunt, she had no idea how to do that.

"Better close your mouth, honey. You might catch a fly." Aunt Jean chuckled as she turned and left.

Nova heard her talking to Dayton down the hall but couldn't make out what they were saying. She stuck her head out of the door just as they stepped into her parents' room. Nova debated whether or not to tiptoe down the hall and listen at the door, but she thought better of it.

She grabbed her suitcase and began placing her clothes in the dresser. Her room had two closed doors, one to the left and one to the right of the bed and nightstands. Nova opened the door on the left and found stairs that she assumed led to the attic. The space was dark, and the stairs were rough wood. Nova quickly closed the door and felt the hairs stand up on the back of her neck. *Creepy.* The second door opened into a cheerful bathroom with a large window, flowered wallpaper, a claw-footed tub, and a walk-in closet.

"This is more like it," Nova whispered. She could definitely get used to this.

Down the hall, Marshall was talking excitedly about something. He came running into her room just as she stepped out of the bathroom.

"I'm having a riding lesson tomorrow morning!" he announced. "Justin's gonna teach me how to ride! He trains all of Aunt Jean's horses. She said after I learn, I can go out on trails and everything!"

"That's great, kiddo." Nova gave her little brother a hug. "Then maybe you can teach me."

"Sure!" Marshall replied. "You want to go to the barn with me?"

"Yeah, I'll go. Give me a minute to change, okay?"

"Okay! Meet me downstairs." And with that he was off, bounding down the hall.

When they arrived at the barn, a tall young man with red hair came striding up. Nova noticed a scar that zigzagged from above his eyebrow to just below his jawline. She wondered if he had been injured riding horses, and she made a mental note to talk to her parents about their decision to let her accident-prone little brother have riding lessons.

"I'm Justin. You must be Nova and Marshall. Your great-aunt says you want to learn to ride."

"Yes, I do!" Marshall replied excitedly.

"Not me. I'll just watch," Nova said quickly.

"Are you sure? I'm a pretty good teacher." Justin grinned.

Nova shook her head. "Maybe later."

Justin laughed. "Well, let me know if you change your mind." He directed his attention to Marshall. "Ready to saddle up, big guy?"

"Yes!" Marshall was literally jumping up and down.

The two of them headed into the barn. A horse was patiently standing in the cross ties and he tossed his head when they walked up. Nova thought he looked too big for Marshall, but he seemed friendly enough and nuzzled Marshall's shoulder.

"This is Hobo, Bo for short. He's one of the gentlest horses you'll ever meet." Justin reached in his pocket and pulled out a piece of apple. "And he has a sweet tooth."

Bo took the apple out of Justin's hand and munched on it while Justin put the saddle on his back and tightened the strap that kept it in place. "First you cinch the girth, then put on his bridle," Justin explained. He unhooked the cross ties and pulled a bridle over Bo's head, placing the bit in his mouth. Bo seemed completely comfortable with the whole process and gave Justin a nudge with his muzzle.

"He likes you." Marshall was in awe.

"Yeah, we've been buddies a long time." Justin rubbed Bo between the eyes, and Bo lowered his head.

"How long have you been here, Justin?" Nova asked.

"Oh, about ten years, I guess. Your uncle Bill built me an apartment over the stables. When I got married two years ago, my wife loved it out here so much we decided to stay. Your aunt's been like a mother to Connie and me."

"You live in the barn?" Nova spoke before thinking. She could feel her cheeks turning red. "I'm sorry. I'm sure it's nice. Don't mind me. Sometimes I just open my mouth to change feet."

Justin laughed. "Don't feel bad. It does sound strange to live in a barn. It's great though, much nicer than a lot of apartments in town." Justin led Bo out of the barn. "Okay, Marshall. Let's see what you've got."

Marshall's exuberance seemed to have left him, and he stood there looking uncertain.

"It's okay, buddy. Just put your left foot in the stirrup and throw your right leg over."

Marshall did as Justin directed and instantly found his enthusiasm again. "This is awesome!"

Justin led Bo up to the riding ring and closed the gate after them. Nova was impressed with Justin's patience and knowledge. After ten minutes of instruction, he had Marshall trotting around the ring.

"You're a natural, big guy!" Justin called as Marshall trotted by.

After about an hour, Justin decided that Marshall had had enough and unlatched the gate. This time, Marshall guided Bo out of the ring and down to the barn without any help. He was immensely proud of himself. After he dismounted and led Bo into the barn, Justin's wife seemed to appear from nowhere, carrying glasses of lemonade. She looked as though she was about to have a baby any minute.

"Connie, I could've come up and gotten that. I don't want you up and down those stairs so much," Justin chided her fondly.

"I'm going crazy sitting around doing nothing." She smiled at Nova and Marshall. "Besides, I had to come down and meet these two. Your aunt has been so excited since your dad called her and said you were coming." Connie busied herself handing out lemonade. "I have some peanut butter cookies in the oven if anyone's interested."

"I'll help you with those," Nova offered. She followed Connie to the tack room where all the saddles and bridles were kept. When she stepped inside, Nova took a deep breath. "I love the smell in here."

"That's the leather. It does smell good, doesn't it?"

Connie smiled at Nova and motioned her to the back of the room where she opened a door, exposing a stairway that led up to the apartment. Nova followed her up and was surprised to find a modern space with a living room, two bedrooms, and a cozy eat-in kitchen. Connie had covered the kitchen table with a red-checked tablecloth and the chairs had matching red cushions. The apartment smelled wonderful from the cookies.

"I can't believe how nice this is!" said Nova without thinking. "I'm sorry. That was rude. I just meant, well, since you live over a barn. It's a really nice barn though...I'm just making it worse."

Connie looked genuinely amused and assured Nova that she knew exactly what she meant. "When Justin asked me to marry him, he said he wanted to live out here, but I thought there was no way I'd ever want to live over a barn. I couldn't believe he wanted me to. I'd never actually been in his apartment. I figured it would be pretty rustic, no place for a married couple. But I came out here and fell in love with it. Honestly, it's much nicer than my apartment in town was."

"I think it's wonderful. When is your baby due?"

"Three more weeks. I hope he's not late. I'm about to explode." She laughed.

Nova smiled. "I bet Aunt Jean's excited."

"Oh, she is. She's like Justin's mom since his parents died."

"I'm sorry about his parents. How long have they been gone?"

"It's been a little over ten years. It was a car accident.

Justin was hurt pretty bad, but his parents were killed instantly. That's actually how he and I met. Our church youth group visited him in the hospital."

A timer went off, so Connie picked up two oven mitts and took the cookies out of the oven.

"So that's when he started working here? After the accident? He must have been pretty young."

"Oh, he was. Just sixteen. But he didn't come here to work. Aunt Jean and Uncle Bill knew Justin's parents. Justin's dad worked for Bill. They came to the hospital every day to see Justin after the accident. Like I said, he was hurt really bad. He almost lost his sight in one eye. When Justin was well enough to leave the hospital, he came here to live. He had to go to a different high school and leave all his friends, and after losing his parents, that was hard. It worked out though. I lived just down the road, so we ended up in the same school."

"I'm sure he was happy to see a familiar face."

Connie blushed. "I was pretty happy to see him too. After he graduated, he went to the university in Charlotte and got a business degree. He missed this place though. This is home. So Uncle Bill built the apartment so he could have his own space, and Justin started running the business."

"What business?" Nova asked.

"This is a business. We have fifteen horses. Two are National Steeplechase champions. People bring their mares here to breed. We also have our own breeding stock and occasionally sell to other barns."

"That's incredible!"

"It is pretty great. You should see Justin ride." Connie beamed as she loaded a plate with cookies, pulled a platter of sandwiches from the refrigerator, grabbed a bag of chips from the cabinet, and loaded it all on a wooden tray. "Come on, Nova. Those boys must be pretty hungry by now."

"I've got this." Nova took the tray from Connie.

"Thanks. It's getting pretty hard to carry anything

heavy since I already have this one to lug around." Connie said, patting her stomach.

When they arrived downstairs with the food, Bo was back in his stall and most of the other horses had been brought in from the pastures. Marshall was having a ball. Justin had shown him how to throw hay into the stalls through chutes in the hayloft floor. The horses stomped their feet in anticipation as Marshall and Justin moved down the line, dropping the hay.

After lunch, Marshall went along to each stall and filled water buckets with a hose that was attached to a spigot just inside the barn. Then he hosed down the concrete walkway between the stalls while Justin swept out the tack room. Lastly they went down the line again, this time dishing out scoops of oats and sweet feed to each of the horses. Justin explained that he always fed them hay first so they would eat the richer oat-and-sweet-feed mixture more slowly. Marshall soaked it all in.

"I'm gonna be a horse trainer like Justin when I grow up," he announced as they walked back to the house.

Nova headed to her room to bathe before dinner. After drying off, she put on a pair of light blue shorts with a white fitted T-shirt and sandals. Her hair was still wet, but rather than take the time to blow it dry, she pulled it into a ponytail and let some of it fall in loose curls around her face. Nova studied herself in the mirror.

For some reason, the sketch of Alana popped into her head. Obviously they had been fraternal twins and not identical. Nova had inherited her dark eyes, dark wavy hair, and delicate features from her mother. Alana had been a pure Grant, not only in coloring, Nova was willing to bet, but in personality too. Even in a sketch, she could see the playful look in Alana's eyes and the humor in her quirky smile. She had been a beautiful child, and Nova imagined that she would have been a lovely teenager too. *I hope I get a chance to meet you, sister.*

When she stepped into the hall a few minutes later, she heard voices and laughter coming from the kitchen. Nova hurried down the stairs and arrived just in time to see Aunt Jean pull a roast out of the oven. Marshall was sitting at the kitchen table, squeaky clean and in his pajamas. He must have been starving, as usual, because he already had his fork in his hand.

"Honestly, Marshall, all you do is eat!" Celeste exclaimed.

Aunt Jean noticed Nova's arrival and said, "Well, aren't you a pretty thing!"

Nova blushed. "Can I help with anything?"

"No thanks, honey. Just have a seat."

Aunt Jean bustled around the kitchen and soon had the carved roast beef, mashed potatoes, green beans, fried squash, and biscuits on the table. When she finally sat down, they all held hands, and she thanked God for bringing her family back together.

When Nova opened her eyes, she saw tears rolling down her aunt's face. *I know just how you feel, Aunt Jean.*

CHAPTER 20

Nova awoke some time during the night to hushed voices in the hallway. She strained to hear what they were saying, but she couldn't make anything out or even tell for sure who was talking. She climbed out of bed and tiptoed to the door. Her dad was talking to someone.

"Not now. Let her sleep," he said softly.

"She has to be told, Day." It was Aunt Jean.

"I know."

"It's more dangerous if she *doesn't* know. You can't give someone a loaded gun with no instructions on how to use it."

"Or how not to," he whispered.

There was nothing else after that. Nova heard footsteps fading away. She walked back to her bed and sat down, suddenly wide awake. Was her dad having second thoughts about letting her in on the family secret? Was that what they were arguing about? She picked up her watch from the night table and looked at the time. One thirty in the morning.

Nova lay down and stared at the ceiling. Maybe she should have confronted them in the hallway. No matter. She had no intention of letting them leave her out. She closed her eyes and pictured her sister splashing in the pool in another life, letting the scene play over and over in her mind until she fell into fitful sleep.

Nova was standing on the riverbank, slightly in the water. She felt the cold slowly soaking into her jeans, creeping up her calves. The mangled Mustang floated toward her, upside down. Nova could see someone was trapped inside. She called out to her dad, but there was no answer. The car continued to drift closer and closer, until finally Nova could see long golden hair floating in the flooded car. Alana!

Nova woke in a cold sweat. The sun was already streaming in through her window and someone was knocking on her door.

"Nova, are you awake?" It was her mother.

"Come in, Mom." Nova shuddered as she sat up and pushed her hair out of her eyes.

"Good morning!" Celeste said cheerfully, but her expression changed when she noticed Nova's flushed cheeks. "Are you all right?" She felt Nova's forehead. "You don't have a fever."

"I'm okay. I had a bad dream, that's all."

She frowned. "Tell me about it."

"I don't really remember it that well. I'm okay, really. Did you want to tell me something?"

Her mom looked uncertain. "Aunt Jean asked me if I'd like to go into Willow with Connie this morning. She wants to get a few things for the nursery, and I thought I'd scope out the antique shops. I don't have to go though."

"No, you should go! I'm probably gonna be lazy today and maybe go down to the barn later. I know you love antiques, Mom. Go with Connie."

Her mother still wasn't sure, so Nova promised not to overdo it.

"I might just sit on the porch and drink lemonade all morning." Nova smiled. "Really, Mom, I don't plan on doing much. Go to Willow."

She seemed satisfied and hurried out to meet Connie. Nova pulled on jeans and a T-shirt and hurried downstairs. Marshall and Dayton were at the kitchen table, eating eggs and bacon. Aunt Jean was happily bustling around the kitchen, frying more bacon and buttering toast.

"We'll all weigh a ton when we leave here," Nova said.

"Nonsense. You're young." Aunt Jean grabbed a plate and ordered Nova to sit and eat.

"Yes, ma'am." Nova saluted. She sat beside her dad and nudged his arm. "How'd you sleep?"

"I slept great," he answered. "How about you?"

"I kept thinking I heard people talking in the hall," she whispered.

He turned toward Nova and gave her a "not now" look, then he cleared his throat. "Marshall, you'd better get going if you want another riding lesson. I saw Justin out there a while ago, saddling a horse for you."

Marshall crammed the last piece of bacon into his mouth and shot off the bench, grabbing a pair of boots.

"Where'd he get those?" Nova asked.

"Oh, we have boots of all sizes lying around." Aunt Jean laughed. "We can find some to fit you too if you're interested."

Nova held up her hands. "No thanks." She watched Marshall pull on his boots and tear out of the door toward the barn. "I hope he doesn't scare the horses."

Dayton sounded worried, "Do you think he'll be okay? I mean, Justin will watch him, right?"

"He'll be fine. And the horses are used to kids. So it looks like it's just the three of us for a while. Dayton, why don't you and Nova go sit out in the garden? It's a beautiful day." She looked pointedly at him.

"Yes ma'am." He smiled, grabbing his cup of coffee. There were plenty of chairs and a cushioned porch swing on the covered veranda, but he motioned for Nova to follow him down the steps to a stone path that took them into the garden. Nova had no idea what the names of any of the flowers were, but she was sure they were the most beautiful she'd ever seen. She was about to say so when he wheeled around to face her.

"Nova, let's agree on one thing," he whispered. "We aren't going to ask Aunt Jean to travel back on our behalf. At some point, that may come up. But just because she knows more than we do doesn't make it right for her to take this on. We're just talking, getting information on an incredible ability that we all share. Nothing more. Agreed?"

"Is that what you two were talking about in the hall last night?" Nova asked.

"Yes. And believe me when I tell you that Aunt Jean can be very stubborn."

"I don't think we have to worry. She doesn't seem like the time-traveling type." Nova chuckled, but her dad's serious expression didn't change.

"Don't be fooled by her Southern lady persona. She graduated from MIT."

Nova's mouth dropped open. "Seriously?"

"Seriously." He finally smiled.

"Okay, Dad. We won't let her do anything but teach us about our gift."

"Good girl." He put his arm around her, and they continued down the path.

"This is so pretty."

"Aunt Jean definitely has a green thumb," he agreed.

"This must be a ton of work. I don't see how she keeps up with it, or the house."

"She has someone who comes in a couple of times a week to help in the house and a lawn service does the grounds, but I think she tends this garden herself."

"Ethan's mom would love this place."

"Ethan?" Aunt Jean had managed to slip up behind them. Nova wondered how much of their conversation she'd overheard. "Is this a friend or a boyfriend?"

"Boyfriend." Nova blushed.

"A boyfriend!" Aunt Jean chuckled. "I'll have to hear all about him!"

She led them farther down the path until they came to a vine-covered gazebo in the middle of the garden. Flowerpots filled with colorful blooms hung from the edges of the roof, and the interior was furnished in white wicker chairs with mint green and light blue cushions.

Nova marveled at the tranquility and beauty of this hidden spot. It was almost magical. She half expected to see fairies flitting among the blossoms and elves peeking out from the flowerpots. "Aunt Jean, I've never seen anything like this. It's like something out of a story book."

"Thank you, honey. It took a few lifetimes to get this right."

Once again, Nova's mouth dropped open. She looked at her dad and whispered, "Did she just say what I think she said?"

"My hearing is fine, by the way," Aunt Jean pointed out. "I guess we all know why we're here, so let's sit down and get to it. You can feel free to talk; no one will hear us."

Nova had no idea how to begin. All of a sudden, time travel seemed like a ridiculous thing to ask about. She looked at her dad for help, but he looked equally taken aback.

"Day, if you can't talk about it with me, who can you talk to?" Aunt Jean prodded.

Dayton cleared his throat. "Nova, Aunt Jean and I talked some last night after you were in bed. She, uh...I mean, I filled her in on what's happened and, well..."

"Oh for heaven's sake, Day, spit it out! Nova, you and your dad want to know about the Grant family gift. First of all, let me tell you that I intended to honor my sister's wishes and never discuss any of this with you. But when I found out that you and Dayton had already traveled, I knew it would be dangerous *not* to talk to you.

"No one in our family knows who first discovered our ability to travel back in time. We've been able to do it for as long as anyone remembers. I don't know how many people possess the ability, but there are probably many more who aren't even related to us. It's a wonderful *and* terrible talent. Sometimes things work out and lives are changed for the better. Look around you. This didn't all happen by accident. Sometimes it takes more than once to get it right. You learn new things and apply that knowledge the next time around. Bill worked for a living and had some pretty hard times before he figured things out. Look at what he ended up being able to accomplish. All of this." She gave them a moment for her words to sink in.

They were both hanging on her every word.

"But sometimes going back causes a tragedy that can't be undone no matter how much you try. That's what happened with my sister, Kate. She was so bitter afterward that she vowed never to use the ability to time travel again. She was convinced that nothing good could come from it. She cut ties to all of her family because she never even wanted to hear about it again. And she was determined that you would never travel, Day. She wanted your life to be *normal*." Aunt Jean's eyes misted over. "I missed her so much after our argument. I always thought we'd get back together some day."

Nova thought about the letters, wishing she'd brought them with her. "She wrote to you, Aunt Jean. I found a stack of letters she never mailed. She missed you too."

Her aunt's eyes filled with tears. "I'd love to see those letters."

Nova looked at her hands. "I'm sorry I didn't bring them. I'll send them to you, I promise."

"Thanks, honey."

No one said a word for a few minutes.

Aunt Jean cleared her throat and continued. "Kate and I were close when we were young. She was delicate but full of fun. And we both loved that our family had the gift. My mother thought it was something that could be controlled, and she taught your uncle Bill, Kate, and me everything she knew about traveling through time. You see, Nova, the good Lord made time a lot more *fluid* than you'd think. Most of us see time as a set thing. Once a minute ticks by, it's gone forever. But that's not really the way it is. Time is something you can grab hold of and pull back. The problem is, when you pull it back, you'd better be very careful what you change. It takes planning, and even then you can cause a change that has an impact on things you never even thought of. Do you understand?"

"Sort of, Aunt Jean. But what about what happened to Dad and me? He came *forward* nine months. He didn't plan it; it just happened. And when he came forward, my life changed too. You say you can remember everything before and after you traveled?"

"Yes, of course."

"Then why can't Dad and I remember? We only remember the life before he came forward."

Aunt Jean raised her eyebrows. "Ah, well, that's the difference isn't it? What your dad did was special. I've traveled many times, but never ahead of where I'd already been. See, it's one thing to go back briefly. My mother called that a 'visit.' Maybe you just need to make an *adjustment* – one little thing that won't impact everything else. So you hop back for a moment then return to where you were. But going ahead into a future beyond where you'd been…" She shook her head. "It's really quite amazing. It makes sense though. If time is moveable, then it can move both ways. It stands to reason that you'd be able to go beyond where you are, as long as you don't try to go farther than your lifetime. I mean, you couldn't jump ahead, say, two hundred years." Aunt Jean laughed.

"But to answer your question, I can remember everything because I went back and relived it. Your dad went back the first time he traveled. He relived the day you and Alana were born and all the time after that. That's why he had such a hard time coping. He remembered the other life that included his other daughter. But this time, he jumped ahead, and when he did, lots of things in the past had to change. You and your dad can't remember that life because, technically, you weren't there to live it. Going forward, beyond where you've been, seems to have its own set of rules, but one thing seems to be the same. Traveling causes things to change, no matter which direction you go."

"But why would that be?" Dayton asked. "Why would going forward change anything in your past?"

Aunt Jean appeared to think for a minute before answering. "I guess it would depend on how big the thing was that was changed or prevented by you going forward. If it was a little thing, not much from your past should change. But if it was a big thing, you might wake up to a completely different life. It's like yanking a wrinkle out of a rug. If it's a small wrinkle, most of the furniture on the rug stays in the same place. If it's a big wrinkle, everything on the rug moves."

"So I was right!" Nova exclaimed. "I told Ethan that some of the things in my past had to change so that my dad being alive would make sense!"

Aunt Jean raised her eyebrows. "So you've talked to Ethan about this?"

"Well, yes." Nova looked at her hands again. "Only because I had no idea what was going on in the beginning. He's been great."

"Well, what's done is done. But in the future, it's best to remember that this is a matter for the Grant family only," Aunt Jean warned.

"I'm sorry. I won't talk to anyone else about it. I

promise."

"That's all right, honey. I know we can trust you. Anyway, what was I saying? Oh yes. How many things change is based on how big a wrinkle you're pulling out of the rug."

"But if that's true, more things should have changed. I mean, Dad getting killed in a wreck was a big thing."

"Well, yes and no." Aunt Jean frowned. "Yes, it was a major tragedy, but no, the event itself wasn't that big. Your life was already set up to have him around. Your dad being alive just kept things on a normal course. So if you think about it that way, it wasn't that big a change. Enough to move the furniture a little, but not enough to cause it to fall off the rug."

"What about Alana? Bringing her back would definitely be a big wrinkle," Nova pointed out. "We're talking about almost sixteen years without her."

Aunt Jean said nothing at first. She just sat there as if her mind had gone off somewhere, finally shaking her head to bring herself back. "Some of the furniture is going to fall."

Everyone was silent for a minute.

Nova looked at her dad. "But I still want to try. Don't you?"

He frowned. "I don't know, firefly. It would kill me if I lost anyone else. What if my mother was right? What if it just causes more tragedy?"

"But you'll *know* about Alana's heart. You'll get help for her this time. And you can make sure Mom gets to the hospital before anything bad happens."

"I knew about Alana's heart last time too. And all I did was lose her five years earlier."

"That won't happen this time! And if it does, you'll just go back again and again until you get it right!" Nova cried.

"Listen to me, child!" Aunt Jean said. "You can't just keep going back. It takes something out of you every time. I don't know how to explain it, but the more times you travel, the harder it gets to go back to a specific time. Your aim isn't as sharp."

"Then it has to be me," Nova said resolutely. "If the ability gets weaker every time you travel, it's reasonable to assume that I would be the strongest. I've never traveled on my own. Both of you have."

"Let's not get ahead of ourselves," Dayton cautioned. "We all know you can't go back because you'd be a baby too. So that means you'd have to go forward in time, and like Aunt Jean said, moving forward to a time when Alana is alive would be a big wrinkle and too much would have to change. I won't approve that. It's too dangerous."

"I have to do something! We're talking about my sister!"

"Nova—"

"Listen, both of you," Aunt Jean interrupted. "You act like it's easy to travel through time. It's not. You don't just decide to do it and step through a door. It takes planning and preparation. You have to be sure of where you're going and what you're going to do differently when you face the event you've aimed for. Even a fleeting loss of focus can have disastrous effects."

"So tell us how to do it," Nova said quietly.

Aunt Jean looked uncertain about sharing any more. "We're just *talking* about it right now, is that agreed?"

"Yes, Aunt Jean," they said practically in unison.

Nova leaned forward and waited. Aunt Jean still seemed uncertain, but after a couple of minutes of awkward silence, she began.

"All right. You have to first go back in your mind to the event you intend to change. Think about what you did that put you on the path you're on now. Sometimes it's a big thing, but many times it's a small decision you made at a crossroads in your life. You went left instead of right, figuratively speaking. Once you've determined where you need to *land*, so to speak, you think about how a different direction will affect the rest of your life. Will it make things better or worse? For example, you wouldn't change a marriage if it meant you'd also lose your children that came from that marriage. You have to think about the repercussions. Most of the time, that's where it ends. You decide it's not worth it, so you go on with the life you have." She paused, letting her words sink in.

Several birds chirped frantically overhead, as if discussing their impression of the startling conversation among the humans in the garden. Nova smiled. Was the idea that animals could have discussions about such things any more unbelievable than time travel? Nova looked up as she fidgeted with a loose piece of the wicker, jutting out of the armrest. Her aunt was watching her, a knowing look on her face.

After another minute or so, Aunt Jean seemed satisfied that they'd had enough time to process what she told them and she continued. "If, in spite of all the potential ramifications, you still want to travel back to correct your path, then be firm in your conviction. Go to a peaceful place, remove all distractions, and totally relax. You have to put yourself into a meditative state. Forget about everything but the event you want to travel to. You must actually be able to feel your brain honing in on it, like looking through the scope of a rifle and aiming at something far away. Wait until you have it clearly in sight, then will yourself to go there as if you're the bullet being fired at the object, or point in time. Focus every bit of energy you have on that point. When it happens, you can actually *feel* it. It's a sensation similar to going over a dip in the road and floating for a split second, then being sucked through a narrow tunnel. It's not an unpleasant experience, just unsettling." Aunt Jean looked at Dayton. "What did you think of when you had your accident?"

"I thought about Nova," he answered.

"Be more specific, Day."

"I thought about when she was little, sitting across from me at my desk in the office. She was coloring." He looked at Nova. "Then I thought about her the way she is now, sitting across from me with her feet up on the desk, laughing and talking. I had promised to take her along on one of my research trips when she finished the school year. I thought about being at my desk in the office, making plans, waiting for Nova to come bursting in so I could share them with her. I didn't want it to be over. I didn't want to die and not be there when she came through the door. All that went through my head in a split second."

"You were thinking about a future you weren't going to have?"

"Yes." He got up and paced. "And then I was sitting at my desk in the office. Just like that. I was completely freaked out. I thought I'd gone crazy. Then it hit me what had happened. I knew I'd traveled, but I thought I'd gone back in time, not forward. That was when I noticed my desk calendar was nine months ahead. Why nine months?"

Aunt Jean thought for a moment. "Hmm. I suppose, for reasons we don't know, that was exactly where you needed to land in time for all the necessary pieces to fall into place. Time travel is a perfectly orchestrated event. Everything happens for a reason. We might not know what those reasons are, but it always works out the way it's supposed to. What happened then?"

"I was afraid to leave the office. I didn't know what I'd have to deal with, so I just sat there until Ethan started pounding on the door."

"Ethan?" Aunt Jean looked at Nova.

"I'd had a rough morning too. Lots of things were different, and I had a meltdown at school. That's when I found out about Ethan being my boyfriend. He came home with me. When I saw Dad's car in the driveway, I passed out."

Aunt Jean laughed. "Well, it sounds like a pretty good switch to me. You got your dad back and a boyfriend too."

Nova didn't think it was so funny. She crossed her arms and sat back in her chair.

Aunt Jean stopped laughing but still smiled warmly at Nova. "Oh, honey, you have to keep your sense of humor if you're going to get through this life."

Nova uncrossed her arms and leaned forward again. "Aunt Jean, there's something that doesn't make sense. Dad traveled forward almost nine months in a split second, but I lived those nine months without him. I thought he was dead that whole time. We all did. My life didn't change until the moment he landed in his office. Why?"

Aunt Jean thought for a moment. "Traveling is a solitary event. You can't take someone else with you, so you didn't travel with him when he yanked the rug." She chuckled. "You're furniture just like everyone else, honey. You're just furniture that's... aware. See, non-travelers go about their lives thinking they're on a steady march through time, from birth to death. They don't realize their lives are changing course along the way. But fellow travelers always know, especially if they're close emotionally or physically to the person doing the traveling. When your dad jumped forward, things changed for everyone, but you were the only one who knew it, because you were the only other traveler who was close to him. So even though you had to march through those nine months with everyone else, when your dad left the timeline that had him in the river and joined the timeline we're in now, you noticed the change."

"Noticed is an understatement," Nova remarked.

"I'm sure." Aunt Jean smiled.

"I have one more question."

"Only one?" Aunt Jean leaned her head back and laughed.

"Okay, I have lots of questions." Nova shook her head. "But just this one for now. If you've traveled back several times, why are you still the age you should be? I mean, if you went back ten years to change some event, wouldn't you then be ten years older than you should be for that time? And wouldn't the same go for traveling forward?"

"That's a good question. I know it's confusing, but if I went back, say ten years, I'd be the age I was at that time when I got there. My age would always be determined by where I landed on the timeline." She put her hand on Nova's knee. "I know it's a lot to take in, honey." Aunt Jean turned her attention to Dayton. "Tell me what happened when you tried to save Alana."

He looked stricken. "Why?"

"I just want to know the details. How did it go wrong?"

He shook his head, clearly not wanting to talk about it again.

"Day, I have a reason for asking. I know it's hard to relive it, but trust me."

He sighed, then shared his nightmarish experience of the first time he traveled. He talked about the first five years with Alana, how bold and full of life she'd been. They'd had no idea that her heart was a ticking bomb. When he shared that fateful day at the pool, losing her, and how he barely got through it. Even harder for him to talk about was the fact that going back had caused her birth to be more traumatic and ultimately fatal.

When he was finished, Aunt Jean had tears running down her face. "So unnecessary. If you had known how to do this thing right, it might have turned out exactly like you'd hoped it would."

"What do you mean?" he demanded.

"I mean, I think we may be able to do something about it."

Nova's heart jumped into her throat. "You'll help us, Aunt Jean?"

Aunt Jean winked. "We'd better head back to the

house. I want to get a turkey in for tonight, then we should go down to the barn and see what Justin's been teaching Marshall."

Aunt Jean stood and started up the path. They had no choice but to follow her.

CHAPTER 21

For the rest of the day, Nova helped out at the barn. Marshall's riding lesson had been a great success and Justin had again declared him a "natural." When Dayton strolled down later in the day, Marshall spent a half an hour trying to talk him into buying a horse when they got home.

"Why don't we just take this one with us?" Nova asked sweetly.

Marshall jumped up and down. "Can we take him, Dad? Can we take Bo?"

He was not at all amused. "You're not helping, Nova. See what you started?"

"Sorry, Dad." Nova giggled.

"Marshall, we can't get a horse right now, but maybe we can find a place that gives riding lessons near our house. How would that be?" he asked.

"Okay, I guess," Marshall grumbled.

Justin took his cue and handed the hose to Marshall. "Time to water the horses, big guy."

Marshall's mood lightened considerably, and he dragged the hose down the main aisle of the barn, stopping at each stall to fill the bucket with fresh water.

"He's a great kid," Justin said. "I wish I had him here all the time."

"I wish we weren't so far away," Dayton agreed, "but we'll be back. You can count on it."

Before long, it was time to trudge up to the house for dinner. They had mucked out stalls, fed and watered the horses, and stacked a new load of hay in the loft. Nova was bone-tired, but Marshall looked as if he could do it all over again.

"Marshall, I think you've found your calling," Nova said as they got to the kitchen.

Aunt Jean took one look at them and shooed them upstairs to get cleaned up. When Nova stepped in front of the mirror in her bathroom, she could see why. Bits of hay covered nearly every inch of her and even stuck out of her ponytail. There was a smudge across one side of her face, and she had no idea where that had come from. The hems of her jeans were wet at least six inches up her leg, and her shoes were damp. She'd been too tired to notice, but now all she wanted was to get into a warm bath, wash her hair, and put on some clean, dry clothes. By the time she got downstairs, the others had nearly finished eating.

"Better get in here, honey. Marshall is eating all the food." Aunt Jean teased.

Marshall looked up with a mouth full of turkey. "I'm hungry," he said sheepishly.

Nova sat down and filled her plate. "Like I said, we're all gonna weigh a ton when we leave here."

Aunt Jean seemed genuinely pleased that her cooking was such a hit with this branch of the Grant family. She promised to do some baking the next day.

"Maybe you kids would like to help," she said brightly.

"I'll be at the barn all day," Marshall said.

"I can help you," Nova offered.

"Okay, tomorrow we bake!" Aunt Jean beamed.

For the rest of the evening, they all sat on the porch. Nova and Marshall took the swing, and after about ten minutes, Marshall was sound asleep. Nova rocked her feet back and forth on the wooden decking. The smooth motion of the swing was soothing, and she allowed it to lull her into a peaceful place. She thought about Ethan back at home and wished she could see him. She could imagine him there with her, gliding back and forth, their hands barely touching. That piece of hair that always fell across his forehead would be driving her crazy. She'd suggest they walk to the barn to say good night to the horses and off they'd go, not fooling anyone. Nova leaned her head against the back of the swing, smiling, imagining her time alone at the barn with Ethan.

"What are you smiling about?"

When Nova opened her eyes, Aunt Jean winked. She couldn't possibly know that the smile was for Ethan, but Nova blushed anyway.

"Do you mind if I go on to bed? I'm really tired," Nova asked, feeling her face get redder by the minute.

Aunt Jean chuckled. "You go ahead, honey. Get some rest. Maybe you and I can take a walk tomorrow and I'll tell you the names of all my flowers."

"Sure," Nova said. She let the swing come to a gentle stop so it wouldn't wake Marshall. "See you in the morning."

"Good night, firefly," her dad called as she plodded up the stairs.

"Good night, Dad," she answered.

Nova hardly had the energy to brush her teeth and change for bed. When she pulled back the covers and lay down, the cool sheets felt heavenly. She took a deep breath and slowly let it out, expecting sleep to come instantly. Her body was trying to cooperate, but her mind refused to allow it. Every word from Aunt Jean swirled around her head over and over. It all sounded just too incredible.

Nova thought of the Grandma Kate her aunt had described, fun-loving and fragile and so much like her dad. It was a stark contrast to the imposing figure Nova remembered from her childhood. Her grandmother had seemed serious, even harsh at times.

She pushed the covers back and sat up. It was no use trying to sleep, and she didn't want to go back downstairs. She glanced around the room, her eyes coming to rest on the attic door. A chill ran up her spine at the thought of going up there. It wasn't like the small space in the ceiling at home. This one was a complete unknown. There could be all kinds of creatures up there. She hesitated for a moment, then thought, *How bad could it be?* Swinging her legs over the side of the bed, Nova slid to the wood floor, careful not to make any noise in case Aunt Jean was in the hall outside her door. She'd noticed that her aunt had an unsettling ability to sneak up on people.

When she turned the brass knob, the attic door stuck for a moment before creaking open. She hesitated, listening, but heard no one outside her room. Peeking in, her gaze traveled up the rough wood stairs into pitch black. There had to be a light switch somewhere, but feeling around inside the door proved fruitless. Nova didn't dare turn the lamp on next to her bed for fear that someone would notice and knock on her door. Aunt Jean might not approve of her snooping around in the attic, so it was best not to be discovered.

She stepped into the space just inside the door and felt around the walls again. Still nothing. Looking around with no light would be impossible, and she had no idea how to come up with a flashlight. At least the attic at home had a bulb mounted on the ceiling with a chain dangling down. Nova reached up. Sure enough, she felt a chain. After she gave it a tug, the stairs were bathed in light.

A large cobweb partially blocked the stairs about halfway up, and several others hung from the ceiling. Nova stood there a moment, contemplating whether or not to retreat to the safety of her cozy room. But she was dying to know what was in the attic, so she took a deep breath and climbed the stairs. When she tried ducking under the cobweb, some of it clung to her hair and she stifled a scream before running the rest of the way up.

"This better be worth it." she whispered to no one in particular.

At the top was another chain light. This one illuminated a surprisingly large wood-floored room lined with shelves. The first thing that caught her eye was a porcelain doll perched on the top shelf to her right, seemingly staring right at her.

"Okay, that's creepy." Nova shuddered and looked away.

She scanned the rest of the room filled with antique furniture, stacks and stacks of books, Christmas decorations, old toys, a child's rocking chair, and several large trunks. The shelves were crammed with more books, dishes, figurines, small boxes, empty mason jars, oil lamps, an elaborate wooden train set, and too many other items to take in. There seemed to be a fine layer of dust on everything, a testimony to the infrequency of visitors to this part of the house. Nova felt like an unwanted intruder. She was tempted to turn and leave, but curiosity won out. She decided to start with the closest trunk.

When she threw her weight against the massive lid, it gave way, revealing more dolls with blank eyes staring up at her. Some were in elaborate outfits, stiff from years of being stored in a box in the attic. Others were devoid of any clothing – cloth bodies with painted porcelain heads and limbs. She let out a muted scream before slamming the top closed.

What's with all the dolls? She shivered a little even though the attic was warmer than her room below. Nova pictured the dolls coming alive, creeping down the stairs at night, and scratching on the door. *Great. Now I'll never get to sleep!*

It took her a few minutes to work up the nerve to

tackle the next trunk. It was smaller, and the lid was much easier to lift. Nova cracked it open slightly and peeked inside. Satisfied that there were no more dolls, she pulled the lid up and discovered a veritable treasure chest – cloth bags filled with old coins, a jewelry box, four silver candlesticks, and a pair of ancient binoculars. Inside the jewelry box were several gold necklaces, a locket with a pearl in the center, a compass, an ornate silver letter opener with the letter "E" carved on the side, an old pocket watch, and what appeared to be two wedding rings, one with a blue stone in the middle. *Okay,* this *is the kind of trunk Marshall would like.*

She pulled out one of the bags and dumped the coins on the floor. Obviously very old, many of the coins looked as if they would have been at home on a pirate ship, part of the plunder amassed after years of raiding villages and capturing other vessels. It wouldn't surprise her to find out that these were authentic gold doubloons. *No wonder Aunt Jean is so rich.*

Nova turned her attention back to the trunk and noticed several paintings in the bottom, underneath everything else. She deposited the bags of coins and other items on the floor and carefully removed the first painting. The scene was familiar, possibly the porch at Willow Hill. Something was different though. She stared at the painting, finally realizing that there was no upstairs balcony. Everything else about the house looked the same. She wondered if this was the original house that had been improved upon with each time change. Maybe that was what Aunt Jean had meant when she said that this place didn't happen by accident and that it took several lifetimes to get things right.

She set the picture aside and examined the next one, a portrait of a young couple sitting on the porch of an unfamiliar house. She recognized the young woman – it was Grandma Kate – but Nova had no idea who the man was. He wasn't Grandma Kate's husband, Sheldon, because she'd

218

seen pictures of him over the years. On the step in front of them was a small child, a beautiful little boy with dark hair, holding a tiny hammer. The hairs on the back of Nova's neck stood up. She had no idea who the child was either. It definitely wasn't her blond-haired, hazel-eyed father. Nova scanned the picture and spotted the artist's signature carefully penned in the bottom right-hand corner –

J. G. Huckaby. Nova thought for a moment, then the realization hit her.

Jean Grant Huckaby.

Nova heard voices drifting up from the hallway below, so she quickly put the coins back in their bag, laid the paintings in the bottom of the trunk exactly as they'd been before, and put the coins on top of them. After replacing the other items, she closed the trunk, hurried down the stairs, and climbed into bed just as someone tapped on her door.

Her dad stuck his head inside. "Just wanted to say good night again."

"Good night, Dad," Nova said, slightly out of breath.

He didn't seem to notice and pulled the door shut. Nova turned over on her back and stared at the ceiling, thinking about what else could be in the attic. There was so much to see, and she couldn't wait to get back up there. Maybe next time she'd take Marshall, if she could tear him away from the horses. She wasn't sure that even a trunk full of pirate treasure would do it. Nova smiled, thinking about showing him the coins. He'd flip over those.

Nova's mind drifted back to the conversation with Aunt Jean in the garden. She wanted to learn everything she could about her family history, especially about her family's amazing gift. She marveled at the fact that she may actually be able to transport herself through time. There was so much to take in. She wanted to go over it all in her mind, everything they had talked about, but the trip to the attic had apparently worn her out. She lay quietly in the four-poster bed, finally sleepy. Closing her eyes, Nova felt her body relaxing.

Traveling didn't sound all that hard. Aunt Jean had apparently done it many times. What would be the harm in seeing if she could at least put herself into a meditative state? The soft mattress hugged her body as she took slow, deep breaths...in and out. The windows were cracked open slightly, and the sound of crickets drifted in. Keeping her breathing slow and rhythmic, she attuned her ears to that sound, blocking out everything else. She imagined herself in the garden, walking along the path to the house. Someone was running ahead of her. It was Alana.

She focused on the image of her sister, golden hair and hazel eyes, so much like Marshall. She looked older now, but she had the same playful expression. Nova pictured her running down to the barn, laughing all the way. Alana would have loved the horses. Nova smiled wistfully. She felt as if she was starting to float, almost as if she were suspended over the bed while still enveloped in its comfortable warmth. She emerged from the garden and followed Alana down the hill toward the barn. Her sister looked back, her hair flowing around her face. Nova tried to catch up but couldn't seem to move any faster. *Wait for me!*

Something was happening. She was on the edge of a precipice. All she had to do was step off. Alana's laugh sounded far away. *Step off...*

Suddenly, an overpowering sense of foreboding engulfed her. *What about the chip in the table?* Her whole body tensed.

It doesn't matter about the chip! she screamed in her mind. *It doesn't mean anything!*

But what if it did mean something? Something terrible. Nova stepped back from the precipice. What if the other accident, much more tragic, was also meant to play out? Maybe there was nothing she could do to prevent that. It was only a matter of time. What if she had managed to dodge that bullet, only to travel again and make it happen?

Nova's heart was pounding. She jumped out of bed and stood trembling, terrified at what she'd nearly done. How could she be so stupid! Didn't Aunt Jean say traveling takes planning? Nova took several deep breaths, trying to slow her racing heart. Staring out of the window at the moonlit garden, she wondered if it was really worth the risk. She'd lived her whole life without Alana, so she had no memories to torture her. It was a completely different story with her dad. Losing him again would be devastating.

Nova paced, trying to calm down. *I can't do it. What was I thinking?* She nearly sobbed. *I'm not strong enough.*

Nova pushed open the window and leaned her head out, breathing in the sweet smell of flowers. She felt utterly defeated. Why had she thought she could do this? Saving Alana was all she had cared about, and nothing else had mattered. Now all she felt was fear and resignation. Traveling was too risky. She just needed to be happy with the life she had and forget about Alana. Her dad was alive and her family was happy.

Nova climbed back into bed, still shaking. Sometime later, she managed to fall into a fitful sleep.

CHAPTER 22

Nova awoke to the sound of tapping on her bedroom door. At first she imagined that it was the dolls knocking on the attic door.

"Nova?" It was Aunt Jean.

Nova sat up and rubbed her eyes as her aunt burst into the room.

"You teenagers sure like to sleep, don't you?" She laughed. "We start baking pretty early around here. Are you still planning to help me?"

"Sure, Aunt Jean. Just give me a minute." Nova managed a weak smile.

Aunt Jean frowned slightly. "Are you feeling all right, honey?"

"I'm fine. Just tired, I guess," Nova lied.

"Anything you want to talk about?"

"Not right now." Nova pushed her hair out of her face. "Just give me a few minutes."

"Well, get yourself awake and come on down to the kitchen. We're baking chocolate pies and sweet potato cake."

Nova wrinkled her nose. "Sweet potato cake? Really?"

Aunt Jean threw her head back and laughed. "Don't knock it until you've tried it, honey. It's one of my specialties."

"Okay, sweet potato cake it is. Just don't tell Marshall what's in it."

Nova washed her face and pulled on a clean pair of jeans and a pale pink pullover, then she headed downstairs. Sunlight streamed in through the open windows, bathing the kitchen in natural light. Nova stopped in the doorway, smiling as she watched her aunt flit around cheerfully. How was it possible that they had only met the day before yesterday? Being around her felt so natural, as if they'd always known each other.

Aunt Jean stopped for a moment and smiled at Nova. "It sure is nice having you here, honey. I don't know when I've laughed so much. It can get pretty lonely around here sometimes."

"I love being here too," Nova said.

The two ovens were already preheated and the table was covered with the ingredients that they would need. Aunt Jean put Nova to work grating sweet potatoes while she rolled out dough for the piecrusts. They had never done much baking around Nova's house, and she felt as though she was all thumbs at first, but before long, she had the hang of it.

Aunt Jean chattered pleasantly as they worked, talking mostly about the old days when Matthew, Bill, and Georgia were still living. She also talked about Justin. His parents had been close friends of the family before they died. Nova felt as though there was more to the story than Connie and Aunt Jean had said, but she was hesitant to ask, figuring she'd find out sooner or later if it was important. She finished grating the sweet potatoes and added them to the batter in a large bowl. As soon as the potatoes were mixed in, Nova poured the thick concoction into four round cake pans that Aunt Jean had lined with parchment paper. When the batter was divided equally among the four pans, Aunt Jean popped them into the oven.

The chocolate pies were next. Nova stirred eggs, sugar, flour, butter, and chocolate over low heat while her aunt placed the dough into pie pans and trimmed the edges in a way that left a fluted pattern.

Nova admired her artistry. "Good grief. I'll never be able to do that."

"Sure, you will, honey. Like other things, it just takes practice." Aunt Jean winked at her.

Nova cleared her throat and returned her attention to the chocolate filling. A delicious aroma of cake and chocolate filled the room.

"I might have to try some of this before it goes in the pie shells, Aunt Jean." Nova laughed.

"I always make a little too much for that very reason." Aunt Jean held up two spoons. "We'd better be quick though. If the others come in, we'll have to give out samples and there won't be enough left for the pies."

It suddenly occurred to Nova that her whole family seemed to have vanished. "Where is everybody?"

Aunt Jean chuckled. "Well, you can guess where Marshall is. I think he'd live in that barn if we let him. And he talked your dad into spending the morning down there too. Your mother is helping Connie with the nursery. They all breezed through here a couple of hours before you got up. I'm taking lunch to them later. So it's just you and me until then."

Nova poured the chocolate into the pie shells and carefully placed them in the second oven. Noticing the time, they set about cleaning the kitchen. As Nova worked, she became lost in thought, thinking about the night before. After a while, she noticed that Aunt Jean hadn't said anything for at least five minutes. She looked up to find her aunt studying her.

"Is there anything you want to talk to me about, honey?"

Nova felt the hairs stand up on the back of her neck. How could her aunt possibly know? "I…uh. Not really."

Aunt Jean frowned. "If you can't talk to me about it, who can you talk to?"

She had a point. Nova plopped down on the bench next to the table. Aunt Jean sat down across from her and waited. Nova couldn't bring herself to tell her aunt that she had almost traveled the night before, or at least she thought she had. Instead, Nova told her about the chip in the table and her fear that everything that had happened before could happen again.

"I know it seems like a little thing to be hung up on, but what if it means something?"

Aunt Jean didn't answer for a moment. When she did, she sounded tired. "I can't guarantee the things that happened before won't happen again. A timeline moves along like a river. The current wants to pull you a certain way. If you float down the river exactly the same way every time, you'll probably bump into the same rocks. You'll still end up going where the current wants to take you. If you don't want to go over the same rocks, you have to make a change that will put you on a different course. It can't be a small change, because you'll end up in the same place, going over the same rocks. It has to be a big change. A change that alters your path."

"But how do I do that? I don't want a completely different life. I don't want to lose other people I love. I just want my sister back." Tears ran down Nova's face. "I remember her…Alana. I know it sounds crazy, but I had an image of her pop into my head when I was in my dad's office. It was when we were little and only lasted a second. But it was so clear."

"Amazing," Aunt Jean said quietly. "You must be very strong. You were so young, then you relived your first five years without her. Just amazing."

"It doesn't feel amazing. It feels hopeless. Even if I want to try, I can't go back in time because I was a baby then too. That would be pointless. I'd have to go forward."

"No, you can't go back. And I don't think your dad has it in him to try again." Aunt Jean sighed. "He's so like his mother."

They were quiet for a moment, then Nova asked, "If I try going forward, how far is enough? And how do I keep the rest of my life the same?"

"Maybe you just need to let it go. It would be a difficult thing to pull off. Going forward into your future is something I have no experience with. I don't know what will happen. If I could fix things for you, I would. But the last time I traveled…well, let's just say I wasn't as strong as I'd been before. I nearly lost what I had worked so hard to get. I can't do it anymore. Do you remember me telling you it gets harder and harder? Eventually, you have to stop. Because if you don't…"

"What?" Nova's voice was barely a whisper.

"If you don't, you can lose everything. You have to know when to stop."

"Is that what happened to my grandmother?"

"No," Aunt Jean stated firmly. "Your grandmother never really believed she had the power. Our mother had each of us practice when we were young. The first time, we traveled back to the previous day. Just one day. That doesn't take much out of you. For me, the experience was exhilarating. I couldn't wait to do it again and again. But for Kate, well, let's just say that when it came right down to it, she was afraid. She doubted herself. You can't use the ability if you don't believe in yourself. You have to be absolutely sure of where you're going and be completely focused. That's the most important thing – focus. She couldn't achieve that focus because her mind was clouded by fear and doubt.

"Later on, when she tried to travel back, she caused another tragedy, worse than the one before. After that, she was bitter and angry." Aunt Jean shook her head as her eyes filled with tears. "She blamed herself and eventually the rest of the family. She refused to let any of us help her. I would have done anything to ease her pain, but she made me promise never to mention traveling again. One day, years later, we had a big argument about it and I never saw her again after that."

Nova put her hand on her aunt's arm. "I'm sorry, Aunt Jean."

She didn't know what else to say. She wondered what tragedy her grandmother had caused, but she was afraid to ask. Besides, talking about it seemed so painful for her aunt. Neither of them spoke for several minutes.

It was Aunt Jean who broke the silence. "Nova, you're not like your dad and grandmother. I don't mean to speak ill of them, but it's the truth. My sister was sweet and fun-loving, just like Dayton. But she lacked resolve, always worried about what could happen, especially after she failed the one time. I guess I should tell you…"

"You don't have to if you don't want to talk about it," Nova offered.

"It's probably a good idea to tell you, so you won't make the same mistake. Not that you would. You remind me of your great-grandmother, Evelyn – my mother. You're strong like her. I can tell. It's just that sometimes a person can get so caught up in the idea of changing things that, well, they get ahead of themselves and something goes terribly wrong." Aunt Jean seemed to be far away, thinking about her sister. She pulled herself back to the present and continued. "Kate's first husband, Daniel, died in an accident."

"Her first husband?" Nova was confused. She'd never heard that Grandma Kate had been married twice.

"Yes. He bought the house next to ours. The people who had owned it were old and in very poor health. They passed away just two weeks apart and left the house in quite a state. He planned to fix it up, sell it, and use the money to start a construction business. He was at the house every day. That's how he met your grandmother. They hit it off right away. He was so good-looking, and she had that Grant sparkle." Aunt Jean smiled wistfully. "She was pretty, like you. He asked her to marry him after only a few weeks. Our parents weren't happy about that and refused to pay for a wedding, but Kate and Daniel were determined. They put the repairs on the house next door on hold and used the money to elope. After the wedding, they decided to move in and continue fixing it up. They were so happy."

Aunt Jean's eyes filled with tears again. "After a while, my parents fell in love with Daniel too, especially when the baby came." She dabbed her eyes with her apron. "He was a precious child, and our parents absolutely doted on him. They loved having Kate, Daniel, and the baby right next door. Daniel worked so hard on that house. He was determined to make it perfect for his family. He thought he could handle all the work himself. Little Danny Jr. would follow him around with a toy hammer. It was the cutest thing you ever saw." She shook her head sadly.

"Wait!" Nova gripped her aunt's arm. "Toy hammer! That's who the people in the painting were with Grandma Kate! Daniel and Danny Jr.!"

Aunt Jean stared at Nova, clearly taken aback. "Painting?"

"In the attic." Nova wasn't sure how her aunt would feel about her going through her old things.

"When were you in the attic?" Aunt Jean asked.

"Last night. I couldn't sleep. In one of the trunks, there was a painting of a young family on a porch. I didn't recognize the house, but I recognized Grandma Kate. There was a man holding Grandma Kate's hand and a little boy with a toy hammer. You painted it, didn't you? I saw your signature on the bottom."

"Your dad's not the only artist in this family." Aunt Jean smiled. "I wanted to remember, but after a while, it was just too painful. I put it away and never looked at it again. Maybe it's good that you found it. Daniel and the little one should be remembered." Aunt Jean's expression was hard to read. "There's a lot of Grant history in that attic. Maybe I should go with you next time. I haven't been up there in years."

Nova grimaced. "What's with all the dolls?"

Aunt Jean threw her head back and laughed. "Awful little things, if you ask me! Georgia collected them, but frankly, they always gave me the creeps. I couldn't wait to get rid of them when she passed. But I guess I felt guilty about it, so I put them in the attic instead."

"I imagined them coming down the stairs during the night." Nova shuddered.

"Oh dear Lord! I'll have to get rid of them for sure now." Aunt Jean shook her head, still laughing.

"Tell me more about what happened to Grandma Kate's first family." Nova was anxious to get back to the story.

"Well, like I was saying, we all loved Daniel and the baby. Everything in Kate's life seemed ideal. Loving husband, beautiful child, family close by…then it all fell apart. Daniel was on the roof, nailing shingles, and fell off. He died instantly – broke his neck." Tears ran down Aunt Jean's face. "Your grandmother was devastated. We all were. She started talking about traveling right away, but she was emotional and our parents tried to talk her out of it. They told her to wait a few weeks, until she was calmer. Kate promised she would, but she lied. She told me how much she hated the house and never wanted to live there again. She and Danny moved in with us the day of the funeral." Aunt Jean sighed.

"Two days later, Kate traveled. To hear her tell it later, she tried to focus on the morning of the accident, to stop Daniel from climbing up on the roof. But she couldn't keep her mind from wandering. She kept thinking about the house, how much she hated it and wished they'd never moved in. The funny thing is, that old house was the reason she met Daniel in the first place. It had almost burned down four years before, when lightning struck the tree behind it. Kate had seen it from her bedroom window and alerted our father. He was able to get help and put the fire out before it burned the house down. If Kate hadn't noticed the fire that night, the house would have been gone. She never would have known Daniel."

"So what happened?" Nova asked softly.

Aunt Jean lifted the end of her apron and dabbed her eyes. "Right as Kate traveled, her mind went back to that day, the day of the fire, and that's where she landed – a year before she ever met Daniel, two years before she had little Danny, and four years before Daniel fell off the roof. She woke up in her room as she had that night and saw the fire. For the second time, she had to save the house she had come to hate. Then she had to face a whole year before she could meet Daniel again. Kate lived for the day he would come. It was all she thought about. All that time without him and the baby."

"That must have been so hard, waiting all that time and missing her family," Nova said.

"Yes, it was. She didn't think she'd get through it. When the time they met finally arrived, she waited on the porch all day, then the next day, and the next. She sat on that porch every day for weeks, but he never came. Something had happened in that year that changed his path. She tried to find him, but it was no use."

"She never saw him again?"

"No." Aunt Jean shook her head sadly. "Kate had no idea how to find him. She looked through every phone book she could find, but he wasn't listed. She asked around town, but no one knew him. He'd been an only child and his parents were dead, so there was no one left who might know where he was. Looking for Daniel became her obsession, but she never found out what happened to him. And of course, she never had little Danny."

"Oh my God, Aunt Jean. Couldn't she have done

something?" Nova cried. "You said it's possible to go back to where you were before. Couldn't she have done that? Gone back to where she started to try again?"

"It would have been possible to go right back to her starting point, the moment she traveled. If she'd done that, she could have tried again to travel to the day he fell off the roof so she could stop him."

"Why didn't she do that?"

"It's not that she didn't try, honey. Any time you travel, there's a connection between where you start and where you end up. You can feel it if you know what to look for. The problem is, it doesn't last very long, so you don't have much time to make that decision. If you miss the train, so to speak, you're stuck. You have to stay where you are. Kate was distracted by the house fire next door. By the time she realized she needed to return, it was too late. It was like she'd missed the last train out of there. None of us ever knew how to jump into the future without that connection, and the idea of manipulating that future…well, let's just say that as far as we knew, no one had ever done anything like that. So in Kate's new reality, her first little family never existed and that's all she had to work with."

"That's so depressing. Wait…how do you remember Daniel and the baby if they never existed?"

"Because I'm a traveler too. It's fuzzy, but some parts are clear. That's how it is when someone close to you travels and you also have the gift. The old life feels like a dream, but one you don't forget. The painting you saw…I did that from memory. You never forget the people you knew. They stick with you."

"Or become your imaginary friend," Nova said quietly. "Well, I guess Marshall doesn't have it. He doesn't seem to remember anything from before."

"Maybe not, but he's still young. You never know."

"Yes, but *I* remember and I was only five when Alana died."

"Nova, I think that's because you're special – stronger than most."

"When I first saw Alana's picture, I could see her in my mind, splashing in the pool. Do you remember Alana, Aunt Jean?"

"I wish I did, honey. But we weren't in touch with your family then."

"I'm sorry Grandma Kate cut us off from all of you. I guess I can understand how afraid she was though. I feel so bad for her."

"I know. Me too." Aunt Jean smiled. "Whatever happens, I want you to know I have faith in you."

Nova's stomach knotted up. She wished she shared her aunt's confidence. "What if you're wrong about me? What if I mess everything up?"

"There's always that possibility, honey. But if you're careful, traveling can accomplish amazing things, like bringing people you love back to you. I've done it myself."

"So why aren't Uncle Bill and Aunt Georgia here? And your husband, Matthew? They couldn't have been very old when they died."

"I guess you could say they just got tired. I had a lot of years with them, a lot more that you realize." She chuckled. "Eventually you wear out and have to quit. It's just time to let nature take its course."

"When did Grandma Kate marry my grandfather?"

"When she couldn't find Daniel, Kate became depressed. She didn't ever want to leave the house. She kept hoping he'd show up. After about six months, our mother sent her to stay with our relatives in Charleston for the summer. That's when she met a handsome young doctor, Sheldon Samuels. He was such a good man. He'd done some work with other doctors for the World Health Organization, and when he met my sister, he'd just returned from West Africa. They were married the next spring, and he left almost immediately for Africa one last time. He wanted to see the people he'd helped, to make sure they were going to be all right."

"He sounds amazing."

"He was, honey. Kate understood him wanting to go back, but after what had happened to her other family, she was frantic, especially when she realized she was expecting another baby. Kate hadn't wanted any more children after losing Danny, but there she was – without her husband and pregnant. A few days before Sheldon was scheduled to leave Africa, he got sick. The other doctors had already left, and by the time he sent for help, it was too late. He never came home."

"Oh my God." Nova didn't know what else to say. She'd always known that her dad hadn't known her grandfather, but she'd never heard the details.

Aunt Jean patted Nova's arm. "Kate moved away after that. She wanted to start over with the baby someplace new, where she didn't know anyone. We all tried to talk her out of it, but she couldn't be swayed. She wanted to raise her son to have a normal life, away from traveling. We were all heartbroken. I think she felt badly about hurting the family though, because she decided to keep the Grant name and give the baby Samuels as a middle name, after his father."

Aunt Jean smiled wistfully. "Dayton truly brought the old Kate back. She absolutely adored him. I went up to see them in New Hampshire, and I can tell you, he was Kate's whole world. I brought up Sheldon a couple of times, but Kate refused to talk about him or anything to do with the past, except to say that traveling always made things worse and she wasn't about to lose this baby too. Over time, she reestablished contact with the family, but she was adamant about not traveling again and never wanted her son to either. She wouldn't allow the subject to come up. We tried to talk to him about it when he was a boy, but we had to do it when Kate wasn't around. And then, of course, she put a stop to that too. It's such a shame. I think something could have been done about little Alana if he had been trained to control his gift."

"So what should I do?"

Aunt Jean thought for a moment "Come with me." She stood and reached for Nova's hand.

"Aunt Jean, is something burning in the oven?"

"It won't matter, honey. Trust me."

They walked across the veranda and down the stone path through the garden to the gazebo.

"What are we doing?" Nova asked, suddenly a little on edge.

"Time travel 101." Aunt Jean laughed.

Nova's mouth dropped open. "We're traveling?"

"Not we, honey. You."

"Wait…now?"

"Just a little. It'll be fine, I promise. I just want you to see what it feels like."

"But I already know what it feels like! And you better have something for me to throw up in, because I already feel like I'm going to." Nova's heart was racing.

"You won't get sick."

"I did before."

"That's different. It doesn't usually happen when you're the traveler." Aunt Jean was clearly determined.

"What do you mean?"

"Well…have you ever been riding in the backseat and gotten carsick?"

"A couple of times, I guess," Nova answered, trying to quell her growing panic.

"It's kind of the same thing. You don't get carsick if you're the one driving." When they sat in the wicker chairs, Aunt Jean pulled hers up to Nova's and looked her in the eye. "We'll just try something easy. Close your eyes and try to relax."

Nova closed her eyes but couldn't will herself to relax. Her heart felt as if it were going to jump out of her chest.

"Nova, deep, slow breaths." Aunt Jean's voice was soothing. "Nothing will happen to you."

"I'm not sure about this."

"You don't have to do it. We'll just talk. Listen to the sounds in the garden instead. What do you hear?"

Nova slowly calmed down. Her breathing became more rhythmic as she listened to her aunt. "Birds...someone's running a mower – it sounds far away. There's a breeze. I feel it, but I hear it in the leaves overhead too."

"That's good. Now, think about when you woke up this morning—how the sheets felt against your skin, what you heard before you opened your eyes."

"I was still tired because I'd had a bad dream, sort of. The sheets felt so cool and comfortable. I didn't want to get up yet. My window was open, and I could hear the birds in the garden."

"What else?"

"Water...the sprinklers maybe? Then you were knocking on my door."

"That's good. Focus on that."

Nova felt the tension leaving her muscles. The fabric on the wicker chair reminded her of the smooth sheets on her bed upstairs. She listened to the sounds of the garden, the same sounds that drifted in through her bedroom window.

"Think about that moment, the sounds of the garden in the morning...the cool sheets...that first knock." Her aunt's voice sounded far away.

Nova felt her body float. *I'm not traveling. We're just talking.* She took a long breath and felt an odd sensation, like the moment a Ferris wheel begins to descend down the backside and the chair drops out from under you slightly.

Nova's eyes flew open. She was in the four-poster bed. Sunlight spilled in through the window overlooking the garden, and someone was knocking on the door.

CHAPTER 23

"Oh my God!" Nova yelled.

Aunt Jean burst into the room, grinning from ear to ear. "You teenagers sure like to sleep!"

"Did I…?" Nova sputtered.

"Get dressed and come on down. We have more baking to do."

Nova could hear her aunt laughing all the way down the stairs. She flung back the covers and frantically dressed. When she flew into the kitchen, she could barely speak.

"Aunt...Jean." Nova tried to catch her breath.

"Pretty cool, huh?" Aunt Jean smiled.

"That was amazing! I can't believe how easy it was." Nova gushed. "Can we do it again?"

"Hold on. You can't treat it like a carnival ride," Aunt Jean cautioned, still smiling.

"It was incredible! I didn't feel a tunnel though."

"Well, you didn't go back very far, did you?"

"No, I guess not. But I loved it! When can we try again? I feel like I could go anywhere."

"Don't get overconfident. That was just a test." Her aunt chuckled. "I can't believe how quickly you were able to focus. You have a strong gift, honey. We'll talk about practicing again later. Right now, let's get busy. We have to bake those darn pies and cakes again."

"Can't we just talk?" Nova couldn't have cared less about baking.

"We can talk while we work."

"Okay." Nova was disappointed. "That really was amazing though. I guess I wasn't sure I could do it on my own."

Aunt Jean gave her a stern look. "I know you're excited right now. But don't get ahead of yourself. That was just a little jump. It's fun to travel when there's nothing riding on it. When you're trying to change something that happened, something tragic, it's not the same at all."

"I'm sorry. I know it won't be easy."

Her expression softened. "You did good though, honey. I'm impressed."

Nova threw her arms around her aunt. "Thank you, Aunt Jean."

"All right then. Let's get this baking done."

Just then, Dayton came storming in. He glared at Aunt Jean. "What the did you do?"

Aunt Jean stood her ground, a stern look on her face. "Day, calm down—"

"Don't tell me to calm down! What do you think you're doing? We agreed. No traveling!"

"Dad, it was me! Aunt Jean just showed me how." As soon as she said the words, Nova regretted them.

His face turned red. "Aunt Jean, this is inexcusable! You and I talked about this. You agreed not to take matters into your own hands with Nova. She's my daughter, not yours! We're done here. Nova, go upstairs and pack."

"Dad, no! It's not her fault. She was trying to make sure I knew how to handle it, so I wouldn't do something stupid. Please don't make us leave!"

Aunt Jean was frowning at Dayton, completely

unfazed by his outburst. "You listen to me, Dayton Grant." Her tone was smoldering. "Do you want to repeat the mistakes your mother made? She and I had a very similar argument about you, and look what happened. You were cut off from the family and had no idea how to really use a power that could have saved your other daughter. So don't stand there and tell me I made a mistake showing Nova how to travel safely. Do you want her to know how to control it, or do you want her to get slung around from one timeline to another, never knowing for sure where she'll land? That's what will eventually happen and you know it. If she doesn't know how to travel and, more importantly, how *not to*, she'll find herself in the same situation you found yourself in, randomly deposited into another life. You were lucky this last time. When it happens to her, she might not be so lucky."

He sat down and shook his head. "You should have told me before you did it. I was shocked when I realized I was repeating time. I told Justin I had to get to the house. I'm not even sure what I said exactly. I probably sounded nuts."

"Don't worry about him. We'll tell him you weren't feeling well or something." Aunt Jean finally smiled. "We won't do anything else unless you're on board, Day."

"I'm sorry, Dad. We should've asked you." Nova hugged him.

"Day, there's no harm done. Let's just forget this happened and enjoy your visit. Go back to the barn with Marshall and Justin. Nova and I still have baking to do."

He reluctantly stood to leave. "You two behave yourselves. Promise?"

"We promise," Nova assured him.

Aunt Jean just smiled and nodded.

By the time the cakes and pies were done again, it was time to prepare lunch. They busied themselves making turkey-and-pimento-cheese sandwiches until they had at least a dozen piled on a platter. Aunt Jean pulled a bowl of potato salad out of the refrigerator.

When did she make that? Nova wondered. "You're amazing, Aunt Jean."

Her aunt looked pleased. At least for now, everything seemed back to normal. No one would be able to tell that Nova had traveled just hours before. She was amazed at how easily she accepted that reality.

Aunt Jean chattered all the way to the barn, but Nova barely heard a word. All she could think of were the events of that morning. When Marshall saw them coming with food, he climbed down the ladder from the hayloft and sprinted over. Justin set up the picnic table on the lawn, and Connie covered it with a cheerful flowered tablecloth. When they were all sitting, they held hands and Aunt Jean thanked God again for bringing her family back to her. She looked over at Dayton and nodded, smiling.

After lunch, Nova and her dad took a walk through the garden. In this peaceful setting, everything seemed right with the world. He recounted his attempt at a riding lesson, to Nova's amusement, and she told him in detail about her new skill as a baker. They laughed, remembering Marshall's reaction when Nova had revealed that the huge bite of cake he had stuffed in his mouth was full of shredded sweet potatoes. Her dad seemed happy. She felt a stab of pain. She wanted desperately to give him back his other daughter.

He stopped walking and turned to Nova. "I'm sorry I flipped out earlier. I want you to learn how to control...how to travel. I wish we had come here sooner. Don't you?"

"Yes." Nova wasn't sure where he was going with this.

"Maybe if I had contacted Aunt Jean years ago, I would've done a better job of fixing things with your sister. She's right. I would have known what to do."

"Dad—"

"I'm sorry, firefly. I shouldn't have brought it up."

"Are you thinking about trying again?"

He looked uncomfortable. "It's just that...being here

and seeing what they accomplished...I don't know. Maybe. I'm not sure."

Aunt Jean had talked about the importance of believing in yourself. "You have to be sure," she had stressed. Her dad didn't have that confidence. Maybe a lifetime of doubt was just too hard to overcome. Even though he had traveled twice, he'd never had any control. Aunt Jean was right. He wasn't up to it.

It has to be me, Nova decided. *If I don't try, he will, and that could be tragic.*

"I love you, Dad. It's gonna be okay," she whispered as they headed back toward the house.

Nova drifted through the rest of the day, her mind preoccupied with planning. She couldn't talk to Aunt Jean. She surely wouldn't think Nova was ready and would try to talk her out of it. Her aunt might even tell her dad and he'd try to stop her. No, she had to do this on her own.

By the time dinner was over and everyone was on the porch, Nova was utterly worn out. Once again, Marshall fell asleep on the swing beside her. Afraid that she was about to do the same, Nova excused herself and headed upstairs to bed. After changing quickly, she opened the window and crawled into bed.

Maybe she should call Ethan so she could hear him call her "hot girl" one more time, just in case. She took the phone off the night table and started to dial but paused halfway through. Calling him could just mess things up. She set the phone on the bed up against the headboard in case she changed her mind later. So many thoughts were swirling around in her head, but in spite of that, she was oddly calm.

Somewhere in the distance, she heard an owl hooting. She listened for it again, but as minutes passed, all she heard was the sound of a grandfather clock somewhere in the house. It was funny that she hadn't noticed it before. Her mind latched on to the slow *tick, tock, tick, tock.* A slight breeze from the open window touched her face. She imagined that she was back in the garden, lying in the soft grass among the flowers. Their delicate scent filled her nostrils.

Nova could barely hear the clock now. She was completely at peace as she drifted in the space between sleep and consciousness. She felt wonderfully relaxed, as if she were floating in a placid pond in the middle of the beautiful garden. She was sure that if she opened her eyes, she would see stars overhead.

As she hovered in that comforting place, a picture slowly formed in her mind. She couldn't make it out at first, but gradually a face took shape. It was the face of a young girl about Nova's age, with hazel eyes and golden hair. Her mouth curved up at the edges in a familiar smile. It was Alana, but not the little girl in the sketches her dad had drawn. This Alana was as she would have been now, almost sixteen.

"You're so beautiful, sister," Nova said softly.

Alana smiled and motioned for Nova to come with her.

"Where?" Nova called.

Alana motioned to her again to come. Nova heard the sound of laughter in the distance. She heard her dad's voice, along with the rest of the family's. It sounded as though they were all there.

"Happy birthday, Nova and Alana!" someone called.

Alana stepped back, still smiling. Nova focused completely on her sister. *It's like aiming a rifle.* She willed herself to focus on Alana's face. Nothing else existed at that moment. At first she seemed stuck in suspended animation. It was tempting to just stay there, warm and safe. She directed her thoughts again to Alana, and suddenly she was overcome with the sensation of floating. Somewhere in the distance, she heard the faint sound of footsteps. She strained even harder to focus on her sister. *Happy birthday, Alana...*

Gentle hands touched her face. "Let go, honey..."

Suddenly she felt as though she was being pulled impossibly fast through a narrow chute. Alana was at the other end, still motioning to her. Nova called out but made no sound as the tunnel became narrower and narrower, finally enveloping her in the blissful darkness of a dreamless sleep.

CHAPTER 24

Sometime the next morning, Nova awoke feeling slightly disoriented. She pulled the covers over her head and stayed perfectly still, enjoying the cozy warmth of her bed. The house was still quiet, so there was no need to get up. She would just stay there, relaxed and comfortable, until she was forced to rejoin the world.

Nova had a feeling that something had happened, but she couldn't remember what it was. Did she have a dream? She tried harder to recall, but the effort produced no results. She would let it go for now. The bed was so comfortable, and she was enjoying the peace and quiet. Aunt Jean was probably downstairs right now, cooking up some wonderfully delicious breakfast. Nova scooted farther down into the covers. She was getting used to the four-poster bed. It felt like her bed at home.

"Nova!" Her mother's cheerful voice drifted in from the hallway outside her room. "Get up! I made cinnamon waffles."

So *Mom* was cooking this morning? Oh well, Aunt Jean probably needed a break. It couldn't be easy cooking big meals every day for company. Especially when she'd been living alone and had this big house to take care of.

"I'll be there in a minute," Nova muttered, her eyes still closed. But she made no attempt to extract herself from the bed.

"Happy birthday!" Her mom called.

Nova chuckled. *What's she up to? My birthday isn't until next month.*

Nova knew she should get up but couldn't seem to pry her eyes open or will herself to move. She imagined Ethan tapping on her window at home. *Maybe I should call him.* She felt around for the phone but couldn't find it, so she shoved her hand farther up the mattress until her fingers touched the iron headboard. Still no phone.

Nova sighed and burrowed back down in the covers. She was nearly asleep again when a realization jolted her awake. She flung back the covers and sat up. She was home. In her own bed. The room spun as dizziness overtook her. Nova grabbed the headboard, trying to keep from fainting for the second time in her life.

Oh my God! What happened? What did I do? She struggled to get her brain to cooperate. *Think!*

She remembered the talk with Aunt Jean in the garden. She remembered baking and their conversation in the kitchen. She remembered going to the garden with her dad and having dinner afterward with the family.

Did all of that really happen? Nova's heart was racing. It felt as if it were coming out of her chest. She fought to keep from falling apart and screaming for help. *I traveled! It's my birthday, so did I go backward or forward?* She tried to slow down her breathing so she wouldn't pass out.

Nova realized that she was gripping the headboard so hard that she was actually losing feeling in her fingers. She pried her hand loose and cautiously slid off the bed until her feet touched the familiar wood floor. Slowly she stood, still feeling unsteady. *I have to find Dad. He has to be here.*

She was wearing boxers and a T-shirt, but not the

ones she had put on the night before at Aunt Jean's. She didn't recognize these. Nova looked around her room. Most of it was the same, but everything appeared to have moved just a little.

She managed the four steps it took to reach her dresser. Grasping one of the brass handles, she pulled open the top drawer and grabbed a pair of jeans and a shirt she didn't recognize. The mirror that had been over the dresser was gone, replaced by a shelf crammed with books. Nova glanced around the room and saw a large wall mirror beside her door. A small dressing table was pushed against it, littered with brushes, makeup, hairbands, and various other things she'd expect to see on a vanity.

Nova stepped in front of the mirror and nearly passed out. Her hair was about four inches longer than it had been the night before. Slowly, her hand shaking, she felt the side of her head. The stitches were gone. She backed up and sat on her bed again, tempted to crawl back in and never get out. *Okay, Nova. Get a grip or you'll never get through this.*

She took a deep breath and stepped in front of the mirror again, examining her reflection. Other than her hair being longer, she looked exactly the same, no older and no younger. She must have traveled ahead about a month to her sixteenth birthday. Normally, she would have been excited about turning sixteen. She would have wondered if her parents had bought her something great, like a car. But under these circumstances, she couldn't have possibly cared less.

It took her about fifteen minutes to pull herself together, but the result was pretty good. Her hair fell in freshly brushed waves down her back, and her jeans and light blue top were probably a *normal* outfit for her. *I look okay for a time traveler.*

Nova opened her bedroom door and listened, praying her dad was there somewhere and not back in the river. She could smell the cinnamon waffles her mom had made for breakfast but didn't hear anyone in the kitchen. They could be sitting at the table eating, or maybe they had given up on her and gone somewhere. Probably not though, since it was apparently her birthday.

There was no sound coming from Marshall's room and the door was closed, so Nova tiptoed past it so she wouldn't wake him and made her way up the hall to her dad's office. The door was closed but not locked. She turned the knob, opened the door, and gasped. The wood shelves and desk were gone, replaced by a room much like her own but painted a crisp white. An iron headboard exactly like hers towered over a bed that was perfectly made with a fluffy comforter and throw pillows. A small wooden nightstand was next to the bed and a mahogany dresser stood against the bed on the other side. Across the room were a desk and two cozy chairs covered with pink flowered fabric. A bookcase on the desk was filled with books and framed photos.

Nova walked over to it and looked at the pictures. Two little girls were hugging each other with a Christmas tree behind them in one. Another was of the same little girls, a few years older, sitting on a pier somewhere. They were dangling their feet in the water and laughing.

Tears rolled down Nova's cheeks. "This is Alana's room," she whispered, spellbound.

Nova didn't notice the footsteps behind her until a pair of hands clamped firmly over her eyes. "Surprise!"

Nova wheeled around, still crying. Her sister, her beautiful sister, was standing right in front of her. Alana stopped smiling but not before Nova noticed that the corners of her mouth curved up slightly, just like Marshall's. Her hair was a deeper gold than it had been when she was little, but long bangs hung loosely over her face, gently framing the same expressive hazel eyes.

"Alana!" Nova barely choked out.

Suddenly Alana's arms were around her, hugging her tight. "What's wrong?"

Nova couldn't stop crying. She had no idea what to

say anyway.

Alana grabbed Nova's shoulders and pushed her away slightly so she could look her in the eyes. "Is this about Steven? Has he been bothering you?"

Nova racked her brain, trying to think of a Steven from school. Nothing. She shook her head.

"Well, what then?" Alana demanded.

Nova couldn't think of anything believable to explain her hysterics, so she finally managed to nod. "It's Steven."

"That jerk! What did he do now?"

"Nothing really…I…I'm just…" Nova couldn't seem to get her brain, or her mouth, to work. She was completely mesmerized by her sister.

Alana pulled her into another hug. "He's a loser. You did the right thing breaking up with him."

"I know. He was a loser." She decided to go with it.

"Well, all is well, little sister. Dry your eyes. I have a surprise for you later!"

"I'm not sure I can take any more surprises," Nova said truthfully.

Alana studied her sister. "Hmm. David's coming over in a few minutes to take me to breakfast for my 'sweet sixteenth.'" She grinned. "But I can cancel if you need me. Twin sister trumps boyfriend, you know."

Nova smiled. *Twin sister!* She took so long to speak that Alana picked up the phone from her nightstand to call David and cancel their breakfast date.

Nova shook herself mentally. "No, don't cancel. I'm fine. Really. Go have fun with David."

Alana beamed. "Okay! But I'll be back before lunch, 'cause that's you and me, okay?"

"Okay."

Alana flitted around the room, brushing her shoulder-length hair and looking for her purse. "I already looked in the driveway, so don't bother. No cars. Mom and Dad are being very secretive though, so something's up. Oh, and Mom fixed *homemade waffles*." She wrinkled her nose. "I've never been able to figure out how taking them out of the freezer and popping them into the toaster makes them *homemade*." She laughed.

Alana continued to chatter the whole time she was getting ready. Nova couldn't concentrate on what she was saying, but she loved every second of sitting in her sister's room, listening to her talking about inconsequential things.

Finally, Alana looked at her watch and exclaimed, "Oh my God! David will be here any second!"

She took Nova's hand and sprinted up the hall to the kitchen. Their parents were standing at the table, holding balloons and grinning from ear to ear.

"Happy birthday!" they shouted in unison, just as a familiar-looking young man who Nova assumed was David came in through the back door.

"Happy birthday!" he added.

Nova smiled and started to say hello, but she found herself picked up off of her feet and swung around in a circle instead.

"Happy birthday, Nova!" He laughed. "You want to come with Alana and me to get breakfast?"

"Oh yes, come!" Alana grabbed Nova's arm and tried to drag her out the door with them.

"Wait! I made waffles!" cried Celeste, obviously insulted that her effort wasn't being noticed.

"I'll stay here, Alana. But thanks," Nova said.

She looked over at her dad, and he winked at her. Nova couldn't wait to talk to him, but she knew that would come later, when they were alone. For now she wanted to enjoy being here with her family.

Alana leaned toward Nova and whispered, "Don't forget, I have a surprise for you later."

And with that, she was out the door with David. Nova couldn't stop smiling.

"Sit down, birthday girl," Her dad grinned.

As she pulled out her chair, Nova glanced at the table and laughed. No chip. Her mom gave her a curious look.

"Sorry. I just thought of something funny." Nova smiled awkwardly.

Over the next half an hour, she managed to down four waffles, which pleased her mother immensely. The atmosphere in the kitchen was festive, and Nova felt happier than she'd ever been. The only thing that could make this day any better was...Ethan! She jumped up, explained that she wanted to check something in her room, and dashed down the hall.

Her dad was right behind her, and he motioned silently for her to be quiet before he closed her door and turned to face her. They just stood there for a moment, looking at each other.

Finally he said, with a great deal of admiration in his voice, "Firefly, I can't believe you did this!" He took her in his arms and hugged her tight. Nova could hear his heart beating.

She looked up at him. "Alana's amazing. Can this all be real?"

"It's real," he assured her. "She's just like I've imagined her all these years, so full of life. And yes, she's amazing. But so are you. I don't think you realize how special you are. What you were able to do is nothing short of a miracle."

"I think Aunt Jean helped me. I think she came in my room."

"However you managed it..." He seemed stuck on the words. "You don't know what this means to me. When nothing happened at Aunt Jean's, I thought—"

"Wait, what?" Nova stepped back, confused.

"Yeah. Nothing happened. I mean, we talked about it a lot for the whole twelve days we were there. But then...nothing."

"Dad, we were just there a few days, not twelve. Then

last night I traveled."

"We've been home over two weeks." he looked stunned. "I went camping with Marshall last weekend."

Nova backed up and leaned against the dresser, thinking. Then it made sense. "It's just like before, when I had to live the nine months without you. I didn't change until the morning you came back."

"Yes, but, you were here."

"I was?" Nova couldn't comprehend that she'd actually been home over the past two weeks. Or at least, some version of herself had been. If she'd been here, shouldn't she have some memory of it? After all, she remembered the rest of the timeline before Aunt Jean's. "I can't believe...I was here? How is that possible? To me, it feels like I was just at Aunt Jean's. I mean, shouldn't I have some memory of the last two weeks? Or the extra time at Willow Hill?"

He stood there shaking his head. "It's a crazy thing, isn't it?"

"Yeah."

"There are aspects to this whole time travel thing that are hard to understand.

Let's decide to leave it at that for now," he said. "I just want to enjoy this."

"Okay. This new life is enough to figure out. If I try to cram any more information into my brain, it's gonna explode." She laughed.

He nodded. "I felt like I was having a heart attack when I woke up this morning and saw Alana. Your mom dragged me out of bed and into the kitchen at the crack of dawn. She wanted to be sure we were both there when you woke up. She barely gave me time to pull on some jeans. When Alana came walking into the kitchen, I couldn't even speak at first. Then I must have hugged her for ten minutes. She asked me what the big deal was. 'I'm just turning sixteen, Dad, not becoming a missionary.'" He laughed. "It's incredible."

"So what do we do now?" Nova whispered.

"I don't know. Going forward does have its drawbacks. We'll have to help each other figure out this new life. Sixteen years we won't remember." He shook his head again. "I have a book that's almost finished. I have no idea what it's about, but Jason called early this morning asking for the first draft." He laughed. "It's going to be weird for a while, but we'll at least have each other to lean on. I'm so proud of you."

"Thanks, Dad. Everything's perfect. It's just…" Nova hesitated.

"What?"

"Nothing."

"Have you talked to Ethan?" he asked softly.

"No. I'm gonna call him if…if I have his number."

"Don't you know it?"

"Yeah, but if it's not in my book…"

"Oh, right. You can't very well call him if he doesn't know you." He held her chin and looked her in the eye, smiling. "Let's try to focus on the positives. Even if you're not friends right now, you never know what could happen with you and Ethan. You're just sixteen."

"I know." Nova tried to pull herself together. "I promised him I'd get to know him again if something happened and we weren't friends anymore."

"Well, that's settled then. If he liked you once, he will again, honey. After all, what's not to like? You're pretty awesome. And hey, maybe you'll have his number."

"Yeah, maybe."

"We'll figure out this new life, but it's going to be hard for a while," he said. "Lots of things will be different."

"Different enough, I hope," Nova muttered.

"What do you mean?" He stepped back, frowning slightly. "Is there anything I should know?"

Nova shook her head. "It's just something Aunt Jean

said. It doesn't matter."

He studied her. "Are you sure?"

"I'm sure." Nova smiled, determined not to focus on anything but the fact that her family was finally whole. "Really, Dad, it's not important. I'd tell you if it was."

He looked as though he was about to say something else, but he hesitated before clearing his throat. "I guess I'd better get Marshall up before all the waffles are gone."

Nova gave him another hug, and he left, closing the door behind him. *It has to be here somewhere.* Jerking open the drawer next to her bed, she pulled out her address book and flipped to the page where his name should be. *Please be there...*

No Ethan. Nova's heart sank. She'd known how risky it was to travel, but deep down, she'd thought that somehow he would still be there for her. She pictured him at her window the night before they left for Aunt Jean's, when she promised to get to know him again if something happened. Nova gazed over at the window, wondering if she'd ever see his face there again. She had her sister after all these years without her, but had lost Ethan. She wished with all her heart that she had told him she loved him when he'd said those words to her. She ran her fingers over the back of her hand where a scar should be, but there were no traces of it. No accident with the bus door. No stitches. No Ethan.

Nova sat on her bed for a while, letting it sink in. She'd have to wait until school started back in September to talk to him. That seemed so far away. Even then, there was no telling how long it would take for the opportunity to present itself. And what if he already had a girlfriend? *He said he'd love me no matter when we met.*

Nova got up and paced, finally pushing him out of her mind and focusing on the present. Her dad was alive and so was Alana. She'd managed to bring her sister back. Everything else could be worked out in time.

Nova walked back up the hall and stopped at the

kitchen door. Her mom was humming while she stuck dishes in the dishwasher. Marshall was still nowhere in sight, and now neither was her dad.

"Where is everybody?" Nova asked.

Before her mother could answer, the back door slammed as Alana burst in. "Hi, Mom!"

She grabbed Nova by the arm and dragged her into the kitchen. Alana was very excited about something. She stepped back and quickly looked Nova over.

"Let's see. Okay…yeah…you look great." Alana grinned. "Don't get mad. I have something to tell you that you're probably not gonna be totally okay with, but give it a chance to sink in. Don't decide right away. I mean, I know you don't like surprises…"

"Alana, take a breath," Nova said nervously.

"Right. Okay. Here goes. There's this really hot guy in my English class who had a major crush on you all year. I didn't say anything because you and Steven were going out, but since you're not now, thank God, I told him he could come over and meet you. Today. To be more specific, I said he could come now. He's so nice! Just give him a chance, okay?"

The last thing Nova wanted to do was meet some guy from school, but before she could reply, someone knocked on the back door and Alana ran to open it. As he stepped into the doorway, his dark blue eyes caught Nova's and he smiled, exposing a dimple in his right cheek.

Alana beamed. "Nova, this is Ethan MacGrady."

Nova couldn't move. It was Ethan. Her Ethan. She stared at him, holding her breath to keep from blurting out something completely inappropriate.

Ethan grinned. "Hi, Nova. Happy birthday."

"Thanks." Nova felt completely tongue-tied.

She glanced at her mother, who seemed equally taken with Ethan. Nova and Alana exchanged looks. *Oh my God, is Mom blushing?* Nova laughed then felt her cheeks go red.

"Umm…you want to take a walk?" Ethan offered.

"Sure." Nova looked back at her smug sister as they walked out the door. *I'll never hear the end of this,* she thought, smiling.

She returned home several hours later, amazed at how beautifully everything had worked out. With Ethan back in her life, she felt as though there was nothing else to wish for. She'd just have to remember to hold back a little with him, let things progress naturally even though she just wanted to throw her arms around him and kiss him like before. If she did that now, he'd probably think she was nuts…or worse. Nova was grinning when she walked through the door, thinking about that scenario.

Her mom was in the kitchen, making coffee. "How did it go with Ethan?"

"Good." Nova smiled. It had been better than good. Amazing. The way it must have been before, during the time she couldn't remember.

"Details please!" Celeste laughed.

"Okay, it was perfect. We made out the whole time."

"Nova! Seriously?"

"No." Nova grinned. "The perfect part is true though."

"Well, thank goodness for that." Her mom took the pitcher from the coffee maker and poured the contents into a mug. "Your dad's still in his office. I haven't seen him since breakfast. Here, take him his coffee." Celeste handed her the steaming cup, but Nova didn't move.

"The office?" Nova racked her brain. Alana's room was where the office had been.

Her mother seemed in a hurry, flitting around the room putting the last few things from breakfast away. "I have some quick errands to run. Try not to make too much noise if you go in your room. He has to finish the first draft of his new book. Jason was asking for it."

"Why can't I make noise?" Nova asked, confused.

"You know he can hear everything through the wall. Just be quiet today."

"Through the wall?" But Marshall's room was next to hers, so where was the office?

"Yes, Nova. Just for today. And go ahead and take your dad his coffee. I'll be back in about an hour, then I'll need to steal him for a little while. Party plans!"

Nova had a sudden sinking feeling in the pit of her stomach. She hadn't seen her little brother all morning. If the office was next to her room...

Her mother was nearly out the door when Nova found her voice. "Mom?"

She looked back at Nova. "What?"

"Where's Marshall?"

She looked confused. "Who's Marshall? I can't keep up with all your friends. If he's around here somewhere, I'm sure you'll find him." She laughed, letting the door slam behind her.

The cup slipped from Nova's hand, hit the floor, and shattered into a thousand tiny pieces.

THE END

FORSAKEN
Chapter 1 Preview

Nova stared at what was left of the coffee mug now scattered in a thousand tiny shards across the kitchen floor. Spellbound, she watched as the pool of roasted Colombian coffee with hazelnut cream slowly soaked into her right shoe, turning the nearly white fabric a golden brown. A ridiculous thought crossed her mind—that now she'd have to pour coffee on the other one so they'd match. The rest of the coffee crept across the wood floor in a spiral pattern. Nova was fascinated that the cup could hold enough liquid to produce such an effect.

Something was wrong, but she felt disconnected, as if she were having an out-of-body experience. If she thought about the coffee, she wouldn't have to remember. She could just contemplate the changing color of her shoe, not thinking about what she'd done.

A single stream of coffee broke away from the circle and wrapped around one of the table legs, like a finger grasping for something to hang on to before being sucked back into the murky pool that continued to grow wider and wider. She should probably do something to stop it, but her feet seemed tethered in place while her ferociously beating heart pumped too much blood to her lungs. If she passed out right there on the kitchen floor, how long would it take for someone to find her?

Maybe she'd wake up surrounded by all the people she cared about, like Dorothy in *The Wizard of Oz*. *"It wasn't a dream. It was a place. And you, and you, and you, and YOU were there."* But someone was missing—someone with sandy hair and hazel eyes, who loved horses and video games and never stopped talking...

Made in the USA
Columbia, SC
06 February 2018